MORE MYSTERIES FROM THE
BERKLEY PUBLISHING GROUP...

CAT CALIBAN MYSTERIES: She was married for thirty-eight years. Raised three kids. Compared to that, tracking down killers is easy . . .

by D. B. Borton

ONE FOR THE MONEY	TWO POINTS FOR MURDER
THREE IS A CROWD	FOUR ELEMENTS OF MURDER
FIVE ALARM FIRE	SIX FEET UNDER

ELENA JARVIS MYSTERIES: There are some pretty bizarre crimes deep in the heart of Texas—and a pretty gutsy police detective who rounds up the unusual suspects . . .

by Nancy Herndon

ACID BATH	WIDOWS' WATCH
LETHAL STATUES	HUNTING GAME
TIME BOMBS	

FREDDIE O'NEAL, P.I., MYSTERIES: You can bet that this appealing Reno private investigator will get her man . . . "A winner."—Linda Grant

by Catherine Dain

LAY IT ON THE LINE	SING A SONG OF DEATH
WALK A CROOKED MILE	LAMENT FOR A DEAD COWBOY
BET AGAINST THE HOUSE	THE LUCK OF THE DRAW
DEAD MAN'S HAND	

BENNI HARPER MYSTERIES: Meet Benni Harper—a quilter and folk-art expert with an eye for murderous designs . . .

by Earlene Fowler

FOOL'S PUZZLE	IRISH CHAIN
KANSAS TROUBLES	GOOSE IN THE POND

HANNAH BARLOW MYSTERIES: For ex-cop and law student Hannah Barlow, justice isn't just a word in a textbook. Sometimes, it's a matter of life and death . . .

by Carroll Lachnit

MURDER IN BRIEF	A BLESSED DEATH

SAMANTHA HOLT MYSTERIES: Dogs, cats, and crooks are all part of a day's work for this veterinary technician . . . "Delightful!"—Melissa Cleary

by Karen Ann Wilson

EIGHT DOGS FLYING	COPY CAT CRIMES
BEWARE SLEEPING DOGS	CIRCLE OF WOLVES

CANINE CRIMES

II

Edited by Cynthia Manson

BERKLEY PRIME CRIME, NEW YORK

CANINE CRIMES II

A Berkley Prime Crime Book / published by arrangement with Dell Magazines, Inc.

PRINTING HISTORY
Berkley Prime Crime edition / October 1997

The Putnam Berkley World Wide Web site address is
http://www.berkley.com

ISBN: 0-425-16038-6

Berkley Prime Crime Books are published
by The Berkley Publishing Group,
a member of Penguin Putnam Inc.,
200 Madison Avenue, New York, NY 10016.
The name BERKLEY PRIME CRIME and the BERKLEY PRIME CRIME
design are trademarks belonging to Berkley Publishing Corporation.

PRINTED IN THE UNITED STATES OF AMERICA

10 9 8 7 6 5 4 3 2 1

Table of Contents

Editor's Note

In CANINE CRIMES II we bring you the second in our popular series of mysteries featuring dogs. Once again we have culled material from *Ellery Queen's Mystery Magazine* and *Alfred Hitchcock Mystery Magazine*. It is no surprise that mystery fans, many of whom are dog owners, enjoy reading stories which feature their canine friends.

In this collection, Cyril Hare's fascinating story WEIGHT AND SEE, describes a wife murderer who depends on his dog for an alibi. Mary Kittredge's THE DOG THAT BIT YOU, sets the stage for murder in a kennel. Mary Robert Rinehart's THE DOG IN THE ORCHARD, weaves a dark tale of a man whose ugly secret is exposed because his dog's howling brings him to the brink of insanity.

On a lighter note we have Ron Goulart's HOW COME MY DOG DON'T BARK, in which an actor on the set of a television show is convinced that the dog on the show is trying to kill him. A more traditional relationship between dog and master is seen in THE WATCHDOG, where a man buys a dog to protect himself from a killer on the loose. In Gene KoKayKo's LATE SEPTEMBER DOGS, when a dead woman's body is found on the beach, her dog is the only clue to her murderer.

Suspenseful tales in the CANINE CRIMES collection have been authored by such masters of mystery as Charlotte Armstrong, Ross MacDonald, Margaret Maron, and Robert Campbell. The dog owners among you will appreciate the fact that often in these stories it is man who is the beast.

<< Weight and See >>
by
Cyril Hare

DETECTIVE-INSPECTOR MALLETT OF the C.I.D. was a very large man. He was not only tall above the average, but also broad in more than just proportion to his height, while his weight was at least proportionate to his breadth. Whether, as his colleagues at New Scotland Yard used to assert, his bulk was due to the enormous meals which he habitually consumed, or whether, as the inspector maintained, the reason for his large appetite was that so big a frame needed more than a normal man's supply for its sustenance, was an open question. What was not open to doubt was Mallett's success in his calling. But if anybody was ever bold enough to suggest that his success might have been even greater but for the handicap of his size, he would merely smile sweetly and remark that there had been occasions when on the contrary he had found it a positive advantage. Pressed to further and better particulars, he might, if in an expansive mood, go so far as to say that he could recall at least one case in which he had succeeded where a twelve-stone man would have failed.

This is the story of that case. It is not, strictly speaking, a case of detection at all, since the solution depended ultimately on the chance application of avoirdupois rather than the deliberate application of intelligence. Nonetheless, it was a case which Mallett himself was fond of recollecting, if only because of the way in which that recollection served to salve his conscience whenever thereafter he fell to the temptation of a second helping of suet pudding.

• • •

The story begins, so far as the police are concerned, at about seven o'clock on a fine morning in early summer, when a milkman on his round came out of the entrance of Clarence Mansions, S.W.11, just as a police constable happened to be passing.

''Morning,'' said the constable.

''Morning,'' said the milkman.

The constable moved on. The milkman stood watching him, two powerful questions conflicting in his breast. On the one hand, it was an article of faith with him that one whose work takes him to other people's houses at a time when most of the world is only beginning to wake up should never poke his nose into other people's business; on the other, he felt just now a craving, new-born but immensely powerful, not to be left out of the adventure which some sixth sense told him was afoot. The constable was almost out of earshot before the issue was decided.

''Oy!'' shouted the milkman.

The officer turned round majestically.

''What is it?'' he asked.

The milkman jerked his thumb in the direction of the block of flats behind him.

''I don't know,'' he said, ''but I think there's something queer up there.''

''Where?''

''Number 32, top floor.''

''How d'you mean, queer?''

''The dog up there is carrying on something awful—barking and scratching at the door.''

''Well, what of it?''

''Oh, nothing, but it's a bit queer, that's all. It's a quiet dog as a rule.''

''They've gone out and left him in, I suppose.''

''Well, if they 'ave, they've left a light on as well.''

The constable looked up at the windows of the top story.

''There *is* a light on in one of the rooms,'' he observed. ''Seems funny, a fine morning like this.'' He considered the matter slowly. ''Might as well go up and see, I suppose. They'll be having the neighbors complaining about that dog. I can hear it from here.''

With the milkman in attendance, he tramped heavily up the

stairs—Clarence Mansions boast no lift—to the top floor. Outside Number 32 stood the pint bottle of milk which had just been left there. He rang the bell. There was no reply, except a renewed outburst of barks from the dog within.

"Are they at home, d'you know?" he asked.

" 'S far as I know. I 'ad me orders to deliver, same as usual."

"Who are the people?"

"Wellman, the name is. A little fair chap with a squint. There's just the two of them and the dog."

"I know him," said the policeman. "Seen him about often. Passed the time of day with him. Didn't know he was married, though."

"She never goes out," the milkman explained. "He told me about her once. Used to be a trapeze artist in a circus. 'Ad a fall, and crippled for good. Can't even get in or out of bed by 'erself, so he says."

"Oh?" said the constable. "Well, if that's so, perhaps—" He sucked his cheeks and frowned perplexedly. "All the same, you can't go and break into a place just because the dog's howling and someone's left the light on. I think I'd best go and report this before I do anything."

The milkman was looking down the staircase.

"Someone coming up," he announced. "It's Mr. Wellman all right," he added, as a rather flushed, unshaven face appeared on the landing below.

The constable put on his official manner at once.

"Mr. Wellman, sir?" he said. "There have been complaints of your dog creating a disturbance here this morning. Also I observe that there is a light on in one of your rooms. Would you be good enough to—"

"That's all right, officer," Wellman interrupted him. "I was kept out last night. Quite unexpected. Sorry about the dog and all that."

He fished a latchkey from his pocket, opened the door, and went in, shutting it behind him. The other two, left outside with the milk bottle for company, heard him speak softly to the dog, which immediately became quiet. In the silence they could hear his footsteps down the passage which evidently led away from the front door. They looked at each other blankly. The policeman said "Well," the milkman was already preparing to go back to his round, when the steps were heard returning, there was the sound of the door of a room nearby being opened, and then Mr. Wellman was out of the flat, his face white, his eyes staring, crying, "Come here, quick! Something awful has happened!"

"But this," said Mallett, "is odd. Very odd indeed."

He sat in the office of the divisional detective-inspector, meditatively turning over a sheaf of reports.

"Odd is the word for it," the D.D.I. replied. "You see, on the one hand there seems no doubt that the lady was alive at nine o'clock—"

"Let me see if I've got the story straight," said Mallett. "Mrs. Wellman is found dead in her bed at about seven o'clock in the morning by her husband, in the presence, very nearly, of a police officer and another man. She has been killed by a blow on the back of the head from a blunt instrument. The doctor thinks that death occurred about seven to eleven hours previously—say between eight o'clock and midnight the night before. He thinks also—in fact he's pretty sure—that the blow would produce instantaneous death, or at all events instantaneous unconsciousness. There are no signs of forcible entry into the flat, and Mrs. Wellman was a cripple, so the possibility of her getting out of bed to let anybody in is out of the question. Am I right so far?"

"Quite correct."

"In these circumstances the husband quite naturally falls under suspicion. He is asked to account for his movements overnight, and up to a point he seems quite willing to do so. He says that he put his wife to bed at about a quarter to nine, took the dog out for a short run— What sort of a dog is it, by the way?"

"An Alsatian. It seems to be a good-tempered, intelligent sort of beast."

"He takes the Alsatian out for a short run, returns it to the flat without going into his wife's room, and then goes out again. That's his story. He says most positively that he never came back to the place until next morning when the constable and the milkman saw him going in. Asked whether he has any witnesses to prove his story, he says that he spoke to the constable on night duty, whom he met just outside Clarence Mansions on his way out, and he further gives the names of two friends whom he met at the Green Dragon public house, half a mile from Clarence Mansions—''

"Seven hundred and fifty yards from Clarence Mansions."

"I'm much obliged. He met his two pals there at about a quarter past nine, and stayed there till closing time. He went from the public house with one of them to the nearest tram stop, and took a Number 31 tram going east, or away from Clarence Mansions. His friend went with him on the tram as far as the next fare stage, where he got off, leaving Wellman on the tram, still going away from home. Is that all clear so far?"

"Quite."

"Further than that Wellman wouldn't help us. He said he'd spent the rest of the night in a little hotel somewhere down Hackney way. Why he should have done so he didn't explain, and when asked for the name of the place he couldn't give it. He thought it had a red and green carpet in the hall, but that's all he could remember about it. The suggestion was, I gather, that he was too drunk to notice things properly when he got to the hotel, and was suffering from a bit of a hangover next morning."

"He certainly was when I saw him."

"Things begin to look rather bad for Master Wellman. They look even worse when we find out a few things about him. It seems that he hasn't a job, and hasn't had one for a very long time. He married his wife when she was traveling the country as a trapeze artist in a small circus, in which he was employed as electrician and odd-job man. When a rope broke and she was put out of the circus business for good, her employers paid her a lump sum in compensation. He has been living on that ever since. His accounts show that he has got through it pretty quickly, and it's odds on that she had been wanting to know where it had gone to. It's not very hard to see a motive for getting rid of her."

"The motive's there all right," said the divisional inspector, "but—"

"*But*," Mallett went on. "Here's where our troubles begin.—Wellman is detained for enquiries, and the enquiries show that his story, so far as it goes, is perfectly true. He did meet his pals at the Green Dragon. They and the publican are positive on that point, and they bear out his story in every particular. Therefore, if he killed his wife it must have been before a quarter past nine or after half past ten, which was approximately the time when he was last seen on the Number 31 tram. But Mrs. Wellman was alive when he left Clarence Mansions, because—''

He pulled out one of the statements before him.

'' 'Statement of Police Constable Denny,' '' he read. '' 'At approximately nine o'clock P.M. I was on duty in Imperial Avenue opposite Clarence Mansions when I saw Wellman. He had his dog with him. We had a short conversation. He said, ''I've just been giving my dog a run.'' I said, ''It's a nice dog.'' He said, ''I bought it for my wife's protection, but it's too goodnatured for a watchdog.'' He went into Clarence Mansions and came out again almost at once. He had a small bag in his hand. I said, ''Going out again, Mr. Wellman?'' He said, ''Yes. Have you seen my pals about anywhere?'' I informed him that I did not know his pals, and he replied, ''I expect they're gone on ahead.'' He then said, ''I'm waiting to see if the wife has turned in yet.'' I looked up at the windows of Clarence Mansions, and there was a light in one of the windows on the top story—the window to the left of the staircase as you look at it. I have since learned that that is the window of the bedroom of Number 32. As I was looking, the light was extinguished. Wellman said to me, ''That's all right, I can get along now.'' We had a bit of a joke about it. He then went away, and I proceeded on my beat. At approximately ten thirty P.M. I had occasion to pass Clarence Mansions again. There were then no lights visible in the top story. I did not pass the Mansions again until on my way back from duty at approximately six fifteen A.M. I then observed that the same light was on, but I gave the matter no thought at the time.' ''

Mallett put down the statement with a sigh.

''What sort of a man is Denny?'' he asked.

''Very intelligent and observant,'' was the reply. ''One of the best uniformed men I have. And not too blooming educated, if you follow me.''

''Very well. We have it then on his evidence that Mrs. Wellman, or somebody else in the flat, extinguished the light at a little after nine o'clock, and that somebody turned it on again between ten thirty and six fifteen. I suppose Mrs. Wellman could turn it off and on herself, by the way?''

"Undoubtedly. It was a bedside lamp, and she had the full use of her arms.''

"Therefore,'' Mallett went on, "we are now driven to this—that Wellman killed his wife—if he killed her—after ten thirty, when he was last seen on the tram, and before midnight, which is the latest time which the doctor thinks reasonably possible. Then comes the blow. To test Wellman's story, for what it is worth, we have made enquiries in Hackney to see if we can find a hotel of the kind that wouldn't mind taking in a gentleman the worse for liquor, with a red and green carpet in the hall, and handy to the Number 31 tram route. And the very first place we try, we not only find that they remember Mr. Wellman there but are extremely anxious to see him again. They tell us that he came to their place about half past eleven—which is the time you would expect if he left the neighborhood of the Green Dragon by tram an hour before—persuaded whoever it was who was still up at that hour to give him a room, and next morning was seen going out at six o'clock remarking that he was going to get a shave. He never came back—''

"And he never got that shave,'' interjected the D.D.I.

"True enough. And when the hotel people opened his bag—which Police Constable Denny has identified, incidentally—it contained precisely nothing. So—''

"So we packed him off to the Hackney police to answer a charge of obtaining credit by fraud and asked the Yard to tell us what to do next.''

"In other words, you want me to fix this crime onto somebody who has to all appearances a perfect alibi for it.''

"That's just it,'' said the divisional inspector in all seriousness. "If only the blighter had had anything on him that could have been used as a weapon!''

" 'On Wellman,' '' said Mallett, reading from another sheet of the reports, " 'were found a pencil, a small piece of cork, a pocketknife, two shillings silver, and sixpence halfpenny bronze.' Why,'' he continued, "do we have to go on saying 'bronze' when all the rest of the world says 'copper,' by the way? But the weapon—he could have taken that away in his bag and disposed of it anywhere between here and Hackney easily enough. We shall be lucky if we ever lay our hands on that. The alibi is our trouble. From nine o'clock onwards it seems unbeatable. Therefore he must have killed his wife before nine. But if he did, who was it that turned the light off in her room? I suppose the dog might have done it—knocked the lamp over, or something?''

''There's no trace of the dog having been in the room all night,'' said the other. ''His footprints are quite plain on the carpet in the corridor, and I've been over the bedroom carpet carefully without any result. Also, there seems no doubt that the bedroom door was shut next morning. Wellman was heard to unlatch it. Besides, if the dog turned the light off, how did he turn it on again?''

Mallett considered.

''Have you tested the fuses?'' he asked.

''Yes, and they are in perfect order. There's no chance of a temporary fault causing the light to go off and on again. And Wellman was waiting for the light to go off when he was talking to Denny.''

''Then,'' said Mallett, ''we've got to work on the assumption that someone else got into the flat that night.''

''Without disturbing the dog?''

''A goodnatured dog,'' Mallett pointed out.

''But there are no signs of any entry whatever. I've looked myself, and some of my best men have been on the job.''

''But I haven't looked yet,'' said Mallett.

Number 32 Clarence Mansions was exactly like all the other flats in the block, and indeed in Imperial Avenue, so far as its internal arrangements were concerned. Three very small rooms, looking onto the avenue, opened out of the corridor which ran from the front door. Three still smaller rooms opened out of another corridor at right angles to the first, and enjoyed a view of the back of the Mansions in the next block. At the junction of the two corridors the gloom of the interior was mitigated by a skylight, the one privilege possessed by the top-story flats and denied to the rest of the block. The bedroom in which Mrs. Wellman had died was the room nearest the entrance.

Mallett did not go into this room until he had first carefully examined the door and the tiny hall immediately inside it.

"There are certainly no marks on the lock," he said at last. Then, looking at the floor, he asked, "What is this powdery stuff down here?"

"Dog biscuit," was the reply. "The animal seems to have had his supper here. There's his water bowl in the corner, too, by the umbrella stand."

"But he slept over *there*," said Mallett, nodding to the farther end of the corridor, where underneath the skylight was a large circular basket, lined with an old rug.

They went into the bedroom. The body had been removed, but otherwise nothing in it had been touched since the discovery of the tragedy. On its dingy walls hung photographs of acrobats, dancers, and clowns, and the framed program of a Command Variety performance—memorials of the trapeze artist's vanished career. The crumpled pillow bore a single shapeless stain of darkened blood. On a bedside table was a cheap electric lamp. Mallett snapped it on and off.

"That doesn't look as if it had been knocked over," he remarked. "Did you notice the scratches on the bottom panel of the door, by the way? It seems as though the dog had been trying to get in from the passage."

He went over to the sash window and subjected it to a prolonged scrutiny.

"No," he said. "Definitely, no. Now let's look at the rest of the place."

He walked down the corridor until he reached the skylight.

"I suppose somebody could have got through here," he observed.

"But he would have come down right on top of the dog," the D.D.I. objected.

"True. That would have been a bit of a strain for even the quietest animal. Still, there's no harm in looking."

He kicked aside the sleeping basket and stood immediately beneath the skylight.

"The light's in my eyes, and I can't see the underside of the frame properly," he complained, standing on tiptoe and peering upwards. "Just turn on the electric light, will you? I said, turn on the light," he repeated in a louder tone.

"It is on," was the reply, "but nothing's happened. The bulb must have gone."

"Has it?" said Mallett, stepping across to the hanging light that swung within a foot of his head. As he did so, the lamp came on.

"Curiouser and curiouser! Switch it off again. Now come and stand where I was."

They changed places, and Mallett depressed the switch. The light was turned on at once.

"Are you sure you're standing in the same place?"

"Quite sure."

"Then jump!"

"What?"

"Jump. As high as you can, and come down as hard as you can."

The inspector sprang into the air, and his heels hit the floor with a crash. At that instant, the light flickered, went out and then came on once more.

"Splendid!" said Mallett. "Now look between your feet. Do you see anything?"

"There's a little round hole in the floorboard here. That's all."

"Does the board seem at all loose to you?"

"Yes, it does. Quite a bit. But that's not surprising after what I've done to it."

"Let me see it."

Mallett went down on hands and knees and found the hole of which the other had spoken. It was quite small—hardly more than a fault in the wood, but its edges were sharp and clear. It was near to one end of the board. That end was completely unsecured, the other was lightly nailed down. He produced a knife and inserted the blade into the hole. Then, using his knife as a lever, he found that he could pull the board up on its end, as though upon a hinge.

"Look!" he said, and pointed down into the cavity beneath.

On the joist on which the loose end of the board had rested was a small, stiff, coiled spring, just large enough to keep that end a fraction above the level of the surrounding floor. But what chiefly attracted the attention of the two men was not on the joist itself but a few inches to one side. It was an ordinary electric bell-push, such as might be seen on any front door in Imperial Avenue.

"Do you recollect what Wellman's job was, when he had a job?" asked Mallett.

"He worked in the circus as odd-job man, and—good Lord, yes!—electrician."

"Just so. Now watch!"

He put his finger on the bell-push. The light above their heads went out. He released it, and the light came on again.

"Turn on another light," said Mallett. "Any light, I don't care which. In the sitting room, if you like. Now . . ." He depressed the button once more. "Does it work?"

"Yes."

"Of course it does," he cried triumphantly, rising to his feet and dusting the knees of his trousers. "The whole thing's too simple for words. The main electric lead of the flat runs under this floor. All Wellman has done is to fit a simple attachment to it, so that when the bell-push is pressed down the circuit is broken and the current turned off. The dog's basket was on this board. That meant that when the dog lay down, out went the light in the bedroom—and any other light that happened to be on, only he took care to see that there wasn't any other light on. When the dog begins to get restless in the morning and goes down the passage to see what's the matter— you said he was an intelligent dog, didn't you?—on comes the light again. And anybody in the street outside, seeing the lamp extinguished and lighted again, would be prepared to swear that there was somebody alive in the room to manipulate the lamp. Oh, it really is ingenious!"

"But—" the divisional inspector objected.

"Yes?"

"But the light didn't go off when I was standing there."

"How much do you weigh?"

"Eleven stone seven."

"And I'm—well, quite a bit more than that. That's why. You see, there's a fraction of space between the board and the bell-push, and you couldn't quite force the board far enough down to make it work, except when you jumped. I had the advantage over you there," he concluded modestly.

"But hang it all," protested the other, "I may not be a heavyweight, but I do weigh more than a dog. If I couldn't do the trick, how on earth could he? It doesn't make sense."

"On Wellman," said Mallett reflectively, "were found a pencil, a small piece of cork, a pocketknife, two shillings silver, and sixpence halfpenny bronze. Have you observed that the little hole in the board is directly above the button of the bell-push?''

''Yes. I see now that it is.''

''Very well. If the small piece of cork doesn't fit into that hole, I'll eat your station sergeant's helmet. That's all.''

''So that when the cork is in the hole—''

''When the hole is plugged, the end of the cork is resting on the bell-push. It then needs only the weight of the basket, plus the weight of the dog, to depress the spring, which keeps the end of the board up, and the cork automatically works the bell-push. Now we can see what happened. Wellman rigged up this contraption in advance—an easy matter for an experienced electrician. Then, on the evening which he had chosen for the crime, he put his wife to bed, killed her, with the coal hammer most probably—if you search the flat I expect you will find it missing—and shut the door of the bedroom, leaving the bedside lamp alight. He next inserted the cork in the hole of the board and replaced the dog's basket on top. With a couple of dog biscuits in his pocket, he then took the dog out for a run. He kept it out until he saw Police Constable Denny outside the flats. Probably he had informed himself of the times when the officer on duty could be expected to appear there, and made his arrangements accordingly. Having had a word with Denny, he slipped upstairs and let the dog into the flat. But before he came downstairs again he took care to give the dog his biscuits in the hall. It would never have done if the light had been put out before he was out of the building, and he left the dog something to keep him at the other end of the passage for a moment or two. He knew that the dog, as soon as he had eaten his supper and had a drink of water, would go and lie down in his basket. I expect he had been trained to do it. Alsatians are teachable animals, they tell me. Down in the street he waited until the dog had put the light out for him, and called Denny's attention to the fact. His alibi established, off he went. But he had to get back next morning to remove that bit of cork. Otherwise the next person who trod on the board might give his secret away. So we find that when he came to the flat the first thing he did was to go down the corridor—before ever he went into the bedroom. That little bit of evidence always puzzled me. Now we know what he was doing. He was a fool not to throw the cork away, of course, but I suppose he thought that nobody would think of looking at that particular place. So far as he knew, nothing could work the lights if the cork wasn't in place. He thought he was safe.

"And," Mallett concluded, "he would have been safe, too, if there hadn't been that little extra bit of weight put on the board. He couldn't be expected to foresee *me*."

Which explains, if it does not excuse, the slight but unmistakable touch of condescension with which Inspector Mallett thereafter used to treat his slimmer and slighter brethren.

≪ The Dog That Bit You ≫
by
Mary Kittredge

WATCHING THE CHAMPION dogs gait through their paces at Westminster, one is given no sense of the work it took getting them there. But dogs at the highest levels are a labor-intensive bunch, their basic maintenance being the least of one's troubles. After that come training, grooming, and showing, the exhaustion and expense of travel, and the strain of competition, as well as a degree of presence in the notoriously contentious community of professional dog enthusiasts, not every member of which is always pleasant, nor at all times even entirely sane.

The dogs themselves, by contrast, are undemanding and kind. It is in their nature to forgive. I sometimes think that's why I have devoted my life to them: In their eyes one so rarely encounters reproach. One can almost believe in the possibility of absolution. Under their unaccusing gaze, I live in the illusion, at least, of a state of grace; I can forget the guilt that gnaws me as if I were a bone.

It began on the day of the accident: I had finished early-morning kennel chores and was headed in the van to pick up a bag of wood shavings for the puppies' weaning pen, and after that to get some pellets of dog chow and cans of mixing meat, when the truck swerved out of the opposite lane straight at me. I had enough time to know that I was in trouble, but little more.

The impact, when it came, was a decisive thump that flung me forward into the seat-belt harness, punched my fist through the windshield, and sent metal dog crates crashing all over the cargo compartment. The steering column came up out of the floor to smack me once, hard, in the center of my chest, creating a small, bright explosion of pain.

Next came a period of tranquillity during which I sat peering through the starred windshield of the other vehicle. I was able to make out that its driver was a man, and that he had red hair; soon, though, I became distracted by the acrid smoke billowing from the van's engine area. The driver's-side door wouldn't open, and the far door was blocked by the demolished passenger seat; happily, there were no dogs riding in the van, but that still left me to be incinerated.

Unbuckling my seat belt, I began trying to escape. But the moment I moved, a giant reached down and chopped me viciously in the leg with an axe of pain, and when I looked to see why, I discovered that my ankle was dangling by a forlorn little strip of flesh no thicker than my index finger. Also, I was having trouble breathing.

A fellow in a yellow slicker approached the van's passenger side, carrying a sledgehammer. A shower of glittering glass was followed by a gratifying amount of cool, fresh air, and then by the fellow in the slicker.

He hauled the passenger seat out and came back for me. I remember trying to help him. I remember the look on his smooth young face as he realized: my foot was stuck beneath the brake pedal, trapping me. I remember his eyes, so full of sorrowing decision.

From somewhere in the engine compartment came an ominous crackling sound, as of oil being heated in a skillet. The fellow seized me and I remember screaming as he tore the remaining flesh from the ankle to free me.

But for the life of me, I don't remember the explosion.

Jerking awake, I swallowed the shriek that always came at the end of the terrible dream. Sweating and shaking, I sat in the darkness, listening to the rain drum the corrugated roofs of the dog runs just outside the window.

A cold, wet nose nudged my hand. At home, I would have invited the animal up onto the bed at once, but here the rules were different. "Shala," I whispered, "you belong out in the kitchen."

Her tail thumped entreatingly. I reminded myself that dog hairs, once having invaded the bed's woolen blanket, would be impossible to pick out. The comforter draped over the foot-board, however, posed no such difficulty, and when I had arranged it on the floor she stepped onto it delicately, sighing as she settled. I shoved a pillow in beside her, pulled the rest of the comforter over both of us, and closed my eyes.

This, as any trainer will tell you, is no way to treat an animal. A dog must see you as its leader, not its littermate, in order to obey. On the other hand, Shala was already doing what I wanted her to: breathing easily, smelling of warm, clean dog, her heart beating under my hand. When I woke again it was five A.M., she was gone, and the alarm clock was buzzing steadily at me.

"*Good* morning," Holly Freeman chirped brightly as I trudged into her kitchen and poured myself some strong black coffee.

Holly sat in her wheelchair, drinking a glass of grapefruit juice and frowning at the day's boarder-dog schedule, her leg, in its cast, sticking out of her flannel nightshirt like a big, white log. Two weeks earlier, Holly had been on an outing at the seashore, balancing on some rocks, when a big wave knocked her into a tide pool; en route, her leg met violently with the rocks. Since then her friends had been helping her run a busy boarding kennel, care for her own twelve purebred Labrador retrievers, and raise ten black pups whose bloodlines would put the Windsors to shame.

Allowing myself another hasty gulp of coffee, I lined a dozen dog dishes on the counter and began measuring kibble into them, adding brewer's yeast, vitamins, and other supplements as directed by the list Holly had posted on the refrigerator. Some dogs got cottage cheese, too, and others got mixing meat; luckily the dishes had the dogs' names printed on them so I could keep it fairly straight. As I worked, dogs began gathering around me, jostling me and one another in their anxiety to eat, *eat*, EAT.

Finishing in an instant, they charged in a pack for the back door, which led to a roofed, enclosed concrete run. Following, I waded in among them to the chain-link gate. Beyond, a quarter of an acre of similarly fenced flat-packed earth was muddy with the recent downpours; I let the dogs out into it.

In one corner of the yard gaped an enormous hole where Holly's friend Peter Wilson, another local dog breeder, had nearly finished installing a new dry well; it wasn't strictly legal, but Holly only meant to run washing-machine water into it. Raising and boarding dogs generates a lot of laundry, and she didn't want to overload the septic system on her quasi-suburban property. Remembering that the kennel helper, Kelley Greene, would also be here all day, I made a mental note to try to keep her and Peter out of one another's way; the two had recently broken off a romance—or rather, Peter had broken it off—and the last thing I needed was any sort of dust-up between the two of them.

"Four arrivals and two departures today," Holly announced as I came back into the kitchen. "At least the boarding business hasn't gone to hell along with the rest of my so-called life, but it's going to be another busy morning."

Despite her bum leg, in the few minutes I'd been gone she had managed to get out boxes of cereal, milk, and bread for toast, and was now balancing dangerously but determinedly on her wooden crutches as she tried to remove the eggs from the refrigerator. I scooped up the egg carton, slid it onto the counter beside the stove, and began grabbing dog dishes off the floor before she could accidentally put a crutch tip into one of them.

"You know," I told her, stuffing an empty milk carton into one of the empty kibble bags Holly used for trash receptacles, "it would be more efficient if I just took a hammer and broke the other leg for you, since that's obviously what you're trying to accomplish."

"Oh, all right." She sank back into the chair. "I just hate not being able to do anything, is all."

"I know. It won't last forever." I pulled the trash-filled kibble bag from the garbage can and put another empty bag into the can. There were only two more empty bags available, a sign that Holly needed to order more dog food; somehow, she had balanced her domestic ecology so that her household trash output just about equaled her dogs' kibble input.

Making a note of this on Holly's "To Do" list, I began washing dog dishes assembly-line style, then started preparing the pups' breakfast of ground kibble and warm water, mixed to the consistency of thin gruel. "After all, look at me," I said. "A year ago I wasn't expected to live, and all I got was a stiff leg out of it."

Holly sighed, brushing back her thick red hair. She was fifty, but you'd never have known it to look at her. Some women wait for beauty until they get older, and she was one of them.

"Does it still hurt?" She eyed my ankle, thickly encased in a woolen sock.

Miraculously, the blast had thrown the severed foot clear; it and I had been rushed to the hospital in separate ambulances, and later the foot and I were reunited.

"Sometimes it aches a little," I admitted. The bones never healed right, and eventually I'd had the whole thing fused with enough steel to reinforce a bridge abutment. It didn't move at all, and it throbbed wickedly in rainy weather or when I tried to walk too far, but I was not about to tell Holly that. She felt bad enough already having to ask people to do things for her.

"Anyway," she said, "I really appreciate your help, Rita. I don't know what I would do without you."

I picked up the gruel bowl and a dish containing breakfast for the mother dog. Her meal included a chunk of raw beef, a mound of cottage cheese, canned chicken, and so many vitamins and minerals that we'd dubbed the mixture "atomic dog food."

"You'd just have to ask one of your dozens of other devoted friends to come around," I told Holly. "Do me a favor and sit while I'm gone, please. I'm at your service, but I'm an animal specialist, not an orthopedic surgeon, all right?"

She agreed, and I didn't believe her, but I had no choice; the puppies were hungry. I carried the food out to the puppy palace, a very nice little pre-fab metal building with its own gas heater, running water, and storage for kennel supplies: wood chips, baled straw, bags of dog chow, and all kinds of training equipment from show leads to traffic cones for heeling in figure-eight patterns. One wall was covered with plaques, ribbons, and rosettes from the competitions Holly's dogs had won. Most of the prizes had been awarded to a dog she had co-owned with Peter Wilson. Named AKC Champion Famous Acre's Black-Hearted Pirate, and called "Blackie" for short, he was the only U.S. dual champion in decades, and had sired up-and-coming contenders, too.

Which meant that Blackie had looked gorgeous in a show ring, but at field trials he'd retrieved shot birds out of difficult and confusing terrain like some magical beast, and if you think this combination is easy to achieve in a breeding program, I can only invite you to try it; it is about as likely as winning the Irish Sweepstakes, only a good deal more work.

The puppies shoved their faces into the gruel bowl while their mother inhaled her breakfast and agitated to be let out. She was a grey-muzzled old bitch, sagging from her final stint at puppy production, but with a beautifully shaped head, kind eyes, and a sweet, biddable temperament.

"Go on, Bumbles," I told her, letting her out with the yard dogs. "You've earned a little relaxation."

As the animal trotted off, Kelley Greene's old white pickup truck rattled up the driveway and slammed to a halt, and the young woman swung out in a towering temper.

"Damn that man," she exclaimed, stomping up the steps to the back door. "It's like trying to talk to a stone."

"Albert Russell," I guessed, following Kelley inside. The kitchen was fragrant with the smells of bacon and eggs, toast, and a pot of fresh coffee, all keeping warm on a hot tray; from her wheelchair, Holly blinked innocently and lit up a forbidden cigarette as I filled my plate.

"Yes, damnit, Albert Russell," Kelley fumed, pouring herself a mug of coffee. Kelley was tall, fair, and athletically built, with a thick braid of flaxen hair like a crown on her perfectly proportioned head. As tall as most men, even in jeans, boots, and a flannel shirt, she looked so much like a Valkyrie that when she was angry, I almost expected thunderbolts to fly out of her fingertips.

"How do you people put up with Albert?" she went on. "He's like some evil force. Of course, he isn't as mean to you as he is to me. I'm just a lowly kennel helper."

Holly and I glanced at one another. Blackie had died a year earlier at a local dog club meet when someone had tossed a poisoned tidbit into his exercise pen. Nobody had actually seen Albert do it, but with Blackie out of the way Albert's dogs began winning honors they hadn't had a shot at before, and rumors about the incident had flown thick and fast. But Kelley had been in the middle of a meanly contested divorce then, and hadn't been paying attention to dog-club gossip.

"I told him," Kelley said agitatedly, "I'd take that old dog Beau off his hands so he wouldn't have to have him put down.

I just love that dog. But Albert said he'd still feel too much responsibility. Can you believe it? Responsibility! The man doesn't know what the word means.''

She slammed her mug into the sink. ''Anyway, I've got to get started. Rita, can you call the house dogs inside? I'll pick up the yard and let the boarder dogs out as soon as I've fed them.''

''Picking up the yard'' was Kelley's euphemism for scooping you-know-what, a chore that got done twice a day around here and one I'd have expected her to dislike. But Kelley said she'd taken so much you-know-what from her ex-husband, she could get a job sweeping up after elephants in a circus and still feel that the you-know-what level in her life had substantially decreased.

Also, she was very efficient at it, which gave me about ten minutes to get the dog room vacuumed, the water bowls freshened, the sleeping crates swept out, and clean newspaper placed for the younger animals, some of whom didn't have their bathroom habits down pat yet; once Holly's dogs were in, I would have time to get the kitchen floor mopped. In an hour, boarder dogs would begin arriving and leaving, and by then the place had to look shipshape enough to make the animals' owners feel comfortable about leaving them, which to Holly meant so clean that a brain specialist would feel right at home doing neurosurgery on one of the grooming tables.

The rest of the morning flew by: The dishes got done, the puppies got their kennel cough inoculations, and Holly managed to get herself into the shower with only a little assistance from me; a plastic lawn chair and a hand-held shower nozzle preserved her from that dreaded indignity, the bed-bath. And by ten o'clock, the new boarders were checked into the boarding kennel: Yogi was a gentle, intelligent mastiff who stepped into his enclosure quietly; inside, he accepted a dog biscuit and lay down to munch thoughtfully on it. Jiff and Tuffy were Jack Russell terriers, bouncy and resilient as a pair of bright rubber balls; they thought kenneling was an adventure devised specifically for their amusement. Only Mitzi, the cocker spaniel, showed surliness, a result of being awfully spoiled. Her idea of a good time was piddling on a rug, and everyone disliked her, or everyone except Kelley, who at the first snotty growl out of Mitzi's throat seized Mitzi by her silky scruff and shook her assertively.

"Bad dog. No growl." Snapping a lead onto Mitzi's collar, Kelley popped the dog smartly into heel position, whereupon the animal's snarl faded to a look of relief, and she sat happily.

"She doesn't like having to be the boss," Kelley explained to Mitzi's startled owner, a fortyish businessman with thinning blond hair and a worried expression. "She just feels it's her job to try."

Somebody's got to, Kelley's own expression added, but she did not say it; the poor guy was clueless.

"Y-yes. Well," he ventured, "it's nice to see that someone can control her. I must confess, she's quite a handful when she is at home with me. Barking, chewing things up, and so on."

"Control her, my Aunt Fanny," Kelley said when he had gone. "What does he think she is, a Bengal tiger? I think I'm going to bring old Mitzi, here, to obedience class with me this afternoon. That's what she needs."

Mitzi's eyes grew round as a bulldog's and her ears perked up alertly; if she could, she'd have uttered the word *Yikes!* But she couldn't, so Kelley led her away to the kennel area, and not a moment too soon, as just then the shower in Holly's bathroom hissed off, Peter Wilson's truck rumbled up the driveway, and the telephone in the kennel office began ringing again.

It took me eight years to become a veterinarian, and two more to discover that I'd made a mistake. I liked the animals all right; it was people who got under my skin, treating their pets as if they were humans in fur suits and then wondering why the animals didn't respond the way they wanted them to. Soon after the accident, I retired, having built up my practice and sold it for a tidy sum; I wasn't rich, but with that and the insurance settlement from the driver of the truck that hit me, I wasn't going to be poor any time soon, either.

Which was why, when Holly had her accident, I was there to help with the chores, one of which was overseeing Kelley Greene's first time at teaching afternoon obedience classes.

"Keep moving!" Kelley called to the frightened-looking beginners grimly parading their dogs around the perimeter of the training hall. "Loose lead, everyone; remember that nobody likes to be dragged, and above all, keep the dog's attention!"

"She treats them," said a gravelly voice from behind me, "like utter morons. Which I suppose is what they are, but it's so annoying to have to listen to it."

"Why do you, then?" I inquired. Albert Russell was a tiny, delicately built man in his early thirties, only five feet tall or so and weighing perhaps a hundred pounds. With his short cap of very pale hair and his small, manicured hands like the well-kept paws of some fastidious rodent, he did not look likely to provoke much else but astonishment at his diminutive stature. But Albert's fragile appearance was deceiving: He had an ego like a mountain and the social graces of an avalanche to go with it.

"That's one of Beau's puppies," he replied, pointing at a yellow six-monthster. Albert's kennel churned out Labrador puppies like a factory; he'd kept poor old Beau at stud until the animal's hips got so bad he could barely walk, much less carry on a doggy romance. Meanwhile, of course, Albert felt free to criticize everyone else's breedings to anyone who would listen.

"I told the pup's new owner I'd have a look at the class," he said, "to make sure Kelley stays on track."

And, of course, to squelch any confidence the pup's owner might be developing in Kelley, who from what I could see was a talented teacher with plenty of enthusiasm and a sincere love for the dogs, not to mention patience with the human students. But that was Albert: Cutting other people down apparently made him feel bigger. It was a common fault in humans of any size, but one Albert had raised to the level of an art form.

"About turn!" Kelley called, and most of the owners and dogs reversed and headed in the opposite direction, all except for one poor unhappy human being and his confused samoyed, both of whom dropped out of the parade to watch.

"No, no," Albert shouted, though he had no business interfering. "Don't quit now. Your dog will lose confidence in you if you do."

The man reddened, but otherwise acted as if he hadn't heard. Kelley, too, ignored Albert's astonishing rudeness, while I tried to think of something, anything, that would shut Albert up; it was the man who was in danger of losing his confidence, not the dog. But the only way of silencing Albert involved a great big cork, and unfortunately I didn't have one.

Luckily, another situation distracted him: Outside, Peter Wilson's backhoe roared as he finished up the dry-well hole. Next he would lay pipe and place a catchment basin, and tomorrow fill the hole in with gravel and cover it.

"Poor Peter," Albert said with barely disguised relish. "He was absolutely broken-hearted over Kelley, you know. Personally, I don't see the attraction. But I felt terrible about having to tell him."

"Tell him what?" On the training floor, Kelley had coaxed the samoyed and its owner back into the group and was showing them all how to practice proofing the sit-stay, using a little mechanical animal. The dogs sat, the owners commanded them to stay, and the toy was set loose to skitter across the floor. The idea was to tempt the dog to break the stay, correcting if it did and praising if it didn't.

"Why, what would happen if he married her, of course," Albert said. "He did have a right to know, and it was obvious she wasn't going to tell him."

Most of the dogs in the class tried to chase the small, battery-powered creature, which clapped a pair of tiny cymbals together as it jittered along on fuzzy pink legs. Another toy, also equipped with cymbals but rolling on wheels, scooted in from the opposite corner of the training floor, pulled along by a length of yellow twine that Kelley tugged at strategic intervals, trying to get the dogs to disobey their owners' commands. This gave Kelley the chance to demonstrate humane corrections, which she proceeded to do.

Slowly, I turned to regard Albert, whose face with its long, thin nose, bright eyes, and narrow lips over small, closely spaced teeth resembled that of an inbred collie.

"A humane correction," Kelley Greene told her students, "is strong, fair, and understandable. It lets the dog know *that* he has done something wrong, and *what* he has done wrong. It is not administered so long after the fact that the dog can't understand why he is being corrected; it is administered *at the time*."

"I don't understand," I told Albert. "What *would* happen

if Peter married Kelley? And how would you know anything about it?''

Albert smiled, looking as wise as he could; the collie he resembled had an overbite. In my opinion it also had a case of distemper that required immediate quarantine—or, under ideal circumstances, euthanasia. But that was another story, at least for the moment.

"I have my ways," he said. "And what would happen is, her alimony would stop. Poor child, she must have been wild to get rid of him. Her ex-husband, I mean. You see," Albert told me, speaking slowly and clearly as if I were the child, "her alimony ends if she marries again. She would be, in a word, penniless.''

Outside, Peter Wilson worked his backhoe. He wasn't exactly penniless, but he didn't have many more than two of them to rub together, and I knew his kennel was in financial trouble. I wondered if he'd told Kelley the real reason he'd broken up with her, or trumped up some lie guaranteed to be even more wounding.

"Is that legal?" Kelley's alimony agreement, if Albert's account was true, sounded like something out of the Dark Ages, although almost everything about marriage sounds like something out of the Dark Ages to me.

"It is if you sign it," Albert informed me sweetly. "It is if you're desperate enough, or foolish enough, to sign it."

"Okay, everybody, that's it for today," Kelley called. "All of you have done very well, and I'll see you next week. Practice those recalls, and remember, no unearned biscuits!''

There was a spattering of applause, and the human students began struggling to lead the pulling, panting canines out of the arena in at least some semblance of good order. It's not so much obedience training itself that defeats a lot of dog owners; it's getting the animal in and out of class, an embarrassing, highly discouraging project for many of them until the dog "gets it." "You mean I have to obey here, too?" you can practically hear the animal asking, and sometimes it takes awhile for the human being to answer the question clearly enough.

Albert hurried to catch up with his puppy owner, no doubt so he could rip the daylights out of everything Kelley had done and said in the previous hour, and when Kelley saw Albert she strode after him, probably to try to argue with him about Beau some more. I could have told her it was useless; Kelley loved the old Labrador retriever, but he was definitely past his prime, and when Albert wanted an animal put down, the animal got put down.

Kelley wouldn't have listened to me about that, though, and anyway I didn't get a chance to say anything to her, because when Peter spotted Albert across the yard, he yanked the hand brake on the backhoe and jumped down with fire in his eye.

"I saw what you did, Albert," he shouted as he approached, stepping rudely in front of Kelley. Peter was dark-haired, hot-tempered, and more than a little impulsive, but he was a fervent dog enthusiast and a good fellow at heart, or so I'd thought until now. At least he'd always seemed willing to help when someone needed him, as Holly did at the moment.

"I saw what you did to that animal!" he shouted. "Did you think I'd just turn a blind eye?" he raged at Albert.

"Peter Wilson, have you lost your mind? What in the world are you yelling about now?" Albert put on his battle face: that of the reasonable victim, mildly querying the (again) irrational attacker.

"I am talking," Peter grated as the departing students glanced back curiously, "about beating a dog. Hitting it with a stick, Albert, to punish it, until it howled and lay down. I'm talking about the field trial training yesterday when your Maxie went after the wrong bird, and you know it, too."

"Oh, really." Albert rolled his eyes. The dog club put on training trials so members could practice for the real events, where dogs would compete for hunting titles; being title-hungry, Albert never missed one of these training sessions. "And why, if I was being so cruel to a dog, have you waited until now to scold me about it?"

I glanced at Kelley, whose tipped head expressed curiosity and suspicion. Albert's words sounded confident but his voice sounded nervous, and I thought Kelley heard it also. This wasn't the first time someone had confronted Albert about hitting a dog; as with the poisoning of Blackie, though, no one had been able to prove anything.

"Because you hustled the dog into your van and drove away before I could knock your block off, that's why," Peter Wilson retorted. "And you hung up on me, last night *and* this morning, when I called. Damnit, it wasn't even a correction, you just got mad at the mistake and took it out on the dog, didn't you? Isn't that what you did?''

''Peter,'' Albert said in a tone that made me want to do more than knock his block off; it was the tone of someone who is going to get away with something, if only he can brazen it out. And Albert was an expert at brazening things out. ''Peter, you've been smoking those funny cigarettes again, haven't you? You ought to stop; after all,'' he went on in a voice loud enough to be heard by all, ''you've already been to jail once. I should think that would have been enough. And aside from what the stuff does to your memory, a man with a felony conviction can't be too careful, now, can he?''

''You're the one who'd just better be careful, Albert! You'd better watch your step!''

With a few words, Albert had reduced Peter to idiot rage; it was Albert's own very special talent. Getting into his van, he drove out of the yard as Peter went on bellowing.

''. . . next time I see you,'' he shouted, ''I *will* knock your block off! I'll bash your skull in, Albert!''

And that was how, in front of many witnesses, Peter Wilson threatened to kill Albert Russell, not that anyone really thought of it exactly that way until about sixteen hours later.

Scratch a woman who loves dogs, somebody clever once said, and you'll find a woman who's been disappointed by a man. It was true of Kelley Greene for the rest of the afternoon after the obedience class; seeing Peter lose control of himself the way he had, even if it was in defense of an animal, didn't do anything to raise her opinion of him. Instead, it rubbed her nose once more in the realization that he wasn't the man she'd thought he was.

For the remainder of the day, she hurled herself into her work, taking each boarder dog out for an extra run, giving all the grooming equipment a more-than-thorough cleaning, wiping the whelping box down with disinfectant and disassembling it to stow in the rafters of the puppy palace. Holly had asked her to come back and stay overnight, to give me a break from the early-morning routines, but when Kelley's old white pickup rattled down the driveway that afternoon, I almost wished she wouldn't return at all; her intense unhappiness gave me a headache.

Peter, meanwhile, dug that dry-well hole like a demon; the gravel around the catchment receptacle needed to settle, he said, but otherwise it was ready to be finished in the morning, and covered with topsoil. He took off soon after Kelley, turning down my offer of a cup of coffee and refusing to meet my eyes until the last minute.

"I was telling the truth, you know," he blurted then. "Albert beat that dog. He shouldn't be allowed around animals. If he could do it once, he'll do it again."

"Lodge a complaint with the club," I suggested. "Bring him up on charges."

The dog club dealt harshly with anyone who abused an animal: fines, expulsion, even permanent banishment from competition, a punishment that would cut the heart out of the ribbon-coveting Albert Russell.

But Peter just shook his head. "My word against his. He wouldn't even get a slap on the wrist." His gaze darkened. "And he deserves *much* worse than that."

Peter was right; it was why no charge had ever been lodged against Albert. To make it stick, you needed more than a story; you needed testimony from someone without an axe to grind. And Peter definitely had one of those.

"Peter . . ." I hesitated; it was none of my business. But I had always liked Peter so much, I just couldn't believe that what Albert had said about him and Kelley was true.

So I asked him. "Albert told me you broke up with Kelley when you found out she'd lose her alimony if she married again," I said. "And forgive me, but I . . ."

For a moment, I thought Peter was going to hit me. "Oh, he said that, did he? I suppose he gave you the lowdown on my big drug conviction, too, didn't he? Told you all about what a rotten louse I am, ruined what little reputation I've got left? Damn the man; *damn* him."

He swung away from me, so blind with anger I was afraid to let him get in his truck. "No, Peter, wait. It doesn't matter; I only wanted to . . ."

To what? I asked myself, later. To stir the you-know-what? But the damage was done; he slammed the truck grindingly into reverse and screeched backwards, nearly slamming into the row of trees that stood like the crosspiece of a capital T at the top of the driveway, parallel to the back of the house. Then he sped away who knew where to do who knew what. All I knew was, it wasn't going to be good.

A few minutes later Albert called, sweet as pie, wanting to know if I could come over and give Beau his final shot. He was, Albert said, a good boy but he was in chronic pain, and Albert knew I would make the dog's death easy.

Which was a crock. Beau had outlived his usefulness, first achieving his titles, then becoming an important stud dog whose progeny had put Albert's kennel on the map. But now, although Beau's hips had always cleared x-ray easily—hip x-rays are the main way of ensuring that a dog does not have hereditary hip disease, a major problem among purebred animals—his hips were breaking down.

I thought that with steroids and painkillers, Beau could have another few decent years of life, but it was not my decision to make. Handing the dog over to Kelley was also a reasonable plan. She could provide a fine retirement home for him, and I knew she adored the animal. But Albert was adamant. Beau had lived with Albert, and would die with him; it was Albert's duty to the dog.

Maybe so, but it was also a way of getting Beau out of the picture before his hip troubles became common knowledge and damaged Albert's reputation as a breeder. I'd done Beau's x-rays myself and cleared the resulting films, but not everyone was going to believe that; the dog world was rife with instances of fraud and trickery.

Reluctantly, I told Albert I would give him a call in a few days to set up an appointment for my visit. I wasn't looking forward to it, but on one count Albert was correct: I would make it easy for the dog. I'd made a point of learning to do animal euthanasia in the kindest, most caring manner possible; if there was a canine heaven, Beau would be in it without even noticing that anything unusual was going on.

Just before dinner, Kelley returned with some eighty-pound bags of kibble that Holly had sent her for. Watching out the kitchen window, I observed her hefting the first of them easily from the bed of the pickup and carrying it into the puppy palace. She looked happier than she had, confirming my opinion of the effectiveness of hard physical work as an emotional painkiller. But when she came in, I knew something else must have happened. No amount of work could have put that look of triumphant elation on her face.

"Albert changed his mind!" she practically sang as she stowed two empty kibble bags alongside the trash can. "I just saw him, and he's going to let me have Beau!"

"But . . ." I turned from the stove, puzzled.

"I know, he wanted you to put him down. He told me all about it when I stopped at his place a little while ago. But I talked him out of it!"

"With what, a tire iron?" Holly inquired, rolling her wheelchair into the kitchen doorway. "Albert takes suggestions about as gracefully as a beagle takes housebreaking."

"Well," Kelley admitted, "I didn't exactly talk him out of it. I made a deal with him. I offered to work for free for him next fall when he goes on the show circuit."

I felt my eyebrows rising nearly to my hairline. It was obvious why Albert would accept the offer; going on a show tour was an enormous amount of work, what with transporting the dogs, grooming and caring for them on-site, and keeping straight all the administrative details. What I couldn't see was why Kelley would agree to do it, the more so with the dreadful Albert.

"I know," Kelley said. "You think I hate him, especially since he told Peter how broke I'll be if I get married again. But better I should find out now what a jerk Peter is than later."

Her face grew stubborn. "And I want that dog. He deserves more than the life he's had. And if this is what I have to do to get him, I'll do it, and that's that."

"Well, more power to you, then," said Holly. "Personally, I think a trip to the mailbox with Albert is all the aggravation I could take, but I guess if things get awful, you can always keep that tire iron handy."

I found Holly's remark amusing; I'd often thought Albert needed a smack on the head.

But it wasn't so funny the next morning.

The rain had ended, but all that night the wind thumped and rattled in the roofs of the dog runs outside my window. I tossed and twisted, waking enough to know what time it was, then sinking to sleep again, over and over, my dreams full of the accident, as always. And of what came after.

I lied about not remembering the explosion. I remember it in nightmares: the astonishing sense of being lifted, captured and carried along on a hot, mushrooming burst of air. Something red and yellow whirling alongside me, bright as a child's pinwheel. Then the treacherous air flinging me to earth, slamming what remained of my breath out of me.

I remember the fellow in the yellow slicker, slamming down beside me. Behind us, the van burned hotly. Bits of glass and pieces of metal rained down. The fellow in the slicker didn't move, and when I dragged myself nearer to see why, I saw that a chunk of the van's windshield had taken most of his throat out, releasing a fist-sized gout of blood that flattened and slowed to a dribble, even as I watched.

If I'd taken another route, if I'd left five minutes earlier or later, if I hadn't been hypnotized in the final instant by the sight of the truck arrowing at me like some huge, malignant insect, then he might still have been alive.

Or if I hadn't been drunk. Not falling-down loaded; just moderately anesthetized by a couple of morning belts against the miseries of the coming day: being lonely, disliking my work, all those things. And of course I'd had a hangover, and a hair of the dog always helped, or so I thought then. But by the time the ER people tested my blood alcohol, which they do for all road trauma victims, I'd had so many transfusions that I was stone cold sober, so nobody ever knew.

They found my severed foot near the fellow's right hand. He'd gone back for it in case it could be reattached, as of course it later was.

I woke as if rising up from a drowning episode, wishing for Shala to come in and keep me forbidden company. The clock said 3:30 A.M. Outside, the wind had picked up again, flapping a loose tarp over some lumber Holly had stacked behind the puppy palace and whistling in the chain-link fence. From somewhere else came a rhythmic clinking, tinny and faint; a moment later the dogs began barking, raising an unholy ruckus as if all the burglars in the world were trying to get in.

I was halfway out of bed when everything stopped: The wind died, the odd clinking faded—if indeed it had ever been there; the sound might have been one of the metal gate latches tapping a fence support—and the dogs, grumbling, resettled themselves. I lay back and stared at the ceiling, praying for daylight and the salve of work, the simple forgiveness of dumb animals.

When I opened my eyes again it was seven o'clock, and Kelley Greene had just found Albert Russell lying atop the catchment receptacle out in Peter Wilson's nearly completed dry-well hole.

"The dogs barked," I said. "At three-thirty this morning. We all heard them." Kelley and Holly nodded.

"Anything else?" The police detective looked at all of us, gathered in the kitchen.

"No," I said. "Just the wind rattling things around. But these dogs don't bark at just anything. Not at any of us, for example; only strangers. You, for instance; you must have heard them when you came up the driveway."

It was true; Holly's property felt isolated, being set far back from the road, but she did have neighbors, and keeping a lot of barking dogs on the place would have been a quick way to get her kennel license revoked. The boarder dogs, because they were exercised individually, simply tended not to bark much, and the house dogs got a shot with a high-powered water pistol whenever they flapped their yaps without good reason.

The police detective nodded, turning to Holly. "What about a Mr. Peter Wilson? I understand he's been doing some work for you. Do the dogs bark when he comes around?"

"Yes, but listen," I put in, "Peter didn't mean what he said to Albert yesterday. He got Peter annoyed—Albert was good at that—and Peter popped off at him, but . . ."

The detective frowned. "Seems that in addition to Wilson's other grudges against Russell—something about a poisoned dog and alleged abuse of another one?—Mr. Russell had been talking to some bank managers about Mr. Wilson. Let them know Wilson wasn't going to be getting some windfall he'd been counting on."

"Oh my god," Kelley said softly, looking horrified.

The detective nodded. "So they'd decided to foreclose on him instead of waiting longer for the money he'd been promising them. Seems that when Mr. Wilson gave up the dope trade, he lost a major portion of his income. And doing favors for people," the detective concluded, "doesn't pay the rent."

One of the ambulance guys peered in the door. "All done out here." They'd loaded Albert's body after officers had combed the area around the dry well for anything that might be evidence. In particular, they were looking for Albert's keys, which so far hadn't turned up.

"Okay," the detective told the ambulance guy, "thanks. I'll just be another minute." He closed his notebook.

"So the upshot is," he said to the rest of us—me, Holly, and Kelley, plus an assortment of dogs who wandered into the kitchen, nosed at the detective, and wandered out again, "the upshot is, Mr. Wilson was angry at Mr. Russell, with fair reason. He threatened Russell yesterday, in front of a number of witnesses."

"Yes," I put in again, "but that doesn't mean—"

"And," the detective added significantly, "Wilson's truck was seen leaving Mr. Russell's property yesterday evening, after Miss Greene here had visited Mr. Russell. No one was seen going in or out after that."

"But if Albert was alive when Peter left, then Peter couldn't have—"

"Wilson didn't say Russell was alive when he left." The detective was swarthy and rumpled, wearing a wrinkled shirt and a loose, stained tie that suggested he'd been watching a few too many *Columbo* episodes. On the other hand, he'd absorbed the greetings of a dozen dogs with equanimity, so I couldn't dislike him too much. I disliked what he said next, though.

"Mr. Wilson says Mr. Russell's house was shut up, that the dogs were in their kennels and the doors were locked, but the van was parked in the carport. Not a light on anywhere, Wilson says."

"Somebody might have picked Albert up," said Holly. "If he'd been going out for the evening with someone else."

"Maybe," responded the detective. "But nobody did. At least, not anybody we've been able to talk to. And it seems to me if that's what happened, Mr. Russell would have left a light on so he could see to get in when he got back. And he'd have taken his keys with him. Only, it seems like he didn't."

The implication was clear: Peter had been lying. Albert had been home when Peter stopped by the house, and Peter had killed Albert, then closed the place up to make it look as if Albert had gone out on his own. Sneaking up here to put Albert's body in the dry well would have been a clever move—Peter had, after all, been planning to fill that dry well first thing today—except that while Kelley had been out picking up the yard this morning, she had glimpsed something like a dead squirrel or a raccoon caught in the corner of the chain-link fence near the dry-well hole.

And since the last thing a purebred dog should be eating is the carcass of a dead, possibly even rabid wild animal, she had gone to investigate, discovering Albert's body in the process.

"Have you . . . have you arrested Peter?" Kelley ventured.

The detective looked satisfied. "Read him his rights and sent him downtown for booking. You ladies want to take my advice, you'll get somebody else to fill that dry well in for you. In my opinion, your friend won't be back for quite some time."

And that, it appeared unhappily, was that: Peter had bashed Albert's head in, just as he'd threatened, and now Peter was in jail. And that was where matters would have stayed, were it not for the vagaries of the canine digestive system, in particular the reliable, generally predictable food-processing apparatus of the Labrador retriever.

"Hello," I said irritably into the telephone when it rang a little while after the detective had left. Then I listened with interest for a moment. It was Albert's kennel helper, a stolid, unimaginative young man whom I'd met on several uninspiring occasions, whose major virtue seemed to be that he worked cheaply. Now, though, I wasn't so sure of that, as he described what he had observed in Albert's kennel yard that morning.

"So," the kennel helper concluded, "I thought I'd, like, call you. 'Cause I thought maybe you'd, like, come over here. Like, to see what's going on with them."

Based on what he'd told me, I thought going over there was a very good idea, indeed. So I, like, did.

I once had a Labrador who ate a whole bucket full of bait fish. The only untoward consequence was a cut on his rear end from a swat with the fisherman's cane pole. On the other hand, I have seen Labradors roll over and perform the death scene from *Cleopatra*—not dying, but giving a damned good imitation of it—on account of a minor change in their kibble:

from eighteen to twenty percent fat, say, or from four to five percent fiber.

I didn't know what to think when I saw Albert's dog yard, though. Picking up wasn't going to take care of it, that was for sure. What it needed, actually, was a fire hose; these dogs' guts really didn't like something they had been eating recently.

"I put 'em in separate enclosures," the kennel kid told me when I had finished inspecting the revolting situation. He'd limped over quickly when he saw me arrive, not in pain but as if one of his legs was shorter than the other, and slightly twisted.

Typical Albert. He'd be quick to hire the handicapped if it meant he could pay less in wages, which from the look on this kid's face, I was willing to bet it had: not shifty, but as if he didn't think much of himself and didn't expect anyone else to, either.

"Like, if it's only some of 'em sick, we can know which ones, that way," he explained.

"Good thinking. Have you fed them?"

He nodded. "Half rations. The food's in a bin in the kitchen. I smelled it and it, like, seemed okay. Not rancid or anything."

The dogs themselves moved around their enclosures cheerfully enough. You can pretty much tell by the look on a Labrador's face whether it feels icky or not, and these didn't; even old Beau, a big handsome chocolate guy with none of the pale eye or snipy muzzle that mars so many chocolate Labs, was chipper if a bit stiff. My opinion of the kid went up another notch.

"Okay. Maybe I'll have a look at that food myself, though. I guess you can finish cleaning up the yard."

"Yeah." He hoisted his shovel and bucket.

Inside I found the dog-food bin, a wide, shallow wooden receptacle that held nearly two eighty-pound bags' worth; Albert bred dogs in a big way, with about twenty adult animals on the premises, and they ate a lot of food. The bins' contents smelled sweet and fresh, just as the kid had said, and I saw no sign of infestation in it. I did see, though, why the dogs had gotten tummy upsets: The food in the bin was not Albert's usual brand.

Rolling up my sleeve, I plunged my hand to the bottom of the bin and grabbed a handful from down there. Withdrawing the sample, I discovered that the food at the bottom of the bin *was* Albert's usual kind of kibble.

Which meant that sometime recently the bin had been almost empty and someone had filled it with nearly two bags of the wrong brand of dog food: the brand Holly used, to be precise. And based on what I'd seen outside, I had a feeling that whatever wouldn't fit into the bin had gone instead into the dogs, a Labrador retriever being the world's most efficient disposer of anything even remotely edible, whether it is its usual food or not.

I headed for the door, then changed my mind and took a stroll through the house. There was just the chance that I was wrong, and something poisonous had been left around for the dogs to get into.

Nothing had, though. Like most dog enthusiasts, Albert had been a stickler for cleanliness and order; like many of them, too, he'd had a fair amount of disposable income. The place was beautifully done in Early American antiques, each piece polished and without a speck of dust; the floors glimmered, the windows gleamed, and the air smelled of soapsuds and lemon Pledge.

In the pine-paneled office stood a desk, a chair, and a file cabinet. On the desk lay several checks, signed by Albert and clipped to the bills they were meant to pay, all ready to be put into their envelopes. The walls were covered with ribbons, rosettes, and photographs of Albert at various dog shows, posing with his current canine super-achiever. Over the years, he'd campaigned a dozen or more dogs, each time with great success, especially in field trialing and obedience competitions.

I happened to know that he achieved his training feats with an electric collar—operated by a hand-held remote control, it zaps the dog when he fails to obey a command—a method I think is more than a little bit like operating a Robby the Robot toy. It works, though—in fact, it concentrates the dog's attention wonderfully—and unlike beating a dog with a stick, it is not against the rules.

Go figure. In the file cabinet I found a manila file folder for each of Albert's purebred dogs. Each folder held the dog's documents: eye exam registration, hip clearance certification, the lineage of both parents, and the animal's AKC registration papers. For dogs he had bought, there was also a bill of sale;

animals he sold, of course, would have taken their records along with them.

Except for Beau, whose full name (his AKC papers said) was Am/Can Champion Ringolevio's General Beauregard, plus a string of initials testifying to his prowess at just about anything a dog could attempt. Besides the usual, he was a Canine Good Citizen, a titled Schutzhund competitor, the winner of two nationally advertised dog-food-sponsored beauty contests, and a registered therapy dog. If they'd let dogs onto the track at Indianapolis, I thought, Albert probably would have bought a stock car for the animal.

Instead, he'd been going to put Beau down. The bottom line was, when a dog outlived his usefulness at winning things, he was finished in Albert's book, especially if the dog also had hip trouble.

At least, Albert had been going to put the dog down until Kelley changed Albert's mind. In Beau's folder, along with his certificates, registrations, and commendations, was a fresh bill of sale with Albert's name signed at the bottom of it. In consideration of work to be performed later (schedule attached), Kelley Greene owned AKC Ch. Ringolevio's General Beauregard.

Which meant Albert must have done up the bill of sale after Kelley left, or she would have taken it with her, and (obviously) before somebody murdered Albert. That took Kelley off any possible list of suspects, in the unlikely event more suspects were needed; Kelley had what she wanted out of Albert, and I believed Kelley when she said she didn't hate Albert for breaking up the romance with Peter. She'd had one rotten marriage already and escaping another seemed only to have provoked relief, not a desire for revenge.

Musing over this, I went back outside and found the kennel kid finishing the yard cleanup. "One thing, though," he said. "Everything was locked up this morning when I got here, but I got, like, keys for the whole place? Which is how I let the cops in when they showed up? Except for that building over there."

He pointed at a metal building like Holly's puppy palace. "He—Mr. Russell—never let anyone have a key to that. He kept that key on his own ring, on a loop he snapped on his belt. He was, like, kind of paranoid."

Right, the way Einstein was kind of smart. Albert thought everyone was plotting mischief against him, probably because he was almost always plotting it himself.

I peered in one of the windows of the storage building. In it were all the same things Holly had in hers: kibble bags—of Albert's usual brand, not the alien variety I'd found in the food bin—plus more trophies, training equipment, cleaning supplies, and tools, all lit from above by an enormous skylight. There was a weaning pen in the building, too, and that made me feel uneasy; from where I stood, I couldn't quite see into it.

"Then after the cops, some other guys came," the kid went on. "They were supposed to, like, fix the heater? Only they couldn't, because I couldn't let them in there, either. An' I been, like, wondering what to do about it."

The kid eyed me sideways, apparently hoping I would come up with a solution where he hadn't been able to. I put my hand against the windowglass: warm. Too warm, and none of the windows was open an inch. "Are there puppies in there?"

"Uh, yeah. Seven-weeksters. I tried breaking the lock, but no luck. And the glass, it's reinforced or something? So it's, like, not breakable. They're big enough, so they'll be okay for a while, but . . ." He frowned, waiting for me magically to fix this situation.

I looked around, and damned if there wasn't a nursing bitch locked up in one of the dog enclosures, which meant those pups had been in that building alone since before Albert was murdered. The kid was right: At seven weeks, under ordinary circumstances, they'd survive for a while, maybe until we found a locksmith with a diamond hacksaw for the carbon-steel padlock Albert had put on the door.

But these weren't ordinary circumstances. The building's other door had no outside handle at all; inside, it possessed a latch and a crossbar made from a solid length of 6 × 6 timber. A battering ram might get through it. Eventually.

And it was hot in there. Too hot. I had an awful idea. "Get a ladder," I told the kennel kid, and ran back inside to the telephone.

One locksmith's line signaled busy; on another I got an answering machine. The third was disconnected, and the fourth was answered by a Spanish-speaking lady who did not understand a word I was saying.

Desperate, I dialed Holly's number and Kelley picked up. Swiftly, I described the problem to her. "So did the cops find Albert's keys?" I asked. "Because if they've got them, I need them right away over here."

"No," Kelley replied. "They even dug out a lot of gravel, but they didn't find them."

"Damn; okay, Kelley, thanks anyway." So much for that idea.

"You know what, though," Kelley said thoughtfully. "I wonder if they looked for them at Peter's. I mean, in his truck or around his house. They might not have had time for that yet, and I do still have a key to Peter's place."

"Do it, and bring them if you find them. I've got some pups over here that I think are slow-cooking, and I haven't got much time." I hung up.

By the time I got back outside, the kid had the ladder set up against the building. The roof was pitched, but not at a suicidally steep angle, and a set of wooden steps led down from rafters on the inside, adjacent to the skylight which I'd noticed was closed but unlocked.

Even getting a window open would help, but once the kid got inside, he could open the other door. "Okay," I told him. "Now you just climb up there and . . . oh."

He was shaking his head, pointing to his gimpy leg. "No can do. Sorry, but I've tried stuff like that and it didn't work out too well. The ladder, okay, but not the roof."

I nodded resignedly and started up the ladder myself. A fear of heights is not among my afflictions, and although my own ankle was stiff, the rest of the leg worked; what with the rehab they'd put me through after the reattachment, I could probably have bent steel bars with it. So I made it across to the skylight okay; I would probably have made it down the skylight okay, too, except for the threadlike wisps of smoke curling from around the edges of it as I reached it. Squinting through the glass, I caught a glimpse of orange flame, licking treacherously toward the bales of straw stacked in one corner of the building.

Albert's damned malfunctioning heater had caught fire.

All the courage drained out of me like blood from a severed artery, replaced by something as paralyzing as embalming fluid. Small flames skittered up the back wall of the building, fed by the rosettes and ribbons there.

"The gas!" I shouted down to the kid, who did not yet know what was happening. "The gas cylinder for the heater, outside by the rear wall. It has a valve—shut it off!"

He blinked, got it, and ran as best he could, while the metal roof of the building heated under my hands. I pried up the skylight and fell back, nearly losing my footing as a choking billow roiled up out of it. And then the whole nightmare burst into my waking memory, like some vile creature battering out of its loathsome egg: The explosion, a white-hot hammer of fire, nailing a spike of glass into the throat of the fellow in the yellow slicker who had saved me. His blood, spraying through the air while he tumbled as if weightless; his eyes, so darkly knowing. Begging, pleading with me to help him.

But I had already killed him.

"It won't turn! I can't shut off the gas!" The kid's voice seemed to come from a far distance. Below me, puppies coughed and whimpered in fright, their nails scratching the wooden sides of the weaning pen.

The roof was too hot to stay on any longer. I turned, meaning to return to the ladder; I wanted to save those puppies, but I wasn't going to kill myself to do it. Then, from the corner of my eye, I glimpsed something yellow.

For an instant, I thought it was a yellow slicker, and the idiotic thought crossed my mind that perhaps he was here, that he hadn't really ever died at all. But when I turned, I saw it was only a piece of yellow cloth, a cleaning rag or a dishtowel, fluttering—or I thought it was; I couldn't make it out clearly— on Albert's clothesline, in the utility area by his back door.

The fellow wasn't alive. He'd died saving me. I had taken him out of the world and he wouldn't be back, which left me not a hell of a lot of choice as to who was going to do any saving that needed to get done around here. Or so it seemed at the time.

Which was why, finally, I climbed down through the skylight. As I descended, the smoke thickened until only the puppies' crying let me find them at all. With my eyes streaming and my heart pounding in terror of the fire at my back, I stuffed the creatures into a burlap sack and staggered toward what I prayed was the building's back door. Wind whistled in the skylight opening, sucked in by the flames that had already devoured the straw; now they began crackling in a stack of two-by-fours, flickering up the steps to the rafters.

The beam barring the door wouldn't budge. "Drag the hose over," I yelled, gagging on smoke and not knowing if the kid outside could hear; not knowing, either, what was going to be in flames in the next few instants: the rest of the building, or me.

Somehow I got my shoulder under the beam and lunged upward; a bolt of pain like a hammer hit me, but the beam moved. Gripping the sack, I fell against the door and it swung open, the rush of air fanning the fire to an inferno as daylight dazzled, blinding me.

Then I was outside and the kid was grabbing me, urging me along. "I got the valve closed," he shouted, "but it's gonna . . ."

The building blew, flinging us to the ground where we covered the sack of squirming puppies with our bodies against the rain of debris. In a few moments, nothing remained but a smoking shell, with two-by-fours and wooden steps burning merrily inside.

"Wow," the kid said, sitting up. "You okay?"

"Yeah," I said, wincing. "Shoulder's killing me, but I'll live. How about the pups?"

He opened the sack. Vigorous yelping from within signaled they were okay, too. "I'm gonna, like, put 'em with their mom," he said. "They ain't completely weaned yet, so she can take care of 'em better'n we can."

I thought that if my opinion of this kid notched up any more, we were going to have to build a pedestal for him. Albert might have been a lot of unpleasant things, but he knew how to pick kennel help. The kid clambered up and limped away with the pups toward the dog enclosures, where the wire fence had protected the animals from shrapnel. I got a glimpse of the yellow thing, whatever it was, still fluttering and waving near the house, and then an old white truck pulled into the driveway and Kelley got out, her eyes enormous.

"Oh my God," she said, staring at the burning wreckage. In the distance, I could hear fire sirens approaching. "I found the keys at Peter's place," Kelley said, holding them out to me, "but I guess you don't need them anymore."

"Right," I said. In the slanting sunlight, Kelley looked

healthy and beautiful as always: tall and athletic in jeans and a plaid shirt, pale hair coiled atop her head.

"The police found a bloody rock in the back of Peter's truck just after I got there," she said. "It really looks like he killed Albert."

"Right," I said again, getting up. "Ouch. Give me a hand, will you?" Gripping my elbow, she hoisted me easily.

By then the firetrucks were pulling in, the yard filling up with shouting men carrying fire hoses. The kennel kid was moving the dogs out of further harm's way, and he seemed to have things well under control, so I got out of there before more vehicles could arrive to block the driveway off completely, as it seemed to me there were some things I needed to check on in and around Holly's kennel.

Being in terror for your life is a lot like an electronic training collar: It really does concentrate the mind wonderfully.

Back at Holly's, I looked hard at her bottle of pain pills, then shook out a couple of aspirin instead, and washed them down with a few gulps of diet soda. Then I took a walk around the place, thinking about Albert and Peter Wilson.

It didn't make sense for Peter to have killed Albert; he had already done his worst to Peter, losing him his kennel and his reputation, breaking up his love affair, and shaming him in front of a lot of people who would be sure to remember and talk about it. Peter might have killed Albert to prevent Albert from beating any more dogs, but that seemed an unlikely motive when so many less extreme methods remained to be tried. A really serious formal complaint to the dog club might at least have put the brakes on Albert's tendencies, just by putting him on notice. And Peter, once his fury abated, would have realized that, too.

On the other hand, he might have bashed Albert in a rage, which was, after all, the emotion Albert was best at eliciting. Peter had threatened Albert, his truck had been seen leaving Albert's place, and an obvious weapon had been discovered in the truck bed. Then there was the fact of Albert's body being found in the dry-well hole. It would have been perfect if not for the dead animal Kelley thought she had seen, in the far corner of the dog yard. Fifteen inches of gravel plus half a foot of topsoil, and *voilà*: instant grave.

And the dogs had barked that night, as they never did at familiar people. But they would have at Peter, who had been an infrequent visitor until the dry-well project.

The trouble was, they'd have barked at other things also. And Albert wouldn't have switched that dog food, at least not all at once. He'd have mixed it with the dogs' old kibble a little at a time, adjusting the proportions at each feeding over the span of perhaps a week, to avoid digestive upset.

I followed these ideas out to the puppy palace, where I found a cone of yellow twine and the two toy dogs from obedience class—one mechanical, one on wheels—on the training shelf. Sadly, I cut a long length of the twine and knotted one end of it through the metal loop on the wheeled toy dog's chest.

Then, to try my experiment, I carried the toy to the bottom of the driveway and left it there, hidden in some tall grass. By the time I got to the top of the drive again, I felt the weight of the world on my shoulders, and it stayed there while I walked behind one of the trees Peter had nearly hit the day before, then turned right so that the string formed a right angle: one leg of it parallel to the driveway and the other parallel to the back of the house.

Continuing on that line, still unwinding twine, I went on through the gate in the chain-link fence and along the back of the house until I was standing below the window of the room Kelley Greene had stayed in the night before. A bit of yellow fuzz the same shade as the twine clung to the outside of the window sash; there had been a wisp of it on the tree bark, too.

From their enclosures, the dogs watched, their pretty heads cocked in varying degrees of curiosity as I began pulling in the string carefully—this was the delicate part—and after a moment I heard it: the little toy dog's metal cymbals clinking together, faintly and then more audibly, as—pulled by the length of twine—the toy was drawn up, up the driveway. It was the same sound I'd heard the night before, thinking it was the chain-link fence gate clinking in the wind.

Only it wasn't: not then, not now. The animals in the pens stood up and pricked their ears up. I pulled the twine again: more clinking. The dogs went wild, just as Kelley Greene drove up in her pickup truck with Beau in the seat beside her.

She got out and looked at me, and she knew, but I didn't think she would run and she didn't. All this—the kennels and animals, early mornings and chores, the dogs and the variety of human beings who owned them (or, in some cases, the reverse)—all this was Kelley's life. And I could see in her eyes that she knew what I had learned for myself, to my sorrow, a year earlier: As she had ruined her life in this little place, she had ruined it in the entire world.

"So that Peter Wilson guy, he didn't, like, really kill Mr. Russell?"

It was six in the morning of the following day, and I was out with Albert's kennel helper, picking up Holly's dog yard. The evening before, we'd brought Albert's dogs over and closed up his place; the kennel helper, whose name was Geoffrey, needed a job and we certainly needed him, what with twenty more animals rambling around the property, and I liked Geoffrey. Meanwhile, I'd started Beau on a regimen of steroids, painkillers, and gentle exercise—plus a little obedience work so he wouldn't get bored, mental stagnation being the bane of the retired dog's existence—all of which he seemed to be tolerating nicely.

And Kelley Greene had turned herself in to the police, her confession and arrest being accomplished at almost the same time as Peter Wilson's release. I'd explained it all at least twice already, but Geoffrey hadn't heard everything, yet.

"That's right," I told him as we finished our cleanup and started on the boarder dogs, herding each one into its own large pleasantly airy roofed enclosure. Holly took good care of her guests.

"Kelley went to Albert's that evening to try again to persuade him to let her have the dog she wanted. But Albert was dead set on putting Beau down. They had words about it, out in Albert's dog yard, and when Albert turned his back, Kelley picked up a rock and bonked him with it."

"Mr. Russell was a little guy," Geoffrey observed astutely. "Small enough so you could, like, sort of stuff him most of the way into a dog-food sack, then pull another sack over the open end of the first one, to hide him. That's why the dogs'd had different food: because Kelley needed two sacks."

"Precisely. And Kelley is a big, powerful woman. Next, she printed out a bill of sale for Beau, and forged Albert's signature by copying one of the signed checks on his desk.

Then she carried Albert into Holly's puppy palace under everybody's nose, and slipped out later to dump him in the dry-well hole. She even put the two empty sacks in the kitchen afterwards, right in plain sight.''

"Phew," Geoffrey said. "That's a lot of work just to get an old dog." He shooed a little papillon into its enclosure, then grabbed it up and cuddled it briefly before shutting it into the pen. "Go on, now," he told it, and it yapped happily at him.

"I don't think Kelley planned to kill Albert," I said. "I think Albert just made Kelley lose her temper for a minute. We all," I added quietly, "do things we regret later."

"Yeah," Geoffrey agreed. "But once she'd done it, I guess she didn't feel she had, like, any choice. So she blamed it all on Peter Wilson?"

"Uh-huh." I lugged a couple of water buckets to the faucet at the back of the house, dumped them, and began refilling them with fresh. Ice-cold water soaked my shoes; it always does. Wet feet are among the delights of being a big-time dog enthusiast.

"During the night, to strengthen the notion that Peter had been here, Kelley got the dogs to bark by pulling the toy past them; she'd set it up earlier so she wouldn't even have to leave her bedroom to do it, and the next morning she pretended to see a dead animal so she could 'find' Albert's body. Later, when she went to Peter's house to ask the cops about the keys—she had them all along in case she needed to get back into Albert's, but she couldn't very well tell me that—she put the bloody rock in Peter's truck bed."

Geoffrey considered this while we dragged the buckets to the various dog enclosures, fastening each handle to the chain-link with a metal snap so the dogs wouldn't tip the buckets over. He remained silent as we scooped wood shavings from the weaning pen in the puppy palace and put in clean shavings, and while we spread fresh straw in the muddiest areas of the dog yard; it had rained again the night before.

Not until we had finished the outdoor chores and gone in for a cup of coffee before starting the indoor tasks did he speak again. "That was, like, pretty good what you did. Going in that building when you knew it was probably going to explode, to save those puppies. That was pretty brave."

Geoffrey's limp was due to a badly healed fracture he'd suffered in a pedestrian accident; he'd been hit by, of all things, the dog-catcher's van. I thought that when I got to know him a little better, I might refer him to my own orthopedic surgeon, possibly along with a check to help with the expenses of getting the leg straightened out. After all, I did have a fair amount of money, and that seemed like a good way of spending some of it.

"No," I said to Geoffrey, "it wasn't brave."

Outside, one of Holly's dogs grabbed a scrub brush I'd left on the back step and raced into the dog yard with it, and the others chased after him; moments later they all were covered with mud, and I knew I would be hosing down a dozen Labradors before the evening.

But first there were puppy meals to be fixed and the crates in the dog room to be vacuumed out, exercise areas to be picked up and a crew of boarder dogs to be welcomed or sent home. There were grooming tools to be used and cleaned; field, obedience, and show-ring classes to be held. And there were dogs to be lived among, to be learned from and loved: labor enough for a lifetime, or so I hoped.

"Actually," I told Geoffrey, "I was only repaying a favor. Or starting to; I think it'll take a long time to finish. Or I might never be finished."

Geoffrey just nodded. He was a good kid; worth more, I thought, than whatever Albert had been paying him. I made a mental note to speak to Holly about that, and then I went back to work.

And that would have been the end of the story, except that later the same day I stopped back at Albert's for some of his special-blend puppy chow, so as not to switch the new pups' feed too abruptly. And although I looked carefully for it, and the police had removed all the things they needed much earlier so I didn't think they could have taken it, there was no yellow cloth or anything like one on Albert's clothesline, or anywhere else.

—with gratitude to Constantine Cavafy (1863–1933)

≪ A Long Walk Home ≫
by
Stephen Wasylyk

THE THIRTEEN-YEAR-OLD future major league outfielder had been bouncing a rubber ball off the driveway wall of the sun-splashed yellow brick apartment house for almost an hour. Most of the rebounds returned to his waiting hands. Now and then the ball caught a projecting brick and caromed off at an odd angle, the *whmppf* of the ball and the slapping of his pursuing sneakers loud in the morning stillness.

Across the street, a kneeling Edna retrieved another tulip bulb from her carefully tended bed in the center of the lawn, brushed it off, and handed it to Barney.

"Arctic White."

Impressed into service by his rotund, blue-haired wife to keep the dun colored bulbs separated properly during this bi-annual ritual, Barney repeated the name dutifully as he dropped it into a labeled paper sack.

Whmppf.

The ball zoomed over the boy's blond head and lodged in a tall hedge that separated the driveway from the side lawn of the house next door. Painted white and trimmed in green, the two story stucco sat in a postcard-pretty setting of foundation plantings, full blooming flower beds, and several large oaks. As a further shield against the intrusive ugliness of the apartment house, the back yard was screened from view by an interlocking border of evergreens.

"Golden Towers," said Edna.

Barney turned the bulb over in his fingers. "Yellow."

Thirty years of marriage had taught Edna when to ignore him.

46

Whmppf.

"He'd better hope that ball doesn't go over the hedge and into the Farleys' yard," said Barney. "Mrs. Farley screaming at him will frighten him into taking up poker."

"Not unless she can do it from beyond the grave."

He brushed the dirt from the bulb she handed him. "She's dead?"

"That's the only way to get there. After all, she was ninety-five. She died last week, while you were away playing fisherman."

He dropped the unidentified bulb into the Golden Towers bag. If it turned out to be Regent Red, she'd have a nice surprise. "There was no viewing or funeral?"

"For whom? The only people with an interest were Marcie and Howard."

"A few of the neighbors would have turned up."

She gave a ladylike snort. "Not likely. Why should you care, anyway?"

"Doesn't seem right. The day I left, she was giving a few kids royal hell for making too much noise. Maybe she was the neighborhood irritant, but she managed to get to ninety-five, which is more than most of us do. She deserved a better send-off, even if we came only to applaud."

"Queen of the Night," said Edna.

Barney considered the bulb thoughtfully.

"Sounds like a high-priced call girl."

Edna glared at him.

Whmppf.

The ball came bouncing across the street to where John Henry, silently watching and wondering why the stupid boy insisted on throwing the ball against the wall when a dog was available to chase after and fetch it for him, immediately snapped it up in his teeth, tail wagging, indicating his willingness to play.

The boy stopped short, eyeing him warily. Tail wagging or not, John Henry was big, black, and formidable enough to discourage anyone's disputing ownership of anything he decided to appropriate.

Barney held out his hand. "Give."

John Henry looked at him in disbelief, the sternness in Barney's voice telling him it wasn't play time after all. Reluctantly, he dropped the wet ball into Barney's hand.

Barney tossed it back to the boy with an easy grace he thought his muscles had forgotten.

"Not bad for an old man," he said.

Edna handed him another bulb. "Seems more trouble than it's worth."

"I've been saying that for years."

"Not the tulips," she said wearily. "The boy."

"You've forgotten the imagination of youth. He isn't bouncing the ball off the wall. He's playing center field in the World Series."

She waggled a finger at the bulb. "Pink Glory."

He was tempted to slip it into Arctic Giant.

"Still think that Mrs. Farley's departure should have been observed with a little formality."

She handed him the last bulb and rose, brushing off the knees of her slacks. "Not our business, Barney. And she wasn't just the neighborhood irritant. She was a sharp-tongued, extremely selfish woman and a perfect example of only the good die young."

She waved at the bulb. "Regent Red. Are you sure you didn't mix up any of the colors?"

"Absolutely," he lied. "I'll see you later. I need a haircut before the wedding."

"What about finishing that clock you've been making as a gift for Denise?"

"Maybe I won't give it to her."

"I wouldn't be surprised. You haven't given one away yet."

"Only because I'm not giving my clocks to airheads. They can buy plastic ones in K-Mart."

"I just happened to think, Barney, that Howard waited for Marcie for thirty years. Would you have waited that long for me?"

"Only if you promised not to grow tulips."

He snapped his fingers at John Henry. The dog fell into step at his left heel.

As they reached the sidewalk, the boy made a spectacular one-handed catch, whirled and threw as though trying to catch a runner trying to score.

Barney had no idea of where he imagined home plate might

be because the ball was headed nowhere in particular until it caught a projecting light bracket on the apartment house wall, flew over the hedge into the Farleys' yard, ricocheted from an oak trunk, and headed toward the rear of the house.

John Henry streaked across the street, brushed by the boy, and caught up with the still rolling ball. He spun with it in his teeth. This *had* to be play time.

The boy turned to appeal to Barney.

Barney crossed to the other sidewalk. "John Henry!"

Tail wagging, the dog started back. Halfway, he paused, head moving from side to side, snout low. He dropped the ball and backtracked, nose an inch off the ground, following an invisible trail to a flower bed under a window and then to the back of the house. Intriguing odors always made him forget what he'd been doing.

The door of the house burst open and a stocky, sandy-haired, elderly man ran out, yelling at the boy in a furious, high-pitched voice.

Barney sighed. Mrs. Farley in her prime couldn't have done better.

The boy cautiously backed away and fled. The ball could be replaced. His life couldn't.

John Henry was still roaming the lawn at the side of the house, nose low, tail wagging. Whatever his sensitive nose had picked up, it pleased him.

Barney whistled. The man glanced at him, turned and saw the dog for the first time. Waving his arms and yelling, he charged at the precise moment John Henry decided to obey Barney's whistle.

A hundred pounds of well-muscled black dog coming head on at full speed converted fury into terror in a split second.

The man screamed and threw himself to one side as John Henry streaked by to take his position at Barney's heel.

Barney lifted a hand. "Sorry, Howard."

Howard raised a trembling forefinger and yelled, "You keep him out of here, do you hear, Barney? If I catch him here again, I'll shoot him."

Barney beckoned.

Howard came to within ten feet.

"Don't ever say that again, Howard," said Barney slowly. "Don't even think it."

Howard opened his mouth, saw something in Barney's face, swallowed, and said, "You're right, Barney. I was upset."

"I understand. Mrs. Farley's passing away must have been a shock."

Howard nodded. "Hit Marcie hard. That's why I'm here."

"You don't have to explain. After all, you've been keeping company with her for a long time. Hell, you ought to simply move in. Mrs. Farley just pass away?"

"No, Barney. She fell. Wasn't really much of a fall. Only the last three steps, Marcie said, but at her age it didn't take much. There was nothing I could do. I called the doctor. She's dead, I told him, no sense in even taking her to the hospital. Had to be done, he said. Couple of minutes later the ambulance came. I went with it. Doctor in the emergency room told me she was dead, as if I didn't already know. Whitman, the funeral director, picked her up the morning after the autopsy. I thought she'd hit her head but they said it was her heart. We buried her that afternoon. Marcie didn't want any fuss, you know?"

Barney nodded. "Tell her she has my condolences. And listen, Howard, maybe it's none of my business, but why don't you and Marcie get away from here? Take a long trip together. Don't even wait to get married. I'll keep an eye on the house for you."

Howard looked down the tree-lined street, a weariness in his eyes. "Nice of you, Barney, but we really can't right now. Maybe later."

"The offer is always good. Take care, Howard."

Howard nodded and hurried into the house.

Barney glanced down at John Henry. "Since you've caused enough trouble for the day, do you think you can behave at the barber shop?"

John Henry's tail indicated assent.

Barney walked slowly. He really couldn't blame Marcie and Howard for being in a hurry to bury Mrs. Farley. When he and Edna had bought the house, Marcie had been a pleasant, goodlooking woman and just about ready to marry Howard. Then her mother had a heart attack, so the wedding was postponed. And postponed. And postponed. Some time later, Edna had learned Mrs. Farley had extracted a promise from them that they would never marry as long as she was alive because she needed Marcie. It might have seemed a reasonable commitment at the time, but neither Marcie nor Howard imagined she would live for another thirty years and never release Marcie from that promise.

Barney had no doubt that they had anticipated each year to be her last and so did nothing, and when finally they looked around, most of their lives had quietly passed by.

He had watched Marcie age until she looked older than Edna, had seen Howard arrive faithfully twice a week for their dates, which were spent talking to each other in the living room. Neither ever went anywhere except out to dinner, with Mrs. Farley as a creaking chaperone.

Edna often said Howard was a saint to wait for Marcie that long, but Edna would go to her grave naive about a great many things. Thirty years was a long time for the old woman to hang on. The first few wouldn't have mattered, the next a source of irritation, the last full of so much hate it could have been packaged and sold by the pound. If there was anything saintly about Howard, it was that he hadn't force-fed the old woman the wrong medication at the wrong time years ago.

It was no wonder they had buried her as quickly as they could. In Howard's shoes, he'd have helped dig the grave with a smile on his face.

But Howard wasn't smiling, and that was odd because he certainly couldn't be grief-stricken.

The barber shop was at the end of a small, low brick building that was an island of commercial development in the suburban residential neighborhood.

It also held a small delicatessen, a drugstore, a dry cleaning shop, and a real estate office. A narrow, dreary alley ran behind it, an eyesore and an anathema to the surrounding residents and a magnet for every dog within a mile.

Three months ago, the usual irritations of the alley had become secondary to the presence of a drab, silent, middle-aged woman named Jessie. Institutionalized for years simply because her mental growth had ceased during childhood, she had been released with many others by a judge who ruled confinement was a violation of their rights.

She had appeared one morning and taken up residence in the boiler room which provided heat for the building's tenants;

a slightly built woman of indefinite age who spent most of her day shuffling aimlessly about the neighborhood.

As often as Sergeant Corcoran drove her back to the home she had been assigned to along with four others who had been returned to live in the community, she reappeared, somehow safely negotiating the long walk necessary to reach the alley.

Legal efforts to have her removed had been dropped after the building owner had been prevailed upon to furnish the boiler room as a small apartment, several church groups supplied a cadre of women who looked after her, and a county social worker was assigned to cart her off once a week for a bath, physical examination, and change of clothing.

Offers of more suitable living quarters by a few of the more good-hearted were ignored. Whatever her reasons, Jessie preferred to remain where she was.

Only a few things managed to penetrate beyond the bewildered eyes, one of them John Henry's presence, which always brought a brief, tender head stroking.

Looking forward to that, the dog took off ten yards from the alley and skidded around the hedge that concealed it from the adjacent houses, but when Barney cleared the hedge, he was trotting back and forth uncertainly.

Barney whistled him to his side. "Maybe she went for a walk. You can check again on the way home."

Sal Melchiorre, napping in the barber's chair with his hands tented on his chest, opened one eye.

"About time someone showed up. I was beginning to think I was back in the sixties when it was a crime to get a haircut."

"Fads come and go," said Barney, "and that one isn't due again for another ten years. Where's your assistant?"

"Home with a cold. I didn't want him breathing on my customers. How was I to know I wouldn't have any?"

John Henry settled in the corner, his chin on his paws.

"Looks sad," said Sal.

"He was expecting to see Jessie, but she wasn't there."

Sal always fastened the neck-band as though he was practicing for an eventual strangulation of a customer he didn't like.

"Being away fishing, you may not have heard. Jessie's been gone for about a week."

"Corcoran take her back to the home?"

"Absolutely not. He was in the other day, asking when I'd last seen her. I really didn't know. Seen her go by so often, I didn't pay attention."

The electric clippers buzzed at the nape of Barney's neck.

"Sounds a little odd," he said.

"I don't know. The social worker says it happens. The psychiatrist told her Jessie might have left because she found a place that makes her feel more secure."

The trimmer buzzed around Barney's ear.

"Hear your neighbor died," said Sal. "The old Farley woman."

"So I was informed a short while ago."

"Whitman, the funeral director, told me it was the fastest funeral he ever handled. Would have been faster but the paperwork slowed him down. Ever realize how hard it is to get out of this world, Barney?"

Regarding the heavy-set, gray haired man in the mirror, Barney considered that experience as approaching much too quickly.

"I've never heard of people standing in line to check out as if they were in a supermarket."

"I'm talking about the paperwork the government demands to prove that you're dead. The politicians let no taxpayer go without a fight. Now with people like Jessie, it's different. They couldn't care less."

The scissors clacked steadily.

"I hope no one harmed her, Barney. Corcoran said that there was talk that someone put her in a car and drove her so far away she'll never find her way back."

"I wouldn't like to think of anyone's doing that."

Sal spread warm lather on his nape, around his ears, and below his sideburns. Barney forced his mind elsewhere. Someone that close to him with a straight razor always made him uneasy.

"Neither would I. I didn't like to see her living back there because I think a person is entitled to more out of life. Yet she wouldn't stay in the home and wouldn't have anything to do with the people who offered her a place to live. What do you do with someone like that?"

"See that they have a warm place to sleep and enough to eat until someone comes up with a sensible solution."

Sal put the razor away and combed Barney's hair to coax a few stubborn strands from hiding.

"I used to watch her go by and wonder where she came from and if she had a family who could have taken care of her."

Barney smiled. Sal's thinking usually went no deeper than the daily major league scores.

"What do you think she was like as a kid, Barney?"

"The same as any other until she fell behind, I suppose."

She'd had a black dog, he knew that. The first time she'd seen John Henry, her face had softened and she said softly, "Boomer?" Then the softness was gone, the memory too difficult or painful to hold. The eyes became puzzled and the blankness in the lined face that had no age was back as though understanding was too difficult.

Sal brushed him off. "You look twenty years younger."

"Don't get carried away. You're only a barber, not a magician."

Barney inspected the haircut critically. "Since you didn't scalp me this time, I'll give you the key to success. Grow a mustache, paint the place pink, and change the sign on the window from Sal's Barber Shop to Mr. Salvatore's Hair Styling Salon."

"And if I do, where will you get your hair cut?"

Barney shrugged as he opened the door. "Edna isn't too old to learn how to cut hair."

John Henry made a cursory tour of the alley before catching up to him.

"She's gone," he said, "but don't give up hope. Corcoran might find her yet."

As they approached the house, the dog left his side and headed for the Farleys', tail wagging. Barney let him get there before whistling him back. John Henry had always instinctively avoided the Farley yard because Mrs. Farley hated dogs more than she hated children, but there was a rabbit warren deep under the hedges somewhere and it appeared that John Henry was narrowing down his perpetual search.

Ignoring Edna's comment about his haircut, Barney leaned against the kitchen wall.

"Have you seen Marcie since her mother died?"

"Of course. I went over to express my condolences."

"Did she impress you as being happy now that she and Howard are free?"

She stared at him. "Happy? Good Lord, Barney. Her *mother* passed away."

"A great loss, I'm sure. How *did* she look?"

"If you must know, I thought she looked more worried than grief-stricken."

"Ah," said Barney.

"Ah, what?"

"Howard had the same look. What would those two have to worry about with Mrs. Farley gone?"

"Perhaps being alone together after all these years." She pointed toward his workshop in the garage. "The clock, Barney. If it isn't finished by this time tomorrow, I buy a wedding gift."

The pieces of the clock he had designed for Edna's grandniece lay in the center of his workbench, stained and varnished and needing only to be rubbed down to a glass-smooth luster before being assembled.

He preferred to finish his clocks that way, rather than after assembly when he had to contend with corners, crevices, and projecting surfaces.

Using his felt pad, rubbing oil, and rottenstone, he began to work, the varnish becoming lustrous and smooth, the beautifully grained cherry acquiring deepness and richness; examining each piece critically before setting it aside.

He was almost finished when someone tapped on the door jamb.

Corcoran and a blonde young woman dressed in a tailored dark blue suit stepped inside.

The sergeant sounded apologetic. "Have a minute, Barney?"

"If you don't mind my talking while I keep rubbing. Edna is pushing me for this."

The young woman leaned over the polished pieces, eyes interested.

"This is Miss Eliot," said Corcoran. "She's the social worker handling Jessie's case."

Barney resumed rubbing. "Sal told me she disappeared."

"That's why we're here. I heard you were back from that

fishing trip and thought you might be able to help.''

Barney held the last piece up to the light, sighting across the glare for imperfections. ''Why me?''

''You and John Henry tour the neighborhood twice a day when you take your walks. I thought you might have seen something.''

Satisfied, Barney polished the wood with a dry cloth. ''Not really. We did run into her occasionally but not for some weeks.''

''Did it ever seem to you that there was a pattern to where you saw her?'' asked Miss Eliot.

Dry-fitting the pieces together to be sure everything was perfect before he used the glue, Barney paused.

''What makes you think there might have been a pattern?''

Miss Eliot moved to get a better look at what he was doing.

''Let me tell you about her. Jessie is one of those people we lost because no one knew what to do with her. We don't really know exactly why she was institutionalized when she was a child because her records were destroyed in a fire, but we can guess because we have experience with others. Someone, a doctor or a psychiatrist, determined that her mental age would never progress much beyond the age of five or so. That diagnosis was a tragedy. What was really wrong with her was that she was a very slow learner. Teaching her required time and patience, but she could learn. With the proper instruction, she could have been capable eventually of getting about on her own and of doing simple work.''

Barney reached for his lightweight clamps. ''Could have been?''

''Could have been. She may have been handicapped, but she could still feel, and like all children she depended on those she loved. So she could be hurt. You can imagine how she felt when she was taken away from her family and placed in the institution. Lost. Confused. How could she know why she was there? Then came the fire. The attendants she was close to died in it and it did something to her. There is no question that up until then, she knew her name and where she lived, but afterward she left that behind. Who she was and where she came from went with the people and the lost records, which were never really restored. She was lost through time, ignorance, and bureaucratic incompetence.''

"No member of the family ever checked on her?"

"If there were any; no. With the records gone along with the people who knew her, she became simply Jessie Doe in the files and Silent Jessie to everyone. When she was sent to the private home, she constantly wandered away, perhaps because she has always been something of a rebel. When asked why, she would only mumble that she was looking for something. One day she ended up in that alley, and nothing could make her return. All we could get out of her was the word home. The psychiatrist thought that she was referring to the alley. Recently, I realized that it could mean more than that. This neighborhood might remind her of where she lived as a child and she was wandering around looking for her home. During the years she spent in the institution she probably felt it no longer existed. Released, she realized it did."

The clock assembled and held lightly with clamps, Barney stepped back and eyed it critically. Almost eighteen inches high, the sides below the delicate face dipped and curved gracefully outward to bracket a small gallery.

Miss Eliot's eyes gleamed. "That *is* beautiful." She indicated the gallery. "A small vase with some bright flowers would be perfect here."

Barney smiled. Some people required no explanations.

"Neighborhoods change," he said. "A mind locked away for forty years wouldn't realize that. She might be completely confused."

"She might," said Corcoran. "Want to sell that clock?"

"I don't sell them. I give them away."

Corcoran grinned. "Not according to Edna. She says you have six in the house already."

"Only because when I met the people I made them for, I felt they wouldn't appreciate them. I don't consider them ordinary clocks. Not because they took a great deal of time, but because each is an original. There is only one like it in the world."

"I see your point," said Miss Eliot.

"All of which has nothing to do with Jessie's disappearance." Barney thrust his hands into his back pockets. "Why not ask from house to house?"

"I don't have the men for that," said Corcoran.

"Run a story in the weekly asking for information."

"The paper doesn't come out for three more days," said Miss Eliot.

"*Barney!*"

Edna's voice snapped across the yard.

He poked his head out of the door.

"John Henry is in the Farley yard. Better call him."

Barney sighed. He'd wondered where the self-appointed official greeter was. John Henry had always liked Corcoran.

They walked out to the street slowly.

"Keep your mind working on it, Barney," said Corcoran. "If anyone knows what goes on around here, you do."

"I resent being considered the neighborhood busybody."

"Don't mean that at all. It's just that you seem to have a way of turning up in the middle of things."

The dog was sitting before the Farley door as if he had come to call.

Barney whistled.

John Henry turned, saw Corcoran, and charged across the street. He submitted to a few pats, his eyes on Miss Eliot. Nose away from her blue pumps, he circled her, tail going furiously.

She glanced at Barney. "What's he up to?"

"I have no idea. Where were you before you came here?"

"I stopped by to see if Jessie had returned."

"That's it. Any friend of Jessie's is a friend of his. What are the odds that Jessie originally came from around here?"

"Monumental. The psychiatrist considers my idea pure fantasy."

"But you're not convinced."

She smiled. "Jessie's had no formal schooling, but I suspect she knows a great deal more than anyone gives her credit for, even though it took her a long time to learn it. Why couldn't a few distant memories and a little female intuition have brought her to the right place?"

Barney decided he liked Miss Eliot. "The problem would seem to be, where is she?"

"It's an old neighborhood," said Corcoran. "Big houses, detached garages, always some people away. She could be holed up somewhere."

"How old is she?"

"We don't know exactly," said Miss Eliot. "Take fifty-five

and go up or down a few years.'' She handed him a card. "If you think of anything, please call me.''

He went back to his workbench, took the clock apart, and began reassembling it, this time using the glue, the splines, and the concealed screws, working automatically, his mind elsewhere.

He had the impression that the pragmatic Corcoran was being gracious to the pretty Miss Eliot and believed that if Jessie had curled up with her memories somewhere a week ago, she was now dead, but there was no way to measure the indomitability of the human spirit. There were too many recorded instances of people who survived situations in which they should have died; courage, will power, and sheer stubbornness had nothing to do with learning ability. Jessie could have left the game a long time ago to sit and stare at images no one else would ever see, but she hadn't.

He set the clock aside for the glue to dry and called John Henry for their midday walk.

As he passed the houses, John Henry scouting before him for interesting odors, he realized that this neighborhood was perhaps more stable than many others. There were quite a few families who had been here before he moved in thirty years ago and who would still be here after he had gone.

The tour ended, he found Edna at her desk reviewing her grocery list.

"That goodlooking friend of yours, Mrs. Martino. Still at the hospital?"

"Of course. Why?"

"I think I'll run over and talk to her."

"What in the world for?"

"You've been taking me for granted lately. It's time I had an affair.''

"Good luck," said Edna.

The hospital had reduced all of its early records to microfilm. After he explained why he wanted to go through them, Mrs. Martino ignored the legalities and fed him the maternity ward reels one after another. An hour later, eyes tired and a headache building from deciphering blurred names, he found what he was hoping for, thanked Mrs. Martino, and drove to the municipal building.

After two hours more of eyestrain and headache, he called Miss Eliot.

He and John Henry were waiting for her when she drove up. "Sal, the barber, was talking about paperwork," he said. "Generally speaking, it's difficult to come into the world without a record of it and impossible to leave without forms being filled out. If Jessie was born to someone in this neighborhood, chances were it took place in the local hospital. I checked. I found a Jessica born fifty-eight years ago to a family still here. I asked around. None of the older residents remembered seeing her grow up, and there is no record of her death. What happened to her? Sent to live with a relative?"

"Or in an institution," said Miss Eliot. "Let me have the address."

"Go slowly. This may be nothing or this may be something you won't ever want to remember. You may want to let Corcoran handle it."

"After five years in this job, there are no surprises or shocks left. I don't need Corcoran unless they refuse to talk to me."

"Let's find out," said Barney.

He took her arm and led her to the Farley front door and pushed the doorbell.

Marcie answered, a thin woman with a bony face, gray hair cut short.

Barney took a deep breath.

"You had a sister named Jessica," he said. "What happened to her?"

He had anticipated reactions ranging from complete puzzlement to full blown screaming to outright violence.

He hadn't anticipated Marcie's eyes rolling upward as she collapsed into Howard's arms, probably one of the few times she'd been there in thirty years.

A coldness clamped his chest. A week. A week was a long time. Maybe if he hadn't gone on that fishing trip—

Howard looked up, a dullness in his eyes. "Upstairs. In what she says is her room."

Barney retreated before officialdom arrived, he, Edna, and John Henry overlooking the minor traffic jam caused by Corcoran's cars and the others.

"I still don't believe it," said Edna.

"Then I'll repeat what Howard told me and you can ask questions. Marcie was only eight when two things happened. Her father left one morning and never returned. Shortly afterward, her mother took Jessie away and returned without her. Never explained a damn thing to Marcie except to keep telling her it was the two of them against the world and all they had was each other, which partially explains why Marcie made that promise. She forbade Marcie to ever mention her father or Jessie, and eventually Marcie assumed they were both dead and simply never thought about them. You'll remember when we bought this house she told us her father had died years before."

"Good Lord. Mrs. Farley simply abandoned the child after her husband left."

"Condemned her if you like. No one knows why he deserted them, but I'd place no flowers on his grave, wherever that might be. He helped make her what she was and certainly did nothing for two small daughters. Howard, of course, had never heard of Jessie. About a week ago, she came to the front door. No one knows if she really remembered or simply selected the house at random, even though hitting the right one must have about the same odds against it as winning the state lottery. When Marcie answered the door, Jessie marched right past her, almost scaring her to death. She screamed. Howard came running. Mrs. Farley was coming down the stairs. Don't let anyone ever tell you we've mastered the intricacies of the human mind. Jessie hadn't seen her since she was a child, but she walked up to her and said, 'I'm home, Mother.' A shock like that can drop a healthy forty-year-old, let alone a woman who's lived with a guilty conscience for more than fifty years.

"I suppose that when her mother hit the floor, Marcie knew that Jessie had to be her long-lost sister. Howard figured he couldn't handle everything at one time and the thing to do was get Mrs. Farley buried first. Afterward, they sat over there wondering what to do about Jessie."

"What will happen now?"

Corcoran and Miss Eliot were crossing the street toward them.

"You and I are going to learn that at the same time."

"All over," said Miss Eliot. "She was released from the

institution so that she could live in a home. She now has her own. I'll arrange for everything she needs and stop by once a week to see how she's doing." She smiled. "And don't be surprised at all the Mercedes you'll see. The doctors will be studying this one for years."

"No repercussions for not reporting how Mrs. Farley really died or for keeping Jessie hidden for a week?" asked Barney.

"Only a few official lectures," said Corcoran. "A heart attack at ninety-five could be brought on by a big phone bill, and while there might be a couple of laws they broke, no one wants to spend a week looking for them."

Miss Eliot extended her hand. "Thank you, Barney."

He nodded.

Corcoran waited until she was in the car.

"I walked through the back yard, Barney," he said softly. "I don't think she should ever know."

"Neither do I. Go chase real criminals, Corcoran."

As his broad back retreated, Edna's fingers dug into Barney's arm. "Just what did he mean by that?"

Barney hesitated, even though Edna could be very difficult to live with when she knew he was keeping something from her.

"Funny how things work out," he said slowly. "If Miss Eliot hadn't showed up with her theory that Jessie was looking for her home, I would have never thought John Henry was sniffing anything over there except rabbit scent, because even he can't pick up anything a week old. But suppose it *was* Jessie? That was what made me check the records, and if I hadn't, I think that Jessie would have disappeared permanently."

Edna's eyes went wide. "Do you know what you're saying?"

"Corcoran had the same thought. Instead of being free after thirty years, Marcie and Howard must have felt they had traded one burden for another, and they didn't intend to let the years pass this time. Mrs. Farley survived because they couldn't get rid of her without questions being asked, but if Jessie disappeared, there could be none because no one knew she was there."

"Disappeared?" Edna whispered the word. "How?"

"Howard has handled the heavy garden work for Marcie

for years the way I handle yours, and you've never asked for a flower bed deeper than eight inches, or at the most twelve. Howard has one, freshly dug, that is three feet deep. Tell me what they intended to plant.''

Edna lifted a stubborn chin. ''They were simply replacing the soil.''

Sure they were, thought Barney. His warm-hearted see-no-evil wife wasn't there when he'd walked around the Farley back yard with Howard, listening to the words tumble out in that high-pitched voice and feeling the man's hate for Mrs. Farley, knowing that nothing destroys reason and compassion more than hate and that Howard had lived with it for decades and Marcie all her life.

''Well, Jessie is safe now, so it doesn't matter,'' he said. ''But John Henry did earn himself a nice piece of steak and Miss Eliot admired my clock so much I believe I'll give it to her. We'll buy something else for Denise.''

Staring at the picture postcard-pretty house across the street where two bedroom windows gleamed like a pair of malevolent eyes in the reddish glow of the setting sun, Edna nodded once, which was her way of saying she knew he was right about the pit but she could never bring herself to admit it. Even to herself.

<< The Dog in the Orchard >>
by
Mary Roberts Rinehart

THE MAN WAS sitting on the porch of the farmhouse. He sat very still, a rifle across his knee, his eyes fixed on the orchard and the wheat field beyond it.

The day had been hot. For hours he had watched the heat rising in shimmering waves from the dirt road that led into the farm. Now, however, it was cooler. A slight breeze ruffled the dust which lay thick everywhere, and moving carefully, he got out a bandanna handkerchief and dried his face.

In the wheat field beyond the orchard the dog raised his head with equal caution. He was panting heavily. He wanted water badly, but his eyes were on the figure on the porch. He knew now that it was dangerous to go to the creek or the horse trough. There was a nick out of one ear where a bullet had just touched him, and flies buzzed around it constantly. He could wait until dark. With the patience of his kind, he closed his eyes and slept.

It was twilight when he got to his feet. He had heard the slam of the screen door, and he knew what that meant. But even then he was wary. He stood, his eyes fixed on the house. So he remained for some time. Then at last, crouching low, he moved to the creek and drank. Thus revealed, he was gaunt to the point of starvation, his coat drab and dry. He was still drinking when he heard the car. He stood tense; then, abandoning all caution, he loped eagerly toward it, and the man inside saw him.

"Hello, Rags," he called. "How are you?"

But the dog shrank back at the sound of his voice, and as he retreated, the man looked after him curiously. Looks half starved, he thought. Queer. I always thought Nellie was crazy about him.

He stopped the car in front of the house and got out. There was a lighted lamp inside, and someone was moving about. He got out and clumped up the steps.

"Hi, Foster!" he called. "Got a minute or two?"

There was a silence. Then the man came to the door. He looked uneasy. "I'm getting my supper," he said. "What's wrong, sheriff?"

"Nothing wrong. Just mending my political fences. Election soon."

"Well, I'm for you. You know that."

He moved aside unwillingly, and the sheriff came in. He knew the house well. It was the usual farmhouse of the district, and Nellie Foster kept it immaculate. It was untidy now, however. The kitchen sink was piled with dishes.

The sheriff looked surprised. "Nellie sick?" he asked.

"Nope. Gone to her mother's."

"Where's that?"

"Indiana," said Foster. "Old lady's not well. She's been gone a week now."

"Looks like it's time she came back," said the sheriff, grinning. "That dog of hers looks it, too. Why don't you feed him once in a while?"

Foster was working at the stove. He was a big man, handsome after a fashion, but now slovenly and unkempt. He kept his back to the sheriff.

"Damn thing won't come near me," he said. "I kicked him once, and he didn't like it. Anyhow, he was her dog, not mine." He added grudgingly, "How about supper? I'm going to fry some eggs."

"Fine. I'll wash first."

The sheriff went out onto the back porch. There was a tin basin there, a pail of water and a ladle. He poured out some water and washed, drying his hands on a dirty roller towel and glancing about him as he did so. Certainly the place needed Nellie, with her active body and cheerful face. But he remembered that lately she had not been so cheerful, and that there had been some talk about Foster and the Burford girl on the next farm—a plump and brazen creature with an eye out for a man. Any man.

He shrugged that off. Foster was a solid citizen, a successful farmer. He had his feet on the ground, all right.

Nevertheless, the sheriff watched Foster surreptitiously as he moved around the kitchen. He might fall for a girl. He wasn't old. Not over forty; and the Burford girl had a way with her.

While Foster fried the eggs, the sheriff poured his own coffee. Sitting at the table waiting, he saw the rifle in a corner and eyed it with surprise.

"What's the gun for?" he asked. "Didn't know you had one."

"Bought it a year or two back," said Foster. "Weasels got after the chickens."

The two men ate companionably enough. Mostly the sheriff talked. It was in the middle of an anecdote that the dog barked in the orchard—a bark that ended in a long bloodcurdling wail. Foster stiffened, and the sheriff saw it.

"What's the matter?" he asked. "Is that Rags?"

"Yep. He does it now and then. Someday I'll shoot him if he keeps it up. Damned nuisance."

"Better not do that. He's Nellie's dog. She'd have a fit."

But the sound continued. Out in the orchard the dog was standing, his long tragic face pointed to the sky. But he was weak from hunger, and gradually the sounds died away. He lay down on the ground, and inside the house the sheriff watched the sweat gather on the backs of Foster's hands.

"How long's that been going on?" he asked. "It doesn't sound like Rags. He was a quiet dog."

Foster rose and picked up the plates. "Since Nellie left, mostly. He misses her, I guess. Want some more coffee?"

"No, thanks. I'd better be moving."

But the sheriff was thoughtful as he drove back to town, and as he got ready for bed that night he spoke to his wife.

"Saw Foster this evening," he said. "He says Nellie's gone to visit her mother."

"Then that's why she wasn't at church last Sunday. I wondered."

"Where is the mother?" he asked. "What part of the country?"

"Indiana, I think. Why?"

Well, that was all right. He was probably only making a

fool of himself. He finished undressing, went to bed and to sleep.

Out at the farm, however, there was no sleep. The dog saw to that. He stood in the orchard and bayed his grief and loneliness to the sky. At last, in a frenzy, Foster picked up the gun and went after him. It was hopeless, of course. The dog was not there, and with an oath the man went back to the house, to lie awake waiting for the sound once more.

In the past week it had been like that, as though it were a game between the two, man and dog; the dog winning at night; the man winning by day. But the advantage lay with the dog. At intervals he slept. The man could not, and he was desperate for sleep. He would doze on the porch, his rifle across his knees, waking with a jerk to find his body bathed in sweat and the gun on the floor.

He did not work on the day following the sheriff's visit, and that night after dark he met the Burford girl out by the barn. She was a big girl, handsome and frankly lustful. She put her arms around him, but he was unresponsive.

"What's the matter with you?"

"Nothing. I couldn't meet you last night. The sheriff was here."

She eyed him. "The sheriff? What did he want?"

"Nothing much. Election's coming soon. But he heard that damned dog."

"Why don't you poison him? I've said all along he'd make trouble."

"He's too smart for that. I've tried it. He won't eat around the place. Anyhow the sheriff saw him. He might ask questions. Well, let's forget it." He pulled her to him and kissed her roughly. "Listen," he said. "I'm going to sell this place and get out. You'll come along, won't you?"

"Sure." But there was no conviction in her voice, and he pushed her away.

"You'll come, all right," he told her grimly.

It rained the next two days. The dog lay in the field and shivered. And on the third day the sheriff went into the store which was the local post office. He asked for his mail and chatted with the postmistress.

"Hear Nellie Foster's gone away," he said idly. "Out to Indiana."

"That so? When did she go?"

"A week or so ago. Don't tell me Nellie hasn't written to Foster!"

"I don't remember any mail for him. I don't think he's been in this week."

"He can't be very anxious about her."

"He's pretty anxious about that girl of Burford's. It beats me how a man with a wife will let a girl like that make a fool of him."

"You sound pretty sure."

"I am sure. I've seen them together."

That day the sheriff had a talk with his deputy. "Maybe I'm crazy, Joe; maybe I'm not. I just don't like it. Nellie was a homekeeping woman, and a trip to Indiana would mean something to her. What does she do? She doesn't call up anybody and say she's going. She just goes. It isn't natural."

"Sure sounds queer," said the deputy.

"I think Nellie's dog knows something. And it's my guess that Foster's out to kill him. He's got a gun. It might be a good idea to get out there and look around, anyhow."

They went out through the rain that afternoon. The roads after they left the state highway were muddy, and Foster was evidently not expecting company. As they turned in at his lane he was on the porch, and he had the rifle to his shoulder. He fired before he saw them.

"For God's sake," said the deputy, "what's he doing?"

Then Foster saw them, and his face went blank. He put down the gun and waited for them.

"What's the idea?" asked the sheriff, as he stopped the car. "Getting ready to go to war?"

"There's no law against my shooting rabbits, is there?"

"Weasels and rabbits. You seem to have a lot of varmints around here, Foster."

The sheriff got out of the car, and the deputy followed. They climbed the steps, while Foster watched them with suspicious, bloodshot eyes. He had not shaved, and he had been drinking. Not much. He was still wary.

"What do you fellows want?" he demanded.

"Well, I've got an errand, if you're agreeable. I told my wife about Rag's missing Nellie, and she said she'd like to keep him for a while."

Foster shrugged. "You can have him if you can catch him. He's gone plumb wild. Most ornery dog I ever saw. Won't even eat."

"Where is he?"

"He lies down in the wheat field a lot."

"Well, I'll try," said the sheriff. He turned to go, then stopped. "Better get a license for that gun, Foster. You might get into trouble."

They left him there, gazing after them. Let them get the dog if they could. He needed sleep. All he asked was a chance to sleep. He rubbed his bloodshot eyes and sat down heavily . . .

The two men moved toward the wheat field. Now and then the sheriff whistled and called, but there was no response. The dog had learned strategy. He was crawling away on his belly, his head low, following the furrow so that no ripple of the grain betrayed him. Finally he reached a culvert under the road and lay there, shivering in the water.

The sheriff also knew strategy. He spoke cautiously to the deputy. "Take a good look around, Joe," he said. "Go over to the orchard and whistle. That's where the dog howled from. And look at the ground. See if it's been disturbed any. I'll go on to the field."

He called again, "Here, Rags. Good dog. Come on, Rags."

But the dog lay under the culvert, motionless. He was still there when the two men drove back to town.

The deputy was talkative. "I didn't see anything," he said. "But there's something up. The place looks like Foster hasn't done a lick of work on it for a week. What is it, anyhow? Mrs. Foster have insurance?"

"He couldn't collect without a body. That girl of Burford's, most likely. They've been seen together."

"What about the dog? Did you want him?"

"I had an idea he could tell me a thing or two if I could get him. Unless Foster gets him first."

The sheriff dropped Joe in town and drove forty miles to the railroad junction. Here he questioned the men in the ticket office and around the station, but without result. A ticket for a woman going to Indiana. Well, where in Indiana? The sheriff didn't know. To ask Foster would make him suspicious, so at last the sheriff drove home, depressed and uneasy.

But Foster was already suspicious. He saw the girl that night and told her about the sheriff's visit. "What's bringing him around?" he said angrily. "He didn't want that dog. Hell, that wife of his wouldn't have a dog on the place."

"So what? Shoot him and bury him."

"The sheriff knows he's here. I can't kill him. Don't be a damned fool."

His tone was rough. Already his feeling for the girl was changing. She both drew him and repelled him. If it hadn't been for her, he would be sleeping at night, able to eat. But he needed comfort that night. He tried to kiss her, but just then they heard the familiar bark ending in a wail. The girl drew back and shuddered.

The next day, in his office, the sheriff spent some time in thought. He had nothing but a vague suspicion. Nellie Foster might be safe enough. But there was that picture of Foster, glaring at the dog with bloodshot eyes over the sights of his gun. There was, too, the entire moral and physical disintegration of the man. Something had caused it. But what?

The sheriff had one line to follow. How had Nellie got the message about her mother? The farm had no telephone, so it had come either by letter or by telegram. He went to the post office once more. There was no telegraph station in the village, and messages were telephoned there from the junction.

This time, however, he went in his official capacity. "Just keep this quiet," he said. "Nellie Foster went to Indiana because her mother was sick. Got any idea how she learned that? By letter or telegram?"

The postmistress looked startled. "There's nothing wrong, is there? About Nellie?"

"I don't know. It's a queer business."

"She didn't get a telegram. She might have had a letter. She and her mother wrote pretty steady. There's just one thing—maybe it doesn't mean anything."

"What is it?"

"Foster's trying to sell his farm."

"The hell he is!"

"Matt Saunders has wanted it for a good while. Foster was in to see him today."

The sheriff went away, thoughtful. So Foster was getting out. He didn't like the look of it. Yet when he met Matt Saunders on the street, the matter seemed commonplace enough.

"Hear you're thinking of buying the Foster place, Matt."

"Yeah. Been dickering for it for a couple of years."

"And Foster's selling."

"Looks like it. Nellie wants to be near her mother, somewhere out West."

But the sheriff was still not satisfied. That afternoon he sent for Joe and gave him some instructions.

"Now, mind this," he said. "We're outside the law, and Foster can raise the devil if he sees you. Besides, I have an idea he's dangerous."

"I'll be all right," said Joe.

"If he stays in the house you stay out."

"You bet!" said Joe fervently.

But Foster did not stay in the house that night. At dusk the dog had commenced once more its mournful wail, and when Foster met the girl at the barn he did not even embrace her. He stood off, red-eyed and unkempt, and his voice was hoarse with rage and fear.

"You got me into this," he said brutally. "Now, get me out. Listen to that! There must be some way to get him. He might let a woman get near him."

She nodded. "He might. He might think I was Nellie. See here, get me some of her clothes—things she's worn—and some shoes and stockings. And you'd better bring meat and a rope."

It seemed a sound plan. Foster felt more cheerful as he went back to his house. The weather had cleared, and the moon was out.

He never saw Joe, hidden in Nellie's room, because as Foster started up the stairs, the deputy slid out the window and dropped lightly to the ground. But Foster was beyond fear or suspicion that night. His only thought was the dog. Nevertheless, as he mounted the stairs he was trembling, and in the bedroom, groping in the clothes closet, he made small whimpering noises, strange from his big body.

But the instinct for self-preservation was strong. He found what he wanted, and went downstairs. The girl was on the porch. She had slipped off most of her clothing, and the moonlight made her flesh gleam white and desirable. But he did not so much as look at her. All at once he hated her white body, and suddenly it occurred to him that she hated him, too; that only one thing united them now, and that was fear.

"Where's the meat?"

"I'll get it."

"Well, hurry, you fool. I can't stay out all night."

She was dressed in Nellie's clothes when he came back, and she took the pan of meat without a word.

The dog was lying in the familiar spot in the orchard. He was very weak. He breathed shallowly, his dull eyes closing, then opening with a jerk. But his ears were alert, and his sensitive nose. It was his nose that told him first. Meat, of course, but something else too. He staggered to his feet and stood trembling violently. She was coming. She was coming at last. With a low whimper he ran to her.

"All right," called the girl. "I've got him."

He made no protest, save when Foster came near. Then he showed his teeth. Tied and locked in the barn, he wolfed down his food, and afterwards he slept. But there was no hope in him, and once in the night he howled again. Foster, lying awake, heard him and swore.

It was morning when Joe reported to the sheriff. He looked pleased with himself.

"Get in?" asked the sheriff.

Joe nodded. "Looks like the story's straight, all right," he said. "Foster nearly caught me, at that. But I had time to look around. Her clothes are gone, except the stuff she worked in."

The sheriff grunted. "Either the story's straight, or he's smarter than I thought he was."

Joe grinned. "Well, he wasn't so smart, at that," he said. "Look at this."

He held out his hand, and in it was a plain gold wedding ring.

"In the pocket of an apron," he said. "Like she took it off when she was working. Ain't likely a woman would go on a visit and leave a thing like that."

"No," said the sheriff soberly. "No."

Once more he got into his car and drove out to the farm. Already the atmosphere of the place had subtly changed, and so had Foster. He had shaved and put on a fresh shirt, and the porch had been swept. When the sheriff arrived, he was repairing the chicken-yard fence, and he looked himself again.

"Thought I'd make another try for Rags," the sheriff said.

"He kinda worries me. That is, unless Nellie's coming back soon."

Foster shrugged. "I don't expect her. Her mother's pretty sick."

"You've heard from her, then?"

"Yeah. Had a letter a day or two ago. She won't be back for a while."

"Then I'd better see about the dog."

"Dog's gone," said Foster. "I gave him to that girl of Burford's. She was going to visit some relatives over in Carter County, and she said they'd take him. Left this morning."

The sheriff looked at him. "I think you're lying, Foster," he said. "You haven't heard from Nellie, and you've been trying to kill Rags for a week or more. Why?"

"He was a damned nuisance, that's why!"

"Where's Nellie, Foster?"

"I've told you where she is. You crazy with the heat or what?"

"Where is she? I mean, what town. What part of Indiana?"

Foster looked at the hatchet in his hand, then put it down and straightened. "Now, get this and get it right, sheriff," he said. "I'm having no interference with my affairs. For a man running for re-election, you're making a fool of yourself for nothing. What business is it of yours where my wife is, or my dog either? Now, get the hell out of here. I've got work to do."

The sheriff reflected ruefully on that as he drove back to town. It was true. Nellie might be in Indiana. She might even have forgotten her wedding ring. All he really had was Foster's lie about the letter and a dog howling in the night; and now even the dog was gone . . .

Certainly the dog was gone. Early in the morning the girl had led him out to her car and tied him in the back. But there was no fight left in him. He lay where she placed him, hardly moving through the long hours.

The girl, on the contrary, was cheerful. She felt that she had escaped catastrophe by her own shrewdness. When she thought of Foster, she laughed out of sheer relief.

The dumb fool, she thought. It's the women who have the brains.

She stayed the night at her cousin's farm. The dog stood by

while they looked at him, his head drooping, his tail between his legs. When the children fed him he ate, but only once did he show any emotion whatever. That was when the girl was starting back the next morning.

"Well, good-bye, Rags," she said. "Be a good dog, won't you?"

She leaned down to touch him, and he snarled and showed his teeth.

"Gosh!" she said. "I don't believe he likes me."

The dog was quiet enough after she had gone. The children petted him, and he was gentle with them. But he lay most of the time in his kennel, sleeping and eating. Now and then he moved outside, as though to test his legs. The rope which tied him was long. He would walk a bit, go back and sleep again. At the end of three days he looked better: his coat had improved; his eyes were clear. And that night he started to free himself.

It took him a long time, for the rope was tough; but before dawn he was free. He moved out of the kennel, shook himself and started for home.

Meanwhile, the sheriff had reached an impasse. Nellie had been a reticent woman. His guarded inquiries revealed no one in town who knew where her mother lived. And then one day his case, such as it was, blew up entirely.

Foster received a letter from Indiana.

"It was from Indiana, all right," said the postmistress. "I couldn't make out the town. He didn't give me time to look at it."

"He was here, was he?"

"He was waiting for me to sort the mail. He's been in every morning for three or four days."

"Would you know Nellie's writing?"

"No, but it looked like a woman wrote it."

The sheriff went back to the office and taking out the wedding ring, laid it on his desk. It was still there when the door opened and Foster came in. He looked well, and he was carefully dressed.

"Just thought I'd drop in," he said. "You and I haven't been too friendly, but I guess that was my fault."

"Understand you're getting out."

"Yes. Sold the farm yesterday. I'll be off in a day or two.

Nellie likes it where she is. Anyhow, her mother's pretty old.''

"Then you've heard from her?"

"Got a letter today."

Foster took it out of its envelope and gave it to the sheriff. It was what might be expected, rather stiff and in a woman's hand, and after the sheriff read it he handed it back.

"She doesn't say anything about her wedding ring, does she?" he asked.

"Her wedding ring? What about it?"

"I had an idea she forgot it."

Foster looked uneasy. "Well, what if she did?" he demanded angrily. "She forgot a lot of things. She always did."

"This look like it? It's got her initials inside."

Foster's face lost its color as he saw the ring. "Where the hell did you get that?" he shouted furiously. "If you've been in my house without a warrant I'll have the law on you."

"I am the law around here," said the sheriff. "At least, until after election. Let's see the envelope of that letter."

But Foster stamped out of the office, and the sheriff was ruefully aware that he had overplayed his hand. When Joe came in, he was pulling on his pipe, the ring still in front of him.

"Foster's had a letter, Joe," he said.

"From his wife?"

"From some woman. Maybe Nellie, maybe not. Ever see the Burford girl's handwriting, Joe?"

Joe blushed. "I had a note or two, 'way back," he admitted.

"Know it again?"

"I may have a letter around somewhere," said Joe uncomfortably.

"I'd like to see it. None of my business what it's about. Think you can find it?"

"I'll go home and look."

An hour later the sheriff sat with the letter before him and a deep conviction in his mind. The Burford girl had written Foster's letter; it had gone to someone in Indiana in another envelope and been sent back by request. The sheriff had another conviction too: that Nellie Foster was dead and buried somewhere on the farm. But where? He could not dig over a hundred and sixty acres. He probably had no right to dig at all, without more of a case than he had; and Foster was leaving. In a day or two he would be gone.

If only he had the dog! He grunted. The dog was probably dead, too.

But the dog was not dead. He was not only alive—he was on his way home. It was now, although neither knew it, a race between Foster and himself, between dog and man; the man to close up his affairs and escape; the dog to prevent that escape; the man living in terror, the dog living by sheer determination. But the dog had instinct, the man only his wits.

It was a long distance, and the dog was wary. He traveled mostly by night, resting during the day; but his route was as direct as a homing pigeon's. By what miracle he found his way, no one would ever know.

But find it he did. On the night before Foster was to leave, Joe came into the sheriff's office. The sheriff was sitting there, his feet on his desk.

"Well, I'd better be going home," he said. "No use sitting here worrying."

"Nothing doing, eh?"

"Nothing. Maybe I'm getting too old for this job."

Joe made ready to follow him. Then he remembered something. "Say," he said, "if I didn't know that dog of Foster's was a hundred miles from here, I'd say I'd seen him tonight."

"Rags? You saw Rags?"

"Well, I don't know him well. Looked like him, though. He was heading for Foster's place, and he was about all in."

The sheriff reached into the drawer of his desk and took out an automatic. "Maybe I'm crazy with the heat, as Foster says," he observed. "Again, maybe I'm not. But I think that dog was Rags, and if it was, I'm damned sure I know where he was going. Better come along."

They drove out by the country road. It was a moonlit night, and a mile or so this side of Foster's, they overtook the dog. He was moving along, his head and tail drooping, his whole body showing exhaustion. The men got out of the car and followed him on foot. They were only a few yards behind him when he turned into Foster's lane. But he did not go to the house.

He went directly to the orchard, and once more lifted his long tragic face to the sky and sent out his heartbroken cry.

The two men listened, their nerves strung taut. The wail ended, the dog began to scratch at the earth. He scratched furiously, and Joe caught the sheriff's arm.

"Do you suppose she's been buried there?" he whispered.

"I'm afraid so, poor woman."

The sheriff started toward the house, Joe following him. When they were close by, Foster flung open the door, but he did not see the two men. He stood staring toward the orchard, and as the dog wailed again he made a strange gesture, as a man defeated. Then he went back into the house and slammed the door. The sheriff leaped for the porch.

He got there just too late. A shot rang out inside, and when they entered, Foster was lying dead on the floor.

Hours later, when Nellie Foster's body had been found in the orchard and taken away, the sheriff climbed wearily into his car. Joe drove, and the sheriff sat back, his eyes closed, while at his feet Rags slept the sleep of exhaustion. They were almost home when he spoke.

"You know, son, it's a funny thing about Foster. He wasn't fighting the law. He thought he had the law beat a mile. What he was fighting was this dog."

"And the dog won," said Joe.

"Yes," said the sheriff. "The dog won."

≪ How Come My Dog ≫ Don't Bark?

by

Ron Goulart

THEY COULDN'T USE those final pictures of him. The photos were too much even for *Worldwide Intruder*, which is why the last picture of Kerry Dent to run in that particular tabloid showed him looking tan, fit, and relatively unwrinkled.

It was the other photos in the *Intruder* which caused Dent to do what he did. If it hadn't been for those earlier pictures, and the unflattering little stories and captions accompanying them, he wouldn't have ended up out in San Fernando Valley in such terrible shape.

Well, his wife had something to do with it, of course. And that impossible dog, too.

Dent told me his suspicions concerning his wife when I visited him on the set of his television show late in the spring of last year. I'm sure you know he was married to Sue Bee Brannigan who does all the commercials for Galz Beer. A striking girl, if not overly supportive. He was a shade over 29 years older than Sue Bee.

His suspicions and complaints about the dog I was already pretty familiar with. His feelings concerning Demon were why I was on the Wheelan Studios lot that bright, relatively clear morning. My advertising agency had bought his new show, "Demon & Co.," for our client, the Barx Smoke Alarm. That's the one that barks and howls like a dog to warn you that your house is on fire. Dent's show seemed perfect for Barx and within three weeks of its first airing, "Demon & Co." had shot up to the number three spot in the ratings. Not bad for a television show staring a German Shepherd and a 59-year-old daredevil actor.

The trouble was, Dent had developed the notion the dog was jealous of him. He took to calling me at the ad agency, and eventually at my home in the best part of Santa Monica, to tell me how insanely jealous Demon was of him. Dent was convinced Demon was deliberately flubbing scenes, wasn't growling on cue, was mugging and letting his purplish tongue loll out during Dent's best dramatic moments and, on three occasions at least, nudging him off high places where only the actor's agility and long experience in action films saved him from serious injury. I'm not overly fond of animals, but still I found it difficult to accept most of what Dent told me.

As I approached the indoor set where Dent was supposed to be rescuing, aided by Demon, a country-and-western singer who was marooned in a flood I heard a great deal of snarling, barking, and shouting.

"Out, I want that gink out of here! Let me go, let me smack him in the beezer!"

That was Dent. You couldn't mistake his voice, which had never quite shaken his Bronx childhood.

"Easy, Kerry. Your pudgy face is getting all flushed. It's going to be coronary time if you don't watch it."

I reached the set in time to see Dent break free of the assistant director and key grip who'd been restraining him from charging at Ben Walden.

Walden was a tall, lean, and moderately handsome young man in his late twenties. He set his camera safely on a vacant canvas chair, pivoted, and stepped out of Dent's way.

"Gigolo!" accused Dent, spinning around. "I told you what I'd do with your camera if I ever caught you around me again!"

"Relax, Kerry," suggested Walden. "Your flabby body can't stand such stress."

"Flabby! I'll shove that—"

Dent, his narrowed eyes on the reporter, didn't notice the approach of Demon. He tripped over the dog and landed with a smack on the sound-stage floor.

Walden, snatching up his camera, clicked off six shots of the actor. "Beautiful, beautiful. All your chins are showing nicely." Then cradling the camera in his arms like a football, Walden jogged away.

He was out of the place by the time they got Dent on his

feet again. "Didn't I give strict orders that nobody from the *Intruder* ever be allowed near me?"

The director patted Dent on the shoulder. "The guy slips in, Kerry, he's elusive."

"And you!" Dent kicked out at the dog, missed, and nearly lost his balance.

"Why don't we take five," the director urged. "Pull Dolly out of the tank, Skipper. We'll try the scene again in a few minutes."

"I can do it now," said Dent.

"Few minutes. Go sit down and have a drink."

"I don't drink. I haven't had a drink in three years, no matter what you read in the damn *Intruder*. 'Aging Hasbeen, Looking the Worse for Booze, Totters out of Gollywood Bistro on Arm of Long-Suffering Wife.' You better keep Walden off my set, off the lot. Otherwise there's going to be real trouble." He noticed me then and came hurrying over.

"You're looking well, Kerry," I made the mistake of saying.

"Why shouldn't I look well? I'm in damn fine shape. I do all my own stunts in this halfwit show," he told me, face still flushed. "Which is more than I can say for Demon, my illustrious co-star. He needs a double for all the difficult stuff. Come into my dressing room so we can talk."

I followed him through a doorway and down a corridor. "The client is a little worried about—"

"Did you see what he did just now? Tripped me so I couldn't wind Walden's clock for him."

"An accident, dogs aren't as bright as—"

"And look at this dressing room." He jerked the door open. "Cozy."

"Cozy my fanny! It's tiny. You know who had this dressing room before me? That clunk who starred in *Cybernetic Midget*. Yeah, this is a dwarf's old dressing room." He stalked to a small refrigerator, took out a bottle of Perrier water. "Demon has a kennel the size of Pickfair, while I—"

"The client was worried by the last story in the *Int*—"

"Listen, I'm a part of your life, right?" He gestured at one wall with his glass of sparkling water.

There were framed stills from some of his old movies mounted on the wall. A shot from *The Dancing Pirate*, two

from *Captain Juggernaut*, one from *Fort Gordo*, and a whole
series from *The Avenging Cavalier*, which was Dent's most
popular movie.

"I saw most of your pictures," I admitted, "when I was a
kid."

"Ha, ha. Very funny. You're as old as I am."

"I'm forty-four, you're fifty-nine."

"Forty-four isn't that far from fifty-nine. However, I don't
have the problems you civilians do." He sipped at the water.
"I take care of myself, good care." He patted his chin.
"That's one chin you see, no matter what snide lies Walden
writes in the *Intruder*."

"It's not so much the lies as the photographs. The client
feels—"

"That bum hounds me! He sneaks around and snaps pictures of me when I'm at my worst. He waits for some unfortunate pose, then snaps and runs."

"The picture in this week's tab is particularly unfortunate.
Where you're hitting that blind beggar woman over the head
with her own accordion."

"It only *looks* that way. Because of that wily jerk Walden,"
explained the actor. "I was helping the old bat adjust the damn
thing and *snap* there's Walden and his camera."

"You were caught standing in front of the Naked Nickel-
odeon," I reminded. "With that poster behind you promising
explicit romantic action inside."

"You don't understand what it is to be a celebrity," Dent
said. "I can't take a walk or meet a friend without some nitwit
reporter or photographer popping up and trying to make me
look bad. The worse offender is that—"

"Maybe you should quit strolling in places like the Los
Angeles tenderloin."

Finishing his Perrier, Dent turned to face me. "You recall
the picture of me three weeks ago in the *Intruder?*"

"The one where you're doing a bellyflop in your pool.
Flabby Kerry Does Flop. The client thought—"

"He climbed over the wall of my estate to snap that." The
actor turned his back on me. "At least, I thought that was his
only reason for being there. Now I—well, it's one of those
little everyday troubles you have to live with."

I said, "I don't think the Barx Brothers can live with many

more of your little everyday troubles, Kerry. What is it?''

He gestured at another wall of photos. ''I've had four wives, everybody knows that. I swear the only one I ever cared for is Sue Bee.''

''She's a striking woman.''

''Of course she is. I only marry striking women. Sue Bee is also intelligent. How many people do you know who've read all the way through Proust's *Remembrance of Things Past?*''

''I read it in college, and my wife read it while she was in the hospital with—''

''Never mind,'' he cut in. ''The trouble is, despite her intelligence—well, Sue Bee is being unfaithful.''

I nodded. ''These days, Kerry, with society in a state of—''

''Unfaithful to *me*! And do you know who the guy is?''

''No, who?''

''Him! The jerk with the camera!''

''Ben Walden?''

''That bum with the camera, yes. Walden is cuckolding me.''

''You're absolutely sure?''

''Figures, doesn't it? Explains why he's trying to destroy me in the pages of that filthy rag. Over-the-hill Swashbuckler Makes Feeble Attempt at Comeback. Feeble? He knows we knocked off the two top shows. The network ought to have a few more feeble swashbucklers like me.''

''Wait now,'' I said. ''Do you know for certain your wife's having an affair with Walden, or do you just suppose she is?''

''I know *here*!'' He thumped his handsome chest. ''Look, if you're an artist you *sense* things. I know. Old Man Dent Takes Snooze After Too Much Booze. He's trying to make me look ridiculous in the eyes of Sue Bee.''

''But a woman of her intelligence wouldn't—''

''Just because she's read Proust doesn't mean she wouldn't have an affair with Walden.''

I was silent for several seconds. ''Going to be tough using any of this with the Barx Brothers,'' I finally told him. ''If true, this is a logical explanation for why the *Intruder* seems to be picking on you. But the idea of your wife fooling around will upset them even more than—''

"You can tell the Barx boys to stick some of their smoke alarms—"

"Kerry, let me think about this. I'll see if I can—"

"Always the ad man. You can't react to anything with your *guts*. You have to write memos, take a couple dips in the think tank."

I cleared my throat. "This probably isn't the best time to ask you about the publicity stills."

"What stills?"

"Ones of you and Demon standing under a Barx alarm."

"Tell you what." Dent put a hand on my back. "We can use Demon's stand-in. That dog is an angel, a gem of a hound. Sweet, considerate, the absolute antithesis of Demon. I keep telling them to take Demon out and retire him or something and use the damn stand-in. They won't hear of it, especially Tessica Janes, the bimbo who claims to be Demon's trainer. She's got them all hoodwinked into thinking Demon is unique. He's unique all right, but—"

"Ready to shoot again, Mr. Dent," someone called outside the door.

Dent straightened, smiling. "Don't brood too much about anything that's happened today," he said to me. "I have an uncanny ability for bouncing back. And you're going to see one hell of a bounce any day now."

The agency sent me to Mentor, Ohio, a few days after that encounter with Kerry Dent and I didn't see him again for nearly a month. We'd been test-marketing a new bread in Mentor, a loaf which was 20 percent sawdust and called Lumberjack Bread, and some problems had arisen. Nearly everyone who ate so much as a slice of the experimental bread had come down with a disease closely resembling the flu. There was a definite danger of the media getting hold of the story. We couldn't afford to have the whole country hearing about a new blight known as the Lumberjack Bread Disease.

I was able, with a mixture of diplomacy and bribery, to keep the whole mess hushed up. Working very covertly we got all the test loaves out of the supermarkets and dumped into a handy river. That dumping gave us another problem, since it turned out that Lumberjack Bread was capable of killing fish even with its wrapper on.

As I say, I didn't get back to Los Angeles until a month or more after my meeting with Kerry Dent on the "Demon & Co." set. Not that I hadn't been in communication with him, or rather he with me. Dent, possibly because he knew I'd been a fan of his swashbucklers in my youth, decided I was the one person he could confide in.

The phone in my slightly mildewed Mentor motel room rang at all hours. Dent's complaints were all variations on ones I'd heard before. Sue Bee continued to be unfaithful with Ben Walden of *Worldwide Intruder*, Demon loathed him and was making enormous efforts to sabotage his comeback, Walden was so audacious that when he sneaked into Dent's mansion to woo his wife he managed to snap unflattering photos of the dozing actor. Despite his claims of renewed vigor, Dent seemed to nap a good deal, as the frequent pictures showing up in the *Intruder* attested.

One particularly bleak morning in Ohio, just after my lovely secretary had rushed in to tell me 5000 dead fish had been sighted floating down the river with several loaves of Lumberjack Bread leading the pack, Dent phoned me collect. He claimed he had absolute proof that Demon not only hated him but was actually trying to kill him. In a scene for the eleventh episode of their show the dog was supposed to remove a smoking stick of dynamite from the vicinity of the bound-and-gagged Dent. He swore, and claimed to have witnesses, that Demon switched a real stick of dynamite for the prop one. If Dent hadn't sensed something was wrong and gone rolling over a low precipice he would have been blown up.

I pointed out that real dynamite could just as likely have blown up the dog when he snatched it up in his powerful jaws. Dent told me the dog had deliberately dawdled instead of rushing in to pick up the dynamite stick. Pacifying him as best I could, I went out to do something about all those dead fish.

My last, although I didn't know it at the time, encounter with Kerry Dent took place by accident. I was out in San Fernando Valley to call on a well-known sci-fi writer in Woodland Hills to see if we could persuade him to endorse a new pizza line the agency was involved with. The author, an extremely surly man, was not at all impressed by the Unidentified Flying Pizza and came close to punching me. Feeling very much like someone in an *Intruder* gossip item, I slunk away from his home and dropped into a valley restaurant for a cup of coffee to calm my nerves.

It was a noisy place, because of the prerecorded whip cracking and pistol shooting, and at first I wasn't aware of the hissing.

"Hsst, over here."

It was Dent, wearing a nylon jumpsuit and dark glasses and without his hairpiece. "Are you incognito?" I inquired, joining him in his booth.

"Used to know Whip in his heyday and I stop by here now and then."

Whip Wigransky's Burger Rancho was one of six such spots in the valley. It didn't seem to me that a nostalgia for the old B-Western actor was what had brought Dent here. "You have," I mentioned, "paw prints all over your front."

He glanced down, frowning, and brushed off some of the muddy spots. "Ho, ho," he said.

"You sound happy. I take it those prints aren't the leftovers from another attack by your co-star."

"That dumbunny isn't a co-star. I'm a star and he's only a bit player." Dent appeared considerably more relaxed than he'd been lately.

"I'm glad you're in a jovial mood. I thought maybe the picture in this week's *Intruder* would have—"

"Ho, ho, ho. That sort of guff rolls off my back. Fat Old Actor, Looking Terrible, Escorts Stunning Much Younger Wife to Premiere. Walden'll have to do a lot better than that to dampen Kerry Dent's spirits."

"I'll pass that news on to the Barx Brothers."

"Give them my love."

I watched his partially masked face. "What are you up to?"

"Having a Bar-B-Q Burger, Owlhoot Style," he said, smiling. "That's all."

"You're out here, disguised, looking smug. It's not like you."

"You didn't know me in my heyday," he replied. "I often went around looking smug. Recently I've found a way to return to the happier moods of yesteryear."

"Are you drinking again?"

"You can't drink and do your own stunts and keep a crazed

hellhound from destroying you.'' He chuckled, relaxing even more. ''I was stupid for a spell, now I'm getting all my old smarts back. There was a rock-and-roll tune I used to be fond of years ago. About a guy who suspected his wife was two-timing him. He asks the suspected lover, 'How come my dog don't bark when you come round my door? Maybe it's because you been here before.' I was like that, stupid. Now I see things as they really are. I've devised a plan to bring me complete and total happiness.''

''You haven't gone and joined some lunatic cult?''

''Cults join me.'' He locked his hands behind his head. ''You and the Barx brood need have no fears. In a short time I shall have everything worked out to the satisfaction of one and all.''

''Tessica Janes lives out here in the valley somewhere,'' I said, recalling the fact all at once. ''You haven't been visiting her and making threats?''

''That bimbo and I have little to do with each other,'' Dent assured me. ''She trains Demon, I am forced to act with him. That's our only link.''

''She's a pretty large young woman. Doesn't look as though she could be intimidated.''

''I don't blame Tess for what Demon does. He hates me and plots against me entirely on his own,'' he said. ''Say, look who's coming in. It's old Whip Wigransky himself. Excuse me while I go wrestle with him. It's a long-standing custom.''

''Sure, certainly.'' I sat there, not even turning to watch the good-natured horseplay which was amusing all the other customers. Deep inside I felt very uneasy. I had a premonition something was going to happen, something which would affect the show and annoy the Barx Brothers.

Immediately after this I had to leave town again. There'd been a disastrous fire in the Barx Brothers main factory in Trenton, New Jersey. The place had burned to the ground and not one of the 10,000 smoke alarms sitting in there had so much as yelped. The wire services had picked up the story and both *Newsmag* and *Tide* were sending people in. The Barx Brothers, with the exception of Carlos who refused to come back from Bermuda, met with me for two days while we worked out a rush campaign to counteract the effects of what had happened.

By the time I came up with a copy approach which satisfied us all, except for Jocko who went off to join Carlos in Bermuda, and wrote some commercials three weeks had passed. I was on the plane back to L.A. when the news came through. I learned about it because my stewardess was sobbing and I asked why.

"The poor darling old man," she managed to say between sobs. "He's been a part of my life since earliest girlhood. I simply adored his swashbuckling films and his TV shows and—"

"Wait a minute. You can't be talking about—"

"Yes, isn't it awful? Kerry Dent is dead."

"Kerry Dent is dead?"

"I heard it on the news just before takeoff."

"How did it happen?"

"Oh, it's too terrible."

She was referring of course only to the official version of Dent's passing. Nobody ever released the true story, which was fortunate I suppose. It's possible that Ben Walden knows most of the truth, but he won't be writing it up in the *Intruder*. Not unless he can figure a way to make his own part in the events seem admirable. Which isn't likely.

As you probably know, I don't like to get too involved in affairs of this sort. Since I was curious, though, and since I felt I owed it to the agency to find out why the star of our top-rated show had been torn to pieces, I did some digging.

What follows is, I believe, a relatively accurate account of how Dent met his end. Some of it I've had to guess.

Dent had come up with a plan to remove the two prime sources of grief in his life—Ben Walden and Demon. He was certain Sue Bee would return to him completely when there was no more Ben Walden around. He also believed Demon could be very easily replaced on the show by the stand-in, a much more admirable dog. He figured it would be to the benefit of all concerned not even to let on there'd been a switch. One German Shepherd looked pretty much like another.

He arranged things so he could put his plan into action the night Tessica Janes, Demon's trainer, was not at home. The girl was scheduled to attend a screening of the punk rock remake of *Boys Town* on the night in question. Dent, with the help of Whip Wigransky, had already planted in Ben Walden's mind the idea that Dent was having an affair with Tessica. That fateful night Whip phoned Walden with a tip that the girl was going to skip the screening and spend the night with the aging actor. Dent assumed Walden wouldn't pass up a chance to get pictures of him in such a compromising situation.

Dent had been, very secretly, working out in San Fernando Valley at a seedy dog-training school. That was where he'd been the day I ran into him. The paw prints I'd noticed had come from the vicious German Shepherd that Dent was training. This dog was designed to be a watchdog, eager to kill anyone his master ordered him to kill. Dent was his master.

Actually it wasn't a bad plan. Lure Walden to Tessica's place and set this killer dog on him. The police would find the body of a snooping reporter who'd obviously been torn to pieces by a mad German Shepherd. There would be Demon in his cage looking sheepish.

Even if Tessica claimed the dog had been locked up all night, the evidence of a dead *Intruder* reporter would contradict her.

Dent arrived a half hour before the ten-o'clock assignation time that he'd had Whip pass on to Walden. It was an exceptionally clear night with more stars out than you usually see in Southern California.

Parking his rented van in a wooded area behind Tessica's spread, Dent led his killer dog out of the vehicle and down to the ranch. By diligent spying earlier he knew there was only one old servant to worry about. The man was in his late sixties and slept in a cottage near the main entrance of the ranch. There was a cyclone fence around the three acres, but it wasn't electrified. Dent had no trouble clipping a section out of it.

The police would naturally assume that Walden, hot after a hot story, had done the snipping.

Up to here Dent's plan went well. He crossed onto the ranch grounds with his dog.

There was an arbor to the left of the ranchhouse. He took the German Shepherd there and crouched in the shadows to await Walden.

He debated whether or not he ought to let Demon loose after the killing. He decided it would be safer not to. As he'd already figured out, no matter what Tessica and the old servant might claim, they'd never convince the police that it wasn't Demon who'd done the killing. There were only two collies and a Spaniel in the kennels here. None of them could be blamed. The frame would fit only Demon.

Unfortunately there were three things Dent couldn't have anticipated. For one thing, he couldn't have known that Walden, who was spending some time with Sue Bee, would be late by about 20 minutes. Nor did Dent know that on the evenings when Tessica was away the old servant let Demon loose for a romp around the ranch.

The third thing he couldn't have expected was that his killer dog, while aggressive with people, was fearful of other German Shepherds.

So when the roaming Demon, sensing the presence of Dent and the dog in the arbor, came galloping in there, the killer dog yelped and ran away through the hole in the fence.

Demon then leaped straight at Dent.

I'd always thought Dent was exaggerating about the animosity Demon felt toward him. It turned out, though, Dent was absolutely right.

That dog really hated him.

≪ The Sleeping Dog ≫
by
Ross MacDonald

THE DAY AFTER her dog disappeared, Fay Hooper called me early. Her normal voice was like waltzing violins, but this morning the violins were out of tune. She sounded as though she'd been crying.

"Otto's gone."

Otto was her one-year-old German shepherd.

"He jumped the fence yesterday afternoon and ran away. Or else he was kidnaped—dognaped, I suppose is the right word to use."

"What makes you think that?"

"You know, Otto, Mr. Archer—how loyal he was. He wouldn't deliberately stay away from me overnight, not under his own power. There must be thieves involved."

She caught her breath. "I realize searching for stolen dogs isn't your métier. But you *are* a detective, and I thought, since we knew one another . . ."

She allowed her voice to suggest, ever so chastely, that we might get to know one another better.

I liked the woman. I liked the dog, I liked the breed. I was taking my own German shepherd pup to obedience school, which is where I met Fay Hooper. Otto and she were the handsomest and most expensive members of the class.

"How do I get to your place?"

She lived in the hills north of Malibu, she said, on the far side of the county line. If she wasn't home when I got there, her husband would be.

On my way out I stopped at the dog school in Pacific Palisades to talk to the man who ran it, Fernando Rambeau. The kennels behind the house burst into clamor when I knocked on the front door. Rambeau boarded dogs as well as trained them.

A dark-haired girl looked out and informed me that her husband was feeding the animals. "Maybe I can help," she added doubtfully, and then she let me into a small living room.

I told her about the missing dog. "It would help if you called the vets and animal shelters and gave them a description," I said.

"We've already been doing that. Mrs. Hooper was on the phone to Fernando last night." She sounded vaguely resentful. "I'll get him."

Setting her face against the continuing noise, she went out the back door. Rambeau came in with her, wiping his hands on a rag. He was a square-shouldered Canadian with a curly black beard that failed to conceal his youth. Over the beard, his intense dark eyes peered at me warily, like an animal's sensing trouble.

Rambeau handled dogs as if he loved them. He wasn't quite so patient with human beings. His current class was only in its third week, but he was already having dropouts. The man was loaded with explosive feeling, and it was close to the surface now.

"I'm sorry about Mrs. Hooper and her dog. They were my best pupils. He was, anyway. But I can't drop everything and spend the next week looking for him."

"Nobody expects that. I take it you've had no luck with your contacts."

"I don't have such good contacts. Marie and I, we just moved down here last year, from British Columbia."

"That was a mistake," his wife said from the doorway.

Rambeau pretended not to hear her. "Anyway, I know nothing about dog thieves." With both hands he pushed the possibility away from him. "If I hear any word of the dog I'll let you know, naturally. I've got nothing against Mrs. Hooper."

His wife gave him a quick look. It was one of those revealing looks which said, among other things, that she loved him but didn't know if he loved her, and she was worried about him. She caught me watching her and lowered her eyes. Then she burst out, "Do you think somebody killed the dog?"

"I have no reason to think so."

"Some people shoot dogs, don't they?"

"Not around here," Rambeau said. "Maybe back in the bush someplace." He turned to me with a sweeping explanatory gesture. "These things make her nervous and she gets wild ideas. You know Marie is a country girl—"

"I am not. I was born in Chilliwack." Flinging a bitter look at him, she left the room.

"Was Otto shot?" I asked Rambeau.

"Not that I know of. Listen, Mr. Archer, you're a good customer, but I can't stand here talking all day. I've got twenty dogs to feed."

They were still barking when I drove up the coast highway out of hearing. It was nearly 40 miles to the Hoopers' mailbox, and another mile up a black-top lane which climbed the side of a canyon to the gate. On both sides of the heavy wire gate, which had a new combination padlock on it, a hurricane fence, eight feet high and topped with barbed wire, extended out of sight. Otto would have to be quite a jumper to clear it. So would I. The house beyond the gate was low and massive, made of fieldstone and steel and glass. I honked at it and waited. A man in blue bathing trunks came out of the house with a shotgun. The sun glinted on its twin barrels and on the man's bald head and round, brown, burnished belly. He walked quite slowly, a short heavy man in his sixties, scuffling along in huaraches. The flabby brown shell of fat on him jiggled lugubriously.

When he approached the gate, I could see the stiff gray pallor under his tan, like stone showing under varnish. He was sick, or afraid, or both. His mouth was profoundly discouraged.

"What do you want?" he said over the shotgun.

"Mrs. Hooper asked me to help find her dog. My name is Lew Archer."

He was not impressed. "My wife isn't here, and I'm busy. I happen to be following soy-bean futures rather closely."

"Look here, I've come quite a distance to lend a hand. I met Mrs. Hooper at dog school and—"

Hooper uttered a short savage laugh. "That hardly constitutes an introduction to either of us. You'd better be on your way right now."

"I think I'll wait for your wife."

"I think you won't." He raised the shotgun and let me look into its close-set, hollow, round eyes. "This is my property all the way down to the road, and you're trespassing. That means I can shoot you if I have to."

"What sense would that make? I came out here to help you."

"You can't help me." He looked at me through the wire gate with a kind of pathetic arrogance, like a lion that had grown old in captivity. "Go away."

I drove back down to the road and waited for Fay Hooper. The sun slid up the sky. The inside of my car turned oven-hot. I went for a walk down the canyon. The brown September grass crunched under my feet. Away up on the far side of the canyon an earth mover that looked like a crazy red insect was cutting the ridge to pieces.

A very fast black car came up the canyon and stopped abruptly beside me. A gaunt man in a wrinkled brown suit climbed out, with his hand on his holster, told me that he was Sheriff Carlson, and asked me what I was doing there. I told him.

He pushed back his wide cream-colored hat and scratched at his hairline. The pale eyes in his sun-fired face were like clouded glass inserts in a brick wall.

"I'm surprised Mr. Hooper takes that attitude. Mrs. Hooper just came to see me in the courthouse. But I can't take you up there with me if Mr. Hooper says no."

"Why not?"

"He owns most of the county and holds the mortgage on the rest of it. Besides," he added with careful logic, "Mr. Hooper is a friend of mine."

"Then you better get him a keeper."

The sheriff glanced around uneasily, as if the Hoopers' mailbox might be bugged. "I'm surprised he has a gun, let alone threatening you with it. He must be upset about the dog."

"He didn't seem to care about the dog."

"He does, though. *She* cares, so *he* cares," Carlson said.

"What did she have to tell you?"

"She can talk to you herself. She should be along any minute. She told me that she was going to follow me out of town."

He drove his black car up the lane. A few minutes later Fay Hooper stopped her Mercedes at the mailbox. She must have seen the impatience on my face. She got out and came toward me in a little run, making noises of dismayed regret.

Fay was in her late thirties and fading slightly, as if a light frost had touched her pale gold head, but she was still a beautiful woman. She turned the gentle force of her charm on me.

"I'm dreadfully sorry," she said. "Have I kept you waiting long?"

"Your husband did. He ran me off with a shotgun."

Her gloved hand lighted on my arm, and stayed. She had an electric touch, even through layers of cloth.

"That's terrible. I had no idea that Allan still had a gun."

Her mouth was blue behind her lipstick, as if the information had chilled her to the marrow. She took me up the hill in the Mercedes. The gate was standing open, but she didn't drive in right away.

"I might as well be perfectly frank," she said without looking at me. "Ever since Otto disappeared yesterday, there's been a nagging question in my mind. What you've just told me raises the question again. I was in town all day yesterday so that Otto was alone here with Allan when—when it happened."

The values her voice gave to the two names made it sound as if Allan were the dog and Otto the husband.

"When what happened, Mrs. Hooper?" I wanted to know.

Her voice sank lower. "I can't help suspecting that Allan shot him. He's never liked any of my dogs. The only dogs he appreciates are hunting dogs—and he was particularly jealous of Otto. Besides, when I got back from town, Allan was getting the ground ready to plant some roses. He's never enjoyed gardening, particularly in the heat. We have professionals to do our work. And this really isn't the time of year to put in a bed of roses."

"You think your husband was planting a dog?" I asked.

"If he was, I have to know." She turned toward me, and the leather seat squeaked softly under her movement. "Find out for me, Mr. Archer. If Allan killed my beautiful big old dog, I couldn't stay with him."

"Something you said implied that Allan used to have a gun or guns, but gave them up. Is that right?"

"He had a small arsenal when I married him. He was an

infantry officer in the war and a big-game hunter in peacetime.
But he swore off hunting years ago.''

"Why?''

"I don't really know. We came home from a hunting trip one
fall and Allan sold all his guns. He never said a word about it to
me but it was the fall after the war ended, and I always thought
that it must have had something to do with the war.''

"Have you been married so long?''

"Thank you for that question.'' She produced a rueful
smile. "I met Allan during the war, the year I came out, and
I knew I'd met my fate. He was a very powerful person.''

"And a very wealthy one.''

She gave me a flashing, haughty look and stepped so hard
on the accelerator that she almost ran into the sheriff's car
parked in front of the house. We walked around to the back,
past a free-form swimming pool that looked inviting, into a
walled garden. A few Greek statues stood around in elegant
disrepair. Bees murmured like distant bombers among the
flowers.

The bed where Allan Hooper had been digging was about
five feet long and three feet wide, and it reminded me of
graves.

"Get me a spade,'' I said.

"Are you going to dig him up?''

"You're pretty sure he's in there, aren't you, Mrs.
Hooper?''

"I guess I am.''

From a lath house at the end of the garden she fetched a
square-edged spade. I asked her to stick around.

I took off my jacket and hung it on a marble torso where
it didn't look too bad. It was easy digging in the newly worked
soil. In a few minutes I was two feet below the surface, and
the ground was still soft and penetrable.

The edge of my spade struck something soft but not so penetrable. Fay Hooper heard the peculiar dull sound it made. She
made a dull sound of her own. I scooped away more earth. Dog
fur sprouted like stiff black grass at the bottom of the grave.

Fay got down on her knees and began to dig with her lac-
quered fingernails. Once she cried out in a loud harsh voice,
"Dirty murderer!''

Her husband must have heard her. He came out of the house

and looked over the stone wall. His head seemed poised on top of the wall, hairless and bodiless, like Humpty-Dumpty. He had that look on his face, of not being able to be put together again.

"I didn't kill your dog, Fay. Honest to God, I didn't."

She didn't hear him. She was talking to Otto. "Poor boy, poor boy," she said. "Poor, beautiful boy."

Sheriff Carlson came into the garden. He reached down into the grave and freed the dog's head from the earth. His large hands moved gently on the great wedge of the skull.

Fay knelt beside him in torn and dirty stockings. "What are you doing?"

Carlson held up a red-tipped finger. "Your dog was shot through the head, Mrs. Hooper, but it's no shotgun wound. Looks to me more like a deer rifle."

"I don't even own a rifle," Hooper said over the wall. "I haven't owned one for nearly twenty years. Anyway, I wouldn't shoot your dog."

Fay scrambled to her feet. She looked ready to climb the wall. "Then why did you bury him?"

His mouth opened and closed.

"Why did you buy a shotgun without telling me?"

"For protection."

"Against my dog?"

Hooper shook his head. He edged along the wall and came in tentatively through the gate. He had on slacks and a short-sleeved yellow jersey which somehow emphasized his shortness and his fatness and his age.

"Mr. Hooper had some threatening calls," the sheriff said. "Somebody got hold of his unlisted number. He was just telling me about it now."

"Why didn't you tell me, Allan?"

"I didn't want to alarm you. You weren't the one they were after, anyway. I bought a shotgun and kept it in my study."

"Do you know who they are?"

"No. I make enemies in the course of business, especially the farming operations. Some crackpot shot your dog, gunning for me. I heard a shot and found him dead in the driveway."

"But how could you bury him without telling me?"

Hooper spread his hands in front of him. "I wasn't thinking too well. I felt guilty, I suppose, because whoever got him was after me. And I didn't want you to see him dead. I guess I wanted to break it to you gently.''

"This is gently?"

"It's not the way I planned it. I thought if I had a chance to get you another pup—"

"No one will ever take Otto's place."

Allan Hooper stood and looked at her wistfully across the open grave, as if he would have liked to take Otto's place. After a while the two of them went into the house.

Carlson and I finished digging Otto up and carried him out to the sheriff's car. His inert blackness filled the trunk from side to side.

"What are you going to do with him, Sheriff?" I asked.

"Get a vet I know to recover the slug in him. Then if we nab the sniper we can use ballistics to convict him."

"You're taking this just as seriously as a real murder, aren't you?" I observed.

"They want me to," he said with a respectful look toward the house.

Mrs. Hooper came out carrying a white leather suitcase which she deposited in the back seat of her Mercedes.

"Are you going someplace?" I asked her.

"Yes, I am." She didn't say where.

Her husband, who was watching her from the doorway, didn't speak. The Mercedes went away. He closed the door. Both of them had looked sick.

"She doesn't seem to believe he didn't do it. Do you, Sheriff?"

Carlson jabbed me with his forefinger. "Mr. Hooper is no liar. If you want to get along with me, get that through your head. I've known Mr. Hooper for over twenty years—served under him in the war—and I never heard him twist the truth."

"I'll have to take your word for it. What about those threatening phone calls? Did he report them to you before today?"

"No."

"What was said on the phone?"

"He didn't tell me."

"Does Hooper have any idea who shot the dog?"

"Well, he did say he saw a man slinking around outside the fence. He didn't get close enough to the guy to give me a good description, but he did make out that he had a black beard.''

"There's a dog trainer in Pacific Palisades named Rambeau who fits the description. Mrs. Hooper has been taking Otto to his school.''

"Rambeau?'' Carlson said with interest.

"Fernando Rambeau. He seemed pretty upset when I talked to him this morning.''

"What did he say?''

"A good deal less than he knows, I think. I'll talk to him again.''

Rambeau was not at home. My repeated knocking was answered only by the barking of the dogs. I retreated up the highway to a drive-in where I ate a torpedo sandwich. When I was on my second cup of coffee, Marie Rambeau drove by in a pickup truck. I followed her home.

"Where's Fernando?'' I asked.

"I don't know. I've been out looking for him.''

"Is he in a bad way?''

"I don't know how you mean.''

"Emotionally upset.''

"He has been ever since that woman came into the class.''

"Mrs. Hooper?''

Her head bobbed slightly.

"Are they having an affair?''

"They better not be.'' Her small red mouth looked quite implacable. "He was out with her night before last. I heard him make the date. He was gone all night, and when he came home he was on one of his black drunks and he wouldn't go to bed. He sat in the kitchen and drank himself glassy-eyed.'' She got out of the pickup facing me. "Is shooting a dog a very serious crime?''

"It is to me, but not to the law. It's not like shooting a human being.''

"It would be to Fernando. He loves dogs the way other people love human beings. That included Otto.''

"But he shot him.''

Her head drooped. I could see the straight white part dividing her black hair. "I'm afraid he did. He's got a crazy streak and it comes out in him when he drinks. You should have heard him in the kitchen yesterday morning. He was moaning and groaning about his brother.''

"His brother?"

"Fernando had an older brother, George, who died back in Canada after the war. Fernando was just a kid when it happened and it was a big loss to him. His parents were dead, too, and they put him in a foster home in Chilliwack. He still has nightmares about it."

"What did his brother die of?"

"He never told me exactly, but I think he was shot in some kind of hunting accident. George was a guide and packer in the Fraser River valley below Mount Robson. That's where Fernando comes from, the Mount Robson country. He won't go back, on account of what happened to his brother."

"What did he say about his brother yesterday?" I asked.

"That he was going to get his revenge for George. I got so scared I couldn't listen to him. I went out and fed the dogs. When I came back in, Fernando was loading his deer rifle. I asked him what he was planning to do, but he walked right out and drove away."

"May I see the rifle?"

"It isn't in the house. I looked for it after he left today. He must have taken it with him again. I'm so afraid that he'll kill somebody."

"What's he driving?"

"Our car. It's an old blue Meteor sedan."

Keeping an eye out for it, I drove up the highway to the Hoopers' canyon. Everything there was very peaceful. Too peaceful. Just inside the locked gate, Allan Hooper was lying face down on his shotgun. I could see small ants in single file trekking across the crown of his bald head.

I got a hammer out of the trunk on my car and used it to break the padlock. I lifted his head. His skin was hot in the sun, as if death had fallen on him like a fever. But he had been shot neatly between the eyes. There was no exit wound; the bullet was still in his head. Now the ants were crawling on my hands.

I found my way into the Hoopers' study, turned off the stuttering teletype, and sat down under an elk head to telephone the courthouse. Carlson was in his office.

"I have bad news, Sheriff. Allan Hooper's been shot."

I heard him draw in his breath quickly. "Is he dead?"

"Extremely dead. You better put out a general alarm for Rambeau."

Carlson said with gloomy satisfaction, "I already have him."

"You have him?"

"That's correct. I picked him up in the Hoopers' canyon and brought him in just a few minutes ago." Carlson's voice sank to a mournful mumble. "I picked him up a little too late, I guess."

"Did Rambeau do any talking?"

"He hasn't had a chance to yet. When I stopped his car, he piled out and threatened me with a rifle. I clobbered him one good."

I went outside to wait for Carlson and his men. A very pale afternoon moon hung like a ghost in the sky. For some reason it made me think of Fay. She ought to be here. It occurred to me that possibly she had been.

I went and looked at Hooper's body again. He had nothing to tell me. He lay as if he had fallen from a height, perhaps all the way from the moon.

They came in a black county wagon and took him away. I followed them inland to the county seat, which rose like a dusty island in a dark green lake of orange groves. We parked in the courthouse parking lot, and the sheriff and I went inside.

Rambeau was under guard in a second-floor room with barred windows. Carlson said it was used for interrogation. There was nothing in the room but an old deal table and some wooden chairs. Rambeau sat hunched forward on one of them, his hands hanging limp between his knees. Part of his head had been shaved and plastered with bandages.

"I had to cool him with my gun butt," Carlson said. "You're lucky I didn't shoot you—you know that, Fernando?"

Rambeau made no response. His black eyes were set and dull.

"Had his rifle been fired?"

"Yeah. Chet Scott is working on it now. Chet's my identification lieutenant and he's a bear on ballistics." The sheriff turned back to Rambeau. "You might as well give us a full confession, boy. If you shot Mr. Hooper and his dog, we can link the bullets to your gun. You know that."

Rambeau didn't speak or move.

"What did you have against Mr. Hooper?" Carlson said.

No answer. Rambeau's mouth was set like a trap in the thicket of his beard.

"Your older brother," I said to him, "was killed in a hunting accident in British Columbia. Was Hooper at the other end of the gun that killed George?"

Rambeau didn't answer me, but Carlson's head came up. "Where did you get that, Archer?"

"From a couple of things I was told. According to Rambeau's wife, he was talking yesterday about revenge for his brother's death. According to Fay Hooper, her husband swore off guns when he came back from a hunting trip after the war. Would you know if that trip was to British Columbia?"

"Yeah. Mr. Hooper took me and the wife with him."

"Whose wife?"

"Both our wives."

"To the Mount Robson area?"

"That's correct. We went up after elk."

"And did he shoot somebody accidentally?"

"Not that I know of. I wasn't with him all the time, understand. He often went out alone, or with Mrs. Hooper," Carlson replied.

"Did he use a packer named George Rambeau?"

"I wouldn't know. Ask Fernando here."

I asked Fernando. He didn't speak or move. Only his eyes had changed. They were wet and glistening-black, visible parts of a grief that filled his head like a dark underground river.

The questioning went on and produced nothing. It was night when I went outside. The moon was slipping down behind the dark hills. I took a room in a hotel and checked in with my answering service in Hollywood.

About an hour before, Fay Hooper had called me from a Las Vegas hotel. When I tried to return the call, she wasn't in her room and didn't respond to paging. I left a message for her to come home, that her husband was dead.

Next, I called R.C.M.P. headquarters in Vancouver to ask some questions about George Rambeau. The answers came over the line in clipped Canadian tones. George and his dog had disappeared from his cabin below Red Pass in the fall of 1945. Their bodies hadn't been recovered until the following

May, and by that time they consisted of parts of the two skel-
etons. These included George Rambeau's skull, which had
been pierced in the right front and left rear quadrants by a
heavy-caliber bullet. The bullet had not been recovered. Who
fired it, or when, or why, had never been determined. The dog,
a husky, had also been shot through the head.

I walked over to the courthouse to pass the word to Carlson.
He was in the basement shooting gallery with Lieutenant
Scott, who was firing test rounds from Fernando Rambeau's
.30/30 repeater.

I gave them the official account of the accident. "But since
George Rambeau's dog was shot, too, it probably wasn't an
accident," I said.

"I see what you mean," Carlson said. "It's going to be
rough, spreading all this stuff out in court about Mr. Hooper.
We have to nail it down, though."

I went back to my hotel and to bed, but the process of
nailing down the case against Rambeau continued through the
night. By morning Lieutenant Scott had detailed comparisons
set up between the test-fired slugs and the ones dug out of
Hooper and the dog.

I looked at his evidence through a comparison microscope.
It left no doubt in my mind that the slugs that killed Allan
Hooper and the dog, Otto, had come from Rambeau's gun.

But Rambeau still wouldn't talk, even to phone his wife or
ask for a lawyer.

"We'll take you out to the scene of the crime," Carlson
said. "I've cracked tougher nuts than you, boy."

We rode in the back seat of his car with Fernando hand-
cuffed between us. Lieutenant Scott did the driving. Rambeau
groaned and pulled against his handcuffs. He was very close
to the breaking point, I thought.

It came a few minutes later when the car turned up the lane
past the Hoopers' mailbox. He burst into sudden fierce tears as
if a pressure gauge in his head had broken. It was strange to see
a bearded man crying like a boy. "I don't want to go up there."

"Because you shot him?" Carlson said.

"I shot the dog. I confess I shot the dog," Rambeau said.

"And the man?"

"No!" he cried. "I never killed a man. Mr. Hooper was

the one who did. He followed my brother out in the woods and shot him.''

''If you knew that,'' I said, ''why didn't you tell the Mounties years ago?''

''I didn't know it then. I was seven years old. How would I understand? When Mrs. Hooper came to our cabin to be with my brother, how would I know it was a serious thing? Or when Mr. Hooper asked me if she had been there? I didn't know he was her husband. I thought he was her father checking up. I knew I shouldn't have told him—I could see it in his face the minute after—but I didn't understand the situation till the other night, when I talked to Mrs. Hooper.''

''Did she know that her husband had shot George?''

''She didn't even know George had been killed. They never went back to the Fraser River after nineteen forty-five. But when we put our facts together, we agreed he must have done it. I came out here next morning to get even. The dog came out to the gate. It wasn't real to me—I'd been drinking most of the night—it wasn't real to me until the dog went down. I shot him. Mr. Hooper shot *my* dog. But when he came out of the house himself, I couldn't pull the trigger. I yelled at him and ran away.''

''What did you yell?'' I said.

''The same thing I told him on the telephone: 'Remember Mount Robson.' ''

''A yellow cab, which looked out of place in the canyon, came over the ridge above us. Lieutenant Scott waved it to a stop. The driver said he'd just brought Mrs. Hooper home from the airport and wanted to know if that constituted a felony. Scott waved him on.

''I wonder what she was doing at the airport,'' Carlson said.

''Coming home from Vegas. She tried to call me from there last night. I forgot to tell you.''

''You don't forget important things like that,'' Carlson said.

''I suppose I wanted her to come home under her own power.''

''In case she shot her husband?''

''More or less.''

''She didn't. Fernando shot him, didn't you, boy?''

''I shot the dog. I am innocent of the man.'' He turned to me. ''Tell her that. Tell her I am sorry about the dog. I came out here to surrender the gun and tell her yesterday. I don't trust myself with guns.''

"With darn good reason," Carlson said. "We know you shot Mr. Hooper. Ballistic evidence doesn't lie."

Rambeau screeched in his ear, "You're a liar! You're all liars!''

Carlson swung his open hand against the side of Rambeau's face. "Don't call me names, little man."

Lieutenant Scott spoke without taking his eyes from the road. "I wouldn't hit him, Chief. You wouldn't want to damage our case."

Carlson subsided, and we drove on up to the house. Carlson went in without knocking. The guard at the door discouraged me from following him.

I couldn't hear Fay's voice on the other side of the door, too low to be understood. Carlson said something to her.

"Get out! Get out of my house, you killer!" Fay cried out sharply.

Carlson didn't come out. I went in instead. One of his arms was wrapped around her body, the other hand was covering her mouth. I got his Adam's apple in the crook of my left arm, pulled him away from her, and threw him over my left hip. He went down clanking and got up holding his revolver.

He should have shot me right away. But he gave Fay Hooper time to save my life.

She stepped in front of me. "Shoot me, Mr. Carlson. You might as well. You shot the one man I ever cared for."

"Your husband shot George Rambeau, if that's who you mean. I ought to know. I was there." Carlson scowled down at his gun and replaced it in his holster.

Lieutenant Scott was watching him from the doorway.

"You were there?" I said to Carlson. "Yesterday you told me Hooper was alone when he shot Rambeau."

"He was. When I said I was there, I meant in the general neighborhood."

"Don't believe him," Fay said. "He fired the gun that killed George, and it was no accident. The two of them hunted George down in the woods. My husband planned to shoot him himself, but George's dog came at him and he had to dispose of it. By that time George had drawn a bead on Allan. Mr. Carlson shot him. It was hardly a coincidence that the next spring Allan financed his campaign for sheriff.''

"She's making it up," Carlson said. "She wasn't within ten miles of the place.''

"But you were, Mr. Carlson, and so was Allan. He told me the whole story yesterday, after we found Otto. Once that happened, he knew that everything was bound to come out. I already suspected him, of course, after I talked to Fernando. Allan filled in the details himself. He thought, since he hadn't killed George personally, I would be able to forgive him. But I couldn't. I left him and flew to Nevada, intending to divorce him. I've been intending to for twenty years.''

Carlson said, "Are you sure you didn't shoot him before you left?''

"How could she have?" I said. "Ballistics don't lie, and the ballistic evidence says he was shot with Fernando's rifle. Nobody had access to it but Fernando—and you. You stopped him on the road and knocked him out, took his rifle, and used it to kill Hooper. You killed him for the same reason that Hooper buried the dog—to keep the past buried. You thought Hooper was the only witness to the murder of George Rambeau. But by that time Mrs. Hooper knew about it, too.''

"It wasn't murder. It was self-defense, just like in the war. Anyway, you'll never hang it on me.''

"We don't have to. We'll hang Hooper on you. How about it, Lieutenant?''

Scott nodded grimly, not looking at his chief. I relieved Carlson of his gun. He winced, as if I were amputating part of his body.

He offered no resistance when Scott took him out to the car.

I stayed behind for a final word with Fay. "Fernando asked me to tell you he's sorry for shooting your dog.''

"We're both sorry." She stood with her eyes down, as if the past was swirling visibly around her feet. "I'll talk to Fernando later. Much later.''

"There's one coincidence that bothers me. How did you happen to take your dog to his school?''

"I happened to see his sign, and Fernando Rambeau isn't a common name. I couldn't resist going there. I had to know what had happened to George. I think perhaps Fernando came to California for the same reason.''

"Now you both know," I said.

≪ The Watchdog ≫
by
Barbara A. Smith

THEY'D PULLED THE first victim from his cardboard residence beneath the Pudding River Bridge on June tenth. A transient.

Although no one knew him, the unfortunate hobo quickly became the hottest topic in town. Of course, a headless corpse was always news, especially in a rural community like Ivory Creek. But it wasn't until two weeks later when they found local farmer Joe Baker also sans a place to hang his hat that the townspeople started to panic.

"Ripped right off his shoulders," Art Kimlinger said from his place in line at Big Mike's Hardware Store, suddenly the busiest place in town.

"I heard chewed off," the next man in line offered.

Rusty Hannan grimaced and shook his head. He didn't like having to wait twenty minutes to pay for a gallon of kerosene. "It wasn't no animal."

"Oh, it weren't," Art said sarcastically. "And just what makes you the expert?"

Rusty shrugged. "I don't know of any animal that takes just the head off his prey. The newspaper said there were no marks anywhere else on the bodies."

"Rusty's right," Mike Bradford, owner of the store, said from behind the counter. "Probably one of those cults. Bunch of crazy sons of bitches up in the woods running around naked waving poor old Joe's head on a stick."

"They'll be in for one hell of a surprise if they show up at my place," Art said. He stepped up and dropped two deadbolts on the counter, then pointed at the ammo case. "Give me two boxes of those Winchester double aughts."

Rusty hoped for Art Kimlinger's sake that he was a good shot if the killer did show up at his house. The sixty-year-old farmer, more than a hundred pounds overweight, couldn't walk across the street without stopping to rest. But given a twelve gauge scattergun, he suddenly fancied himself invincible. Rusty knew better. It didn't matter what gun a man packed or how careful he was; when his number came up, he could kiss it goodbye. He'd learned that lesson in Vietnam.

"You ever put a telephone in at your place?" Art asked Rusty.

"Nope."

"Best get one. If this wacko shows up, you'll be wishing you had one."

Rusty didn't bother to answer. Did they really think some killer was going to hang around forty minutes while a county bull drove over from Putnam to arrest him? He'd lived twenty years in his cabin without a phone, he didn't plan on getting one now. If a killer showed up in *his* woods, he had better know them as well as Rusty did.

"Better make that three boxes of shells," Art said.

Rusty chuckled. "How many of them killers you figure there are, Art?"

"Laugh all you want to. I've got a family to think about. Never hurts a man to be prepared."

Since Joe Baker's death, Big Mike's Hardware Store looked like the Putnam shopping mall on the day after Thanksgiving. Every handgun, shotgun, and rifle beneath the counter had sold within a week. Deadbolts, motion lights, personal alarms, pepper spray, even baseball bats, moved briskly. The waiting list for home alarm installations stretched past three weeks. All the citizens of Ivory Creek were preparing for the worst except Rusty Hannan, who'd been prepared for the last twenty years.

Ten-year-old Brendon Kraemer and his nine-year-old cousin Alice would remember this Fourth of July as long as they lived. It was only half a fib because they really were walking to the store for Popsicles. That they intended to stop in a vacant field along the way and set off bottle rockets was the half they left out. The body they found in the grass, clothed in shorts and T-shirt with a Dodgers baseball cap resting between its bloody shoulders, was the part they'd always remember.

Victim number three, Willie Cooper, was the town idiot. While most thought he was retarded, Willie had actually been quite normal until he smashed his three-wheeler into a tree fifteen years earlier at the age of ten. Willie, or Mr. Baseball, as polite townsfolk addressed him, would talk to anyone who'd listen. Annoying, but harmless. And now, dead.

While Willie's death didn't come as a great personal loss to many, it did occur within spitting distance of the town, which concerned everyone. Even Rusty Hannan began to think there might be more to this than just a passing lunatic. Other than the missing heads, the bodies bore no marks or signs of a struggle, which meant they hadn't seen it coming.

Whack!

Ambush.

Once Rusty got a man in his sights, it only took one bullet. But he had to see him coming.

His cabin sat on ten acres of dense Douglas fir, a quarter mile off the main road. He'd built it himself after his discharge from the Marine Corps. Good therapy, the doctors said.

He needed an alarm system that was portable, covered a large area, and sounded an immediate warning. It had to be easy to operate and dependable. Since he didn't have any savings, and didn't qualify for credit, it also had to be inexpensive. He didn't like it, but the answer was obvious.

The closest animal shelter was fifty miles away in Putnam.

Rusty had owned one dog in his lifetime. His border collie, Taffy, died a week before his sixteenth birthday. They'd grown up together, inseparable, but as Rusty grew and matured, Taffy became old and feeble. Instead of all the good years they'd spent together, he mostly remembered her pathetic final days. He'd vowed he'd never own another pet.

But this would be a watchdog, nothing else.

He knew what he wanted before he arrived at the shelter. Low maintenance. Short hair and big enough to knock a man down.

A girl in her twenties, a skinny redhead splattered with freckles, guided him through the kennels. A plastic dogbone-shaped name tag identified her as Annie. She asked lots of questions.

Their entrance to each run brought on a frenzy of barks, ranging from tiny yips to throaty woofs. He hadn't expected to see so many animals. The dogs rushed forward, standing or jumping against the gates, their pink tongues darting through the wire mesh to lick his hand in greeting. Some urinated on the cement in their excitement.

"Is your yard fenced?" Annie asked.

There was a fence along one side of his property. It belonged to a neighbor. "Sure," Rusty replied. "I got a fence."

"And what about shelter?"

"I plan to keep him in the garage at night." He meant the lean-to on the side of the toolshed.

She nodded. "You have thirty days to spay or neuter any animal. The adoption fee covers part of the surgery, plus a veterinary examination. Of course, you're responsible for the vaccinations."

A black Lab caught Rusty's eye. He wiggled a finger through the mesh and called to him, but the dog bowed his head and retreated to the back corner of the run.

"Timid," she said. "Probably been abused. How about this little guy. Dachshunds make great watchdogs."

Rusty grimaced. "I got possums on my place bigger than that. What about this one?"

A tan and black German shepherd approached the gate. He barked once, then settled on his haunches.

"Neutered male," she said. "Animal Control picked him up in the country, out in your direction as a matter of fact. No tags, no identification—hungry, sore feet. Someone probably dumped him."

"Why?" Rusty asked. "Is there something wrong with him?"

Annie smiled faintly and shook her head. She unlocked the gate and stepped inside with the shepherd. "There's nothing wrong with most of the animals in here. It's people who have the problem. He's a big dog, and it costs money to feed a big dog. And then there's the maintenance—brushing, picking up after him in the yard."

"I have ten acres," he said with a shrug.

"You're not planning to let the dog run loose, are you?"

Rusty began to wonder just who was doing who the favor here. "No, but I don't plan to keep him on a leash when I'm out in the woods either. Besides, I got a fence."

Annie snapped a lead on the shepherd's collar and led him through the back door into a fenced exercise yard. Keeping a tight grip, she briskly trotted him around the perimeter before handing the leash to Rusty. "They're cooped up all day. Sometimes they act a little rambunctious at first. Unfortunately, we can't spend as much time working with the older, less adoptable animals."

Rusty walked the shepherd around the yard twice. A couple of tugs, plus a stern *no* corrected most undesired changes in course.

"Looks like he's been on a leash before," Annie hollered. "Probably wouldn't take much to train him."

"Down, boy," Rusty commanded, slapping the dog's rump. "Down."

The shepherd obediently settled to his stomach.

"Now stay!" Rusty dropped the leash and walked away, but the shepherd gave immediate pursuit.

He pointed at the ground and said sharply, "Stay, boy, stay!"

The dog barked repeatedly, springing from side to side in a frenzied game. He'd stop, crouch, his tail briskly fanning the air, then launch into another series of barks and leaps. Each of Rusty's attempts to retrieve the leash met with the same behavior.

"He's probably just excited to be outside," Annie said.

When Rusty finally recovered the leash, he promptly walked the shepherd to the kennel.

"He's been here for five days. We're only required to hold strays for three, but when we have the space we keep them— just in case the owner shows up."

Rusty handed the leash to Annie.

"They usually don't, though," she said.

He nodded.

"I've got a Doberman-Lab mix that just came in this morning. You want to take a look?"

Rusty watched the shepherd, who now stood calmly gazing up at him, tail still whipping back and forth. He shrugged, then said, "I'll take him."

•　•　•

Few people had ever visited Rusty Hannan's cabin. The forty-eight-year-old veteran kept to himself, living off a meager disability pension for a shrapnel wound that still ached at times during the winter months. In the summer, he drove hay trucks and bean pickers for local farmers and earned a few extra dollars selling firewood. His furniture came from garage sales, his clothing from Goodwill, his meals from a can.

He lived a Spartan lifestyle and, until now, a solitary one. He called the dog Twenty-three, the last two digits of his animal shelter identification number.

Twenty-three had remained on a chain for the first week. The sixty-five-dollar adoption fee was considerably more than Rusty had expected to pay, and he didn't intend to pay it twice. The dog's accommodations were equally frugal: a pile of burlap sacks for a bed, a three pound coffee can full of water, and a fifty pound bag of generic food.

Rusty had no idea whether the dog would bark at an intruder if one did show up, but he barked at everything else: coons, possums, squirrels, even birds. It'd already been two weeks since Willie Cooper's death, so maybe the killer had moved on. And maybe he'd shelled out sixty-five dollars for nothing.

When finally given the chance to run loose, Twenty-three often disappeared for hours at a time, especially at night, but by morning he was always back sleeping in his burlap sacks or lying across the back door step. He wasn't allowed in the cabin although he tried to slip inside at every opportunity. His job was to keep watch—outside.

Rusty drove to Ivory Creek every Saturday morning for supplies. He'd left Twenty-three at home the first week, but the following Saturday, when he dropped the tailgate, the dog promptly jumped inside the pickup bed. Rusty tied him to the cab with the shelter leash, remembering Andy Krebs' golden retriever, who had gone over the side into oncoming traffic and was promptly flattened by a bread truck.

Rusty kept a close watch on Twenty-three from the rear view mirror, especially when they reached Ivory Creek. The town was busy, sidewalks crowded, as they usually were on Saturday. He parked on a side street a block from the hardware store. He didn't like leaving Twenty-three where he couldn't keep an eye on him, so he untied the leash and took him along.

The sight of a German shepherd pulling the grizzled six

footer briskly down the sidewalk brought stares from several people standing in front of Big Mike's.

Tom Case fearlessly offered his hand to the dog.

Twenty-three sniffed it and left it intact.

Rusty breathed a bit easier.

"Got you a dog, huh?" Tom asked, rubbing the animal's head. "Probably a good idea considering what's been going on around here."

"Hear anything new?" Rusty pushed on Twenty-three's rear end until he sat.

"You mean about Estelle Morley being killed?" Edna, Tom's wife, asked.

"No! When did this happen?"

"Found her yesterday morning on her patio," Tom said. "Back door wide open. They figure it happened sometime during the night."

Rusty shook his head in disbelief. Estelle Morley's place was about two miles from his. She was seventy-eight years old. "Same as the others?"

Tom nodded. "Head's missing. Torn off like the rest."

"Was her place robbed?"

"Purse was still on the kitchen counter with thirty-seven dollars in it," Tom said. "What jewelry she owned was all there, along with the television set. Hell, she'd even had Mike put deadbolts on all the doors two weeks ago."

"It's just horrible," Edna muttered.

"They found her outside?" he asked.

Tom nodded again. "Less than ten feet from the house. I still say it could be some kind of animal. Hell, it'd be nothing for a cougar to take a person's head off, or a wolf, or even a big dog. There sure would have to be something wrong with it, though. Could be rabid, maybe wounded."

Rusty stared down into Twenty-three's gaping mouth. His tongue lolled aside, exposing his pointed white fangs in a big toothy grin. "But with no other bite or claw marks anywhere else on the body?"

"I know," Tom said with a shrug. "It doesn't make sense."

As the front door to Big Mike's swung open, Twenty-three lunged forward, barking, nearly pulling Rusty off his feet. The two men leaving the store stepped carefully out of reach and backed away from the dog. A deep guttural growl, the first

Rusty had ever heard Twenty-three make, sent everyone else on the sidewalk into the street.

All the commotion brought Mike Bradford running to the door. "Rusty, what the hell is the matter with that dog?"

"Sorry, Mike. I guess he's not used to being around so many people."

"Well, get him away from the store. I can't have him scaring off my business."

Twenty-three continued to bark and struggle against the leash. By now Tom and Edna Case were inside their car with the doors locked.

"Where'd you get that thing, anyway?" Mike shouted from behind the door.

"Animal shelter in Putnam."

"Don't they check those animals for diseases?"

"Sure they do," Rusty said, using every ounce of strength to restrain Twenty-three. "I got papers that show he's healthy. They checked him at the shelter."

Mike peered skeptically through the crack in the door. "What about rabies?"

"He ain't got rabies. I've had him almost two weeks. This is the first time he's been around a lot of people is all. I think he's just excited."

"You're keeping him tied up, aren't you?"

Rusty knew sometimes it was best to say what people wanted to hear. "Sure, all the time. I had to park a block away. I didn't want to leave him in the back of the pickup while I was in the store."

"Best lock him in the cab then," Mike said.

Rusty nodded, then dragged Twenty-three back to the pickup.

The real reason Rusty had never gotten another dog after Taffy's death was that he'd known he would be disappointed. As he was disappointed now. Twenty-three couldn't be trusted around people. Eventually he'd bite someone, a little kid or an old lady, and get Rusty sued. Animals had a lot in common with people, there weren't many who could be completely trusted.

Twenty-three went back on the chain when they reached the cabin. Although he'd eventually calmed down during the ride home, Rusty had begun to worry how far the shepherd strayed during his nightly free periods. People knew where he belonged now. He'd be held responsible for any damages or injuries.

Three days later, County Sheriff Harvey Popp showed up at the cabin.

Twenty-three's frenzied barks alerted Rusty to the sheriff's approach the moment the patrol car turned into the lane. The vehicle rolled slowly past the cabin, then parked in the clearing between the back door and the toolshed. Rusty folded his arms and waited on the step. After making certain the dog was chained, Sheriff Popp stepped from the car.

"Afternoon," he said, touching the rim of his hat.

Rusty nodded. "What can I do for you?"

"I have a few questions about your dog."

"My dog?" Rusty chuckled, then shifted his hands to his pockets. He walked to the shed and shouted at Twenty-three to be quiet, which he did.

Sheriff Popp remained purposely outside the chain's perimeter. "I understand you had a problem with the dog in town the other day."

"He barked at some people. That's hardly a problem."

"Look, folks around here are scared to death. Four unsolved murders make them edgy."

"He barked at some people," Rusty repeated curtly.

"Have you always kept him chained?"

Rusty considered the question carefully before answering. "Mostly."

"Mostly?"

"He's been loose on the property before, but I'm always here."

The sheriff rested both hands atop his gun belt and took a couple of small steps forward. "What about at night? You keep him chained up at night?"

Rusty nodded. "Mostly."

"Now, let me explain a couple of things. The first victim, fella down by the river, was said to have a dog, which we never found. Next, Animal Control over in Putnam tells me they picked up this dog the day after Willie Cooper died, about a half mile away. Finally, Estelle Morley's house is about two miles as the crow flies straight through those trees. So I'm asking you again, do you keep the dog chained up at night?"

"No animal killed those people," Rusty insisted. "If one did, it's damn sure not something I've ever seen before."

Sheriff Popp approached Rusty and the dog but kept a hand poised near his holster. Twenty-three remained silent, seated obediently at Rusty's side.

"Look, I've got to follow through on every lead. The Cooper kid and the transient both had animal hair on their clothing, dog hair. The hairs look like they're from the same animal. The coroner says Mrs. Morley died late Thursday, early Friday. Was the dog loose then?"

"He might have been," Rusty said. "He was off the chain for a couple of nights, but I couldn't swear which ones. Anyway, he was always here when I got up."

Sheriff Popp nodded slowly, then carefully slipped one hand into his jacket pocket, removing a small clear plastic bag. "Suppose you brush a few hairs into this bag for analysis. And until you hear back from me, you keep that animal chained. If I get wind of him running loose, I'll have to pick him up."

Rusty stroked Twenty-three's back, then deposited the resulting loose hair into the bag. Sheriff Popp sealed it and wrote the date on the corner. "What do you call him?"

Rusty shrugged. "Twenty-three."

"Hell, that's not a name, that's a number."

"He ain't a pet, he's a watchdog."

Sheriff Popp recorded the number on the bag and left.

Twenty-three started barking shortly after two o'clock in the morning. Rusty dressed quickly, took his .22 rifle from the closet, and slipped out the back door. He purposely left the cabin dark. The surrounding stand of Douglas fir filtered the moonlight, silhouetting an ominous landscape of murky shapes and shadows. Yet Rusty knew those shapes and shadows; which belonged, and which did not.

Twenty-three growled and lunged against the chain as Rusty sprinted across the clearing for the cover of the toolshed. From there he could watch the lane, and no one, or thing, could approach within thirty feet of his position without being seen. Crouched in the darkness, weapon ready, heart drumming in his ears, he thought of another place, another time. He knew what to do. Stay low, quiet. Get off the first shot.

Phantom incoming rounds and ghostly screams echoed

along with Twenty-three's frantic yowls. Time tempted Rusty to move into the woods, become the aggressor, but he knew patience was his ally. That and the dog, whose reactions should reveal any movement by an intruder. Twenty minutes after he'd started, Twenty-three finally stopped barking. He sank to his belly, head down, and whined.

Rusty approached him carefully. He'd never seen an animal react so viciously, almost maniacally. If Twenty-three had broken loose, there wouldn't be much left of whatever lurked in the woods.

"Good boy," Rusty said, squatting to scratch Twenty-three behind the ears. The dog's eyes rolled up to meet his in an apologetic gaze. "We'll get him next time."

A search of the woods surrounding the cabin revealed nothing. He'd look again during the daylight.

Rusty returned to bed at four o'clock, but sleep eluded him. Sheriff Popp was right—four unsolved murders made folks nervous, including him. He didn't know who, or what, was in those woods tonight. Yet after talking to the sheriff, he had another concern. Maybe there wasn't anything there at all.

"They're German shepherd hairs, all right," Sheriff Harvey Popp said.

Every ear in the Ivory Cafe strained in his direction.

"They can't say if they belong to Rusty's dog, though."

"That animal is squirrelly," Mike Bradford said. "Went crazy for no reason the other day in front of the store. You ought to pick him up. Better safe than sorry, I say."

"That's right," Art Kimlinger agreed between mouthfuls of pecan pie.

"I can't pick up every mutt in the county just because two bodies had dog hair on their clothing. Hell, I bet most people in this room have some kind of animal hairs on them right now. Besides, the coroner said if the killer was an animal, there should be saliva in the wounds. So far he hasn't found any."

"But you think this dog of Rusty's belonged to the first victim, the hobo?" Mike asked.

Sheriff Popp nodded. "Couple of kids used to fish beneath the bridge said the guy had a dog looked just like Rin Tin Tin."

"That's a German shepherd all right," Kimlinger said confidently.

"And where did Animal Control pick this dog up at?" Mike asked.

"Ridge Road," the sheriff answered.

"Ridge Road?" Kimlinger shouted. "That's right next to where they found the Cooper boy. And he had hairs on his clothing, too."

"Willie loved animals," Shirley, the waitress, interjected. "He'd play with any stray dog or cat that came along."

"That's right," Mike said. "So did Estelle, bless her soul. She'd feed any animal that wandered onto her place. Why, if she saw that shepherd standing on her patio, she'd have gone right out there, without thinking a thing of it."

"What are you going to do about this, Harve?" Kimlinger asked.

"I've already talked to Rusty. He's promised to keep the animal chained up."

Mike Bradford shook his head tentatively. "Rusty's an independent cuss. You really think he'll do it?"

"He damn well better," Sheriff Popp said. "I told him I'd cite him, plus take the dog if I got wind of it running loose. Everybody knows he ain't got two nickels to rub together, so I figure he'll listen."

After the third night, Rusty knew he should end it, put a bullet in Twenty-three's head. But each morning he found another excuse not to.

During the day Twenty-three acted normal, following Rusty's movements outside the cabin with eager black eyes that begged for attention. The fits had occurred only at night between two and four o'clock, lasted fifteen to thirty minutes, then mysteriously stopped. Although not foaming at the mouth, he behaved as if he were rabid—barking, snarling, nearly strangling himself in an effort to break free.

Rusty considered telling Sheriff Popp about Twenty-three's bizarre behavior but decided against it. It just wasn't his fault. He'd only adopted a dog from the shelter, tried to do the right thing. Still, people in Ivory Creek would find a way to place the blame on him. There was no proof that Twenty-three had killed anyone. Maybe he was wrong about the dog, too.

He searched the woods all day Friday but didn't find any evidence to make him believe someone had been out there,

especially three nights in a row. That night from the back step
he ate a dinner of fresh sweet corn and tomatoes while
Twenty-three watched from the end of his chain forty feet
away. The dog fanned the air with his tail, ears cupped forward, eyes always intent on Rusty. He'd bark occasionally,
once or twice, wanting attention.

Tomorrow Rusty planned to stop at Mike's hardware store,
eat lunch at the Ivory Cafe, then get a haircut at Jim's barber
shop. If there was any news about the murders, he'd learn it
in one of those three places. Gossip in a small town was more
reliable than a newspaper, faster and cheaper, too. Twenty-
three would remain at the cabin.

Rusty sat outside until darkness reduced the view from the
back step to patches of grey filtered through a forest-green can-
opy of fir branches. Before going inside he filled the food and
water bowls, then roughhoused with the dog for a few minutes.
It was a shame. If it weren't for the temporary bouts of madness,
Twenty-three might have made a pretty decent watchdog.

The barking started at one fifteen, an hour earlier than usual.
Rusty didn't dress and go outside with his rifle as he'd done
the previous nights. He didn't even get out of bed. Within
twenty minutes the noise should stop and he could go back to
sleep. Luckily, his closest neighbor lived a mile away and
wouldn't be disturbed by the racket.

The seizure had grown worse. Twenty-three's barks soon
turned to throat-rattling growls.

At one thirty the chain broke.

Twenty-three crossed the clearing and rammed the back of
the cabin before Rusty's feet hit the floor. Snarling and barking, he scratched furiously at the wood, his fangs ripping at
the frame. Rusty knew the door would hold; that wasn't the
problem. Once the dog gave up on him, he might go after
someone else. There was no choice now but to shoot him.

Following a brief silence, Twenty-three attacked the front
door.

Rusty dressed in thick insulated coveralls from the back of
the closet. They would afford some protection if the dog got
hold of him. If he couldn't get a shot off through a window,
he might have to open the door and take his chances. Leaving
the lights off to preserve his night vision, he sat down on the

edge of the bed and pulled on his work boots. Again the heavy leather offered some protection, and their steel toes could be used as weapons.

About now he was damn glad he'd built the cabin himself, especially the doors—sturdy two inch fir with inch and a half deadbolts from Big Mike's. The only way inside was with an axe or a key. After testing the front door, Twenty-three circled the cabin, stopping to scratch at each window and frame. Rusty waited in the bedroom, rifle raised, but couldn't get a decent angle for a shot through the small high windowpane.

With luck, the seizure would run its course and Twenty-three would simply lie down, whimpering, the way he'd done on previous nights. If not, Rusty would lure him to the kitchen window alongside the back door. The rectangular window consisted of twelve small panes that were eye level with the kitchen table. He could either break out one pane to take his shot or shoot through the glass.

Twenty-three returned to the back door, where he began to dig furiously at the jamb.

Fully dressed, rifle in hand, Rusty walked from the bedroom into the kitchen. The kitchen and front room formed an L shape, the front room facing the main road, the kitchen and breakfast table overlooking the clearing and toolshed in the rear.

Twenty-three lunged against the window the moment Rusty entered the kitchen, but the glass held. He stood on his hind legs, front paws propped against the glass, head at waist level, barking viciously. Rusty would never get a better opportunity for a clean shot. He raised the rifle and took a step backward.

The safety clicked off.

"Put it down and raise your hands," a voice behind him said.

Rusty started to turn.

"Don't! I told you to put it down!"

He cautiously lowered the rifle to the kitchen table, then slowly raised his hands overhead.

"Slow now, make it slow—"

Rusty knew that voice but couldn't place it. "What the hell are you doing in my cabin?"

"Nice and easy, no sudden moves. Turn around."

He couldn't make out the face in the shadows, but saw clearly a revolver aimed at his head.

"Lock your fingers behind your head and kneel down. Do it slow, Rusty."

Once the intruder spoke his name, he finally realized his identity. "Mike? What's going on? How'd you get inside?"

"Aren't you forgetting where you bought your locks? And who cut your spare keys? I thought keeping those key codes would pay off some day. Appears I was right."

"But what are you doing here?"

"Half the folks in town already think that dog's the killer. After tonight they'll all believe it."

Rusty began to lower his hands.

"Keep 'em up!"

"I was gonna shoot him, Mike, honest. I swear I didn't know."

"You dumb hick. You still don't know, do you?"

Mike Bradford stepped forward into the moonlight that filtered through the kitchen window. His right hand leveled a .32 revolver directly at Rusty's head; his left hand gripped a plastic bag and a linoleum knife.

"After they find your body, they'll figure it was the dog all along. I admit I'll miss all that extra business, but I don't really need it any more. Not with Joe and Estelle's loans both paid in full, so to speak."

"You?"

Mike lifted his eyebrows in an innocent shrug. "Sure. I make a decent living from the store, but not enough to make a dent in that eighty thousand dollar balloon payment I owed on the business. The bank finally called the note. Told me to come up with the whole eighty grand or they'd foreclose."

"Art Kimlinger said you inherited that money from a relative."

He laughed and dropped the plastic bag and linoleum cutter on the floor. "Yep, you sure can trust old Art to spread the word. I told Joe and Estelle it would be better for business if local folks didn't know I borrowed the money from them. Forty grand each at twelve percent. The robbers, both got just what they deserved."

Behind Rusty, Twenty-three continued to scratch at the side of the cabin. Mike smiled and shook his head. "That old bum's dog would sure like to get a piece of me."

"So why didn't he?" Rusty asked.

"Couldn't, he was tied up that night, going nuts just like he is now. He must have finally chewed through the rope and took off before they found the body."

Rusty had to keep him talking, wait for a distraction before making his move. Another step closer and he might stand a chance.

"But why kill the hobo, Mike? And Willie?"

"Practice makes perfect," Mike said, grinning darkly. "I popped that old bum, had his head off and bagged in less than a minute."

"Why the heads?"

Mike's eyes glistened as he spoke. "Ballistics, Rusty. No bullet, no bullet hole, no way to trace it back to me. A head's a hell of a lot easier to hide than a body, too. I've been building a fence around my property this summer, so it was just a matter of making a few post holes a little deeper."

Rusty didn't have to ask many questions to keep him talking. Mike appeared to enjoy sharing his scheme.

"The others were all quick. I just said, 'Hi, Joe, how's it going?' Boom! I let him have it. 'Good evening, Estelle. Lovely night out, isn't it?' Kapow! Then, of course, I had to make sure nobody linked any of the victims together. You know, motive. So I had to make them look random. That dumb Cooper kid had been coming in the store bugging me for years. I figure I did the town a favor."

"So it was you out in my woods at night."

"Very good. . . . I had to make sure I could get in without tangling with the mutt. You know, Rusty, you really should have bought a heavier chain. That was close."

"Why don't we just blame it on the dog?" he asked. "I'll back you up."

Mike laughed again. "You must think I'm simple like ol' Willie. Nothing personal, Rusty, but I'm not leaving any witnesses." His arm stiffened as he took aim.

"Wait! How do you plan on getting past the dog on the way out?"

"Hypodermic full of Biotol. I'll stick him through a window. And this time they *will* find saliva in the wounds. And when they find the dog, he'll be covered in blood . . . your blood. Who knows, I might even poke a few pieces of flesh down his throat."

"Mike, wait—"

But he was through talking. He squeezed the trigger.

An explosion of breaking glass corresponded with the crack of the .32. Anticipating the shot, Rusty dived, and at the same time he was knocked forward from behind. Twenty-three yelped and dropped to the floor.

Instinctively, Rusty grabbed the linoleum knife as he tackled Mike Bradford. Mike was a killer, but Rusty was a survivor, trained in hand to hand combat.

They struggled briefly. Mike's second shot lodged in the ceiling as the knife found a home in his throat. He died within seconds.

Rusty switched on the lights and hurried to where Twenty-three lay crumpled on the kitchen floor, whining softly. The bullet had struck him in the right front shoulder and exited above his leg. From what Rusty knew of anatomy, it had probably missed any vital organs but might have broken a bone or two. He pulled two clean kitchen towels from the drawer and applied pressure to the wounds, securing them with strips of electrical tape.

Twenty-three feebly licked at his fingers.

He couldn't call Ivory Creek's veterinarian, Otis Berger, to come to the cabin, so he'd have to take Twenty-three to town. Art Kimlinger was right about the telephone. He'd have one installed first thing next week.

He ran outside to start the pickup, rushing next to the bedroom for a blanket. He carefully lifted Twenty-three and carried him to the pickup, then laid him on the front seat.

"Easy, boy," he said softly, starting down the lane. "You're gonna be fine, just fine. You're a lucky dog, that's for sure. That's a nice clean wound, straight through. You'll be riding around in the pickup and going to town again before you know it."

The dog lifted his head from the seat, then lowered it slowly against Rusty's thigh.

Rusty smiled and stroked his muzzle. "You're a good dog, Twenty—"

He hesitated.

"You're a good dog, Lucky."

≪ On Windy Ridge ≫
by
Margaret Maron

WAITING IS MORE tiresome than doing, and I was weary. Bone weary. "Seems longer than just yesterday those two went up to Windy Ridge," I said. "Two went up, but three were there, you know."

"Now what's that supposed to mean, Ruth?" asked Wayne.

Wayne's my cousin and a good sheriff. What he lacks in formal training, he makes up in common sense and a knowledge of the district that comes from growing up here in the mountains and from being related by birth or marriage to half the county. Our grandmothers were sisters and we've run in and out of each other's houses for forty years. I knew he was wondering if my queer remark came from tiredness or because I half believe some of the legends that persist in these hills.

He walked over to the deck rail and looked down into the ravine, but my eyes lifted to the distant hills, beyond trees that burned red and gold, to where the ridges misted into smoky blue. The hills were real and everlasting and I had borrowed of their strength before.

When I built this deck nearly twenty years ago, I planned it wide enough for a wedding breakfast because Luke Randolph and I were to be married as soon as he came home from Vietnam. It was May, wild vines grew up the pilings, and the air was heavy with the scent of honeysuckle and wisteria the day Luke's brother Tom came over with the crumpled telegram in his hand.

The hills haven't changed since then, but the red cedar planks have weathered to silver gray and Wayne looked at me uneasily across their width.

"You're not going ghostie on me, are you, Ruth? This isn't the first time a man's been shot up on Windy Ridge, and it won't be the last. Hell, Sam's already put in two complaints."

Feisty Sam Haskell owns a small dairy farm on the edge of Windy Ridge, and trying to keep his herd from being shot out from under him every year makes him a perennial source of tall tales. In exasperation once, he'd painted C-O-W in bright purple on the flank of every animal. Two were promptly shot.

Wayne sighed. "That's what puzzles me. Gordon Tyler was a furriner, but Noah knew better than to go into the woods the first day of deer season when all those cityfolk show up, blasting away at anything that moves without waiting to see if it's got two legs or four. Why'd he go?"

"Gordon wanted to try his new rifle, and he talked Noah into it," I said.

Yesterday had been one of those perfect October mornings with barely a hint of frost in the air. We'd just finished a late breakfast here on the deck: Noah Randolph, who was Luke's nephew, my niece Julie, and me. Julie had bubbled like liquid sunshine that morning, her red hair flaming like a maple tree. After a summer of flirting around with Gordon Tyler, she'd finally decided that Noah was really the one she wanted to marry, and her brand new diamond sparkled in the crisp air.

Noah was so much like my Luke—a mountain man, tall and solid, with clear brown eyes and a mane of sandy hair. Not handsome. His features were too strong and open. But a good face. A face you could trust your life with. Or trust with a niece who's been your life for fifteen of her twenty years after her parents died in a plane crash.

They were arguing over the last cheese biscuit when Gordon Tyler came up the side steps carrying a gleaming new rifle. Dark and wiry, he moved with the grace of a panther, and most women found him magnetic.

"I never liked Gordon," I told Wayne.

"Then why did you encourage him?"

"Because Julie didn't appreciate Noah. Remember how I dithered over Luke so long? Wondering if I loved him only because no one more romantic was around? It took that damn war—knowing he could be killed—to make me realize. Julie was me all over again, and Gordon had money, glamor, and the surface excitement she thought Noah lacked. I thought if she got a good dose of Gordon, she'd wake up to Noah's real value.''

"It's usually a mistake to play God," Wayne said.

Which was exactly what I had thought as I fetched Gordon a cup from the kitchen and urged him to pull up a chair and how about a slice of ham? I knew I'd acted shabbily in using him to help Julie finish growing up, and I tried to ease my conscience by being overly hospitable when the pure and simple truth was that I wanted Gordon Tyler to go away. To get off our mountain and out of Julie's life now that he'd served his purpose.

Until then, I'd rather enjoyed the seasonal influx of wealthy people who bought up our dilapidated barns and farmhouses and remodeled them into sumptuous vacation homes. Oldtimers might grumble about flatlanders and furriners and yearn for the days when Jedediah's store down at the crossroads had stocked nothing more exotic than Vienna sausage, but it's always amused me to step around a flopeared hound sprawled beside the potbellied stove and ask Jedediah for caviar, smoked oysters, or a bottle of choice Riesling.

Now I felt like one of the old-timers, and I wished all flatlanders and furriners to perdition, beginning with Gordon Tyler, who'd bought the old Eddiston orchards as a tax shelter and play-pretty last year. We'd heard he'd inherited right much money, and he never mentioned any commitments to work beyond occasional board meetings up north. That gave him a lot of free time. Especially after Julie caught his eye this summer.

Julie said she'd been frank with him about Noah, but I was sitting across from Gordon when Noah and Julie announced their engagement out at Taylor's Inn, and something about the way he went so white and still made me think he really hadn't expected it. The moment passed, though, and he was the first to jump up and offer a toast.

Before the engagement, Gordon had barely noticed Noah; yet in less than two weeks he transformed himself from Julie's rejected lover into Noah's good ol' pal. When Noah could get away from the farm he'd inherited from Luke, they even went squirrel hunting and fishing together.

"It always sort of surprised me that Gordon could shoot so well," said Wayne, "him being a city boy and all."

"Gordon never did anything in public unless he could do it best," I said bitterly. "He always had to win. By hook or crook."

"He won the shooting medal fair and square," Wayne observed.

"Only because the Anson boy couldn't enter."

"Come on, Ruth! You don't think Gordon had anything to do with Tim Anson's falling through his barn roof, do you?"

"I don't know what I think any more," I said crossly. "Gordon was up there with him, pointing out the rotten spots he wanted reshingled. Maybe he didn't know that section of roof was so far gone. All I'm saying is that Tim's the best shot around, and Gordon didn't enter the match till after Tim had broken his arm."

"No, honey," Wayne said gently, "you're saying a lot more than that."

Wayne has known me all my life. Did he realize I'd spent the last twenty-four hours brooding over all that had happened since Julie and Noah became engaged?

When Gordon had interrupted our breakfast on the deck, I'd marked down the faint unease his presence aroused as a product of my own guilt pangs. Unlike Noah and Julie, I wasn't happy that he'd taken their engagement so well. Good-natured resignation seemed out of character.

Yet, as I brought out a fresh pot of coffee, there was Gordon showing Noah his new rifle. All morning the surrounding woods had reverberated with gunshots as deer season opened with its usual bang, and Gordon was anxious to test the gun. "It should stop a whitetail," he said.

"Oh, it'll do that," Noah agreed dryly. His big hands held the expensive, customized Remington carbine expertly, and as he laid his cheek against the hand-carved stock and sighted along the gleaming barrel, a strand of brown hair fell across his eyes. Julie brushed it back with a proprietary hand, her ring flashing in the sunlight.

Gordon's eyes narrowed, but he smiled and said, "I know you don't like to go out opening day, but this may be my only chance. I'm flying to Delaware tomorrow on business, and there's no telling when I'll get back. Of course, if you're afraid to come, I can go alone."

"Common sense isn't fear!" I snapped, and Julie said, "Noah's staying right here. Too many fools show up the first day."

If we'd kept our mouths shut, he probably would have put Gordon off; but with both of us jumping in, Noah naturally stood up, touseled Julie's red-gold hair, and told her to quit acting like a bossy wife.

"How far do you feel like walking?" he asked Gordon.

"Why don't we try Windy Ridge? I saw a nice buck up there the other day."

As Noah grabbed his jacket and started to follow Gordon down the steps, he looked back at Julie. There were times when she could look very tiny and crushed, as if all the sunshine had gone out of her life, and she was doing it then. I'd have sworn that even her hair had gone two shades duller. Hurt tears threatened to spill over her sandy lashes, and Noah returned, wiped her eyes with his handkerchief, and gently cupped her face in his strong hands.

"Quit worrying, honey. I'll wear my orange hunting cap. Nobody's going to take me for a deer, so cheer up and give me a kiss."

Brightness flowed back into her and she kissed him so thoroughly that it took an impatient horn blast from Gordon in the driveway below to tear Noah away.

"You be careful, Noah Randolph!" Julie called. She saw me grinning and smiled ruefully. "Was your Luke as pigheaded as Noah?"

"Never," I lied airily. "Any Randolph can be led around by the nose if you know how."

"Yah! And cows can fly," she gibed, but she was content again and it did give us a chance to work on the wedding. By midafternoon we were well into the invitation list when we heard a car door slam on the drive below.

Julie pushed the papers away and rushed to the rail to peer over. Mild disappointment in her voice, she said, "It's only Cousin Wayne. Gordon's with him, but where's Noah?"

I joined her at the rail and as soon as I saw Wayne's face, my arms went around her instinctively, as if I could shield her from what I knew he would say.

The next few moments were a blur of kaleidoscoping time.

I heard Wayne's words, but they seemed overlaid by those other words twenty years ago.

". . . some trigger-happy hunter (*Vietcong sniper*) . . . up on Windy Ridge (*on midnight patrol*) . . . happened so quickly . . . I'm sorry, Julie." (*Luke's dead, Ruth.*)

"I was up ahead in some thick brush," Gordon said shakily. "There was another party working the west slope, but we didn't think anyone else was up as high as we were. I heard the shot, and when Noah didn't answer, I ran down and found him lying there. Someone went crashing through the bushes. I fired my gun and yelled at him to stop, but he didn't. Thank God for those guys on the west slope. I didn't even know they were there until I heard their dog bark."

One of them was a doctor from Asheville, and he had stanched the wound and applied first aid while the others rigged a stretcher. Together they got him down from the ridge and into a truck. Using CB radio, they had called for an ambulance that met them halfway into Asheville. Even so, it didn't look good.

"He's lost too much blood," Wayne told me quietly.

While Gordon drove us to the hospital, Wayne remained behind to direct the hunt for whoever had shot Noah. It was a forty-minute drive, and Gordon kept blaming himself all the way. "If he dies, it'll be my fault," he kept saying.

"He won't die!" Julie said fiercely.

"Whatever happens, it won't be your fault," I told him. "Noah's a grown man. He went with you of his own free accord."

Tom and Mabel Randolph were in the intensive care waiting room when we arrived, along with her sister and some cousins. The news had traveled fast.

Noah was still in surgery, we were told. There was nothing to do but wait. "And pray," said Mabel Randolph, her eyes swollen from so much crying. "Please pray for him."

Time dragged. There was a snack area next to the waiting room, and hospital volunteers kept the coffee urn filled. More kinfolk arrived to share the wait and to offer the homely comfort of fried chicken, ham biscuits, and stuffed eggs. Everyone kept trying to get Julie and me to eat, but Julie couldn't seem to swallow either.

Six hours after Noah had been rushed into surgery, the doctor came to us, still dressed in his operating greens, the sterile mask dangling from his neck. Clinically, he described the path the bullet had taken through back and lung, just missing the spinal column, but nicking the heart and finally coming to rest in the left lung.

He talked about shock and trauma and blood pressure that wouldn't stabilize, and Mabel Randolph listened numbly until he'd finished, then said, "But he'll be all right, won't he?"

The doctor's eyes dropped and I liked him for that. Till then, he'd been so full of facts and figures that he could have been talking about soybean yields or how he'd gone about mending a stone wall. But he still had enough feeling that he couldn't look a dying boy's mother straight in the face and tell her, sure, he was going to be just fine. "Maybe, if he makes it through the night," he told Mabel, and his voice trailed off.

He seemed relieved when Wayne's sturdy form advanced across the waiting room. "Here it is, sheriff," he said, and gave Wayne a small packet. "I tried not to scratch it any further."

It was the slug he'd removed from Noah's lung, and Wayne passed it over to one of his deputies, who left in a hurry for the state lab.

"We blocked the roads and impounded every gun that came down the mountain," Wayne told us. "Then we did a sweep to make sure nobody was hiding up there."

By morning, Noah's threadhold on life was stretched cobweb thin and Wayne had the lab report. Noah had been shot with a .30 caliber bullet.

Now, I like to trail along behind a pack of bell-voiced coonhounds on a moonlit night, and I can knock a possum out of a persimmon with my .22 as well as anybody, but such things as calibers, rifling, bores, and grains were beyond me. All I knew was that after the roads were blocked, every gun that came down from Windy Ridge, even Noah's old Winchester and Gordon's new Remington, was impounded, and all the rifles that could shoot a .30 caliber load were test-fired.

No match.

"What about the three men who helped carry Noah out?" I asked.

"All cleared," Wayne said.

It had been a long, tense night, and when he offered to take Julie and me home, I was ready to go, but Julie wouldn't be budged.

She promised to nap on one of the empty couches if I'd bring her some fresh clothes that afternoon when I returned. We left with Gordon trying to persuade her to go down to the cafeteria with him for breakfast and Mabel telling her she needed to keep up her strength for Noah's sake.

As we drove home along winding mountain roads, Wayne said, "We found his white handkerchief up there where he fell, Ruth. Warm day like yesterday, a man works up a sweat tramping the woods. Guess he forgot and pulled it out to wipe his brow."

I looked puzzled so he spelled it out for me. "Say you've never done much hunting; say you've got an itchy trigger finger, and you spot something white flickering in the underbrush. You gonna wait till it turns around and shows antlers? Hell, no! A patch of white means a whitetail deer to you, so *bang!*"

At home, I showered and lay down, but tired as I was, sleep was a long time coming. I drifted in and out of troubled dreams in which Noah blended into Luke—Luke in his army uniform manning a lonely sentry post in a thicket of red-berried dogwoods and golden poplars. I saw the Vietcong sniper snaking through the underbrush and tried to cry out, but Luke couldn't hear me. He fell slowly into the leaves, and the sniper covered his face with a white flag.

"But Luke doesn't have a white flag!" I cried, and came awake as the telephone rang.

It was Julie with a list of small items she wanted me to bring. She said they'd persuaded Mabel Randolph to let Gordon take her home for a few hours while she and Tom kept the vigil. There was no change in Noah's condition.

"No change is probably a good sign, don't you think?" Julie quavered. "It means he's holding on."

I said it did seem hopeful, but my heart grieved for what she still might have to face.

My dream of Luke had left me too restless and disoriented to sleep again. Instead, I found myself pacing the deck as I had twenty years ago, until—like twenty years ago—I got into my car and drove aimlessly, until despair finally eased off again and I realized that I was at the end of one of the old logging trails that crisscross Windy Ridge.

The trees had begun to shed, and a cool gust of wind stirred the fallen leaves. I got out of the car and walked up a slope where Luke and I had often walked together. Squirrels chattered an alarm, a pair of bobwhites exploded into flight at my feet, and, from farther up the ridge, a dog greeted me with sharp, welcoming barks.

I thought I knew every dog in the area, but I couldn't place the pointer that came crashing down the hillside so recklessly. For some reason, dogs lose all dignity with me. I'm not particularly fond of them, but through the years, I've become resigned to having them act the fool whenever I'm around. This one was no exception. He came prancing through the leaves, paw over paw, as if I were his long-lost friend, and tried to jump up and lick my face.

"Down, boy!" I said sternly and he sat obediently enough. He was white with the usual rust-colored markings, flopears, and intelligent brown eyes. His long, thin tail whipped the air to show me how happy he was for company, and I remembered that Gordon said he'd heard a dog bark just before Noah was shot. This dog, probably. He wasn't wearing a collar, but I was willing to bet he belonged to the party that helped Gordon with Noah, though I'd never heard of anyone using a pointer to hunt deer.

"Your people go off and leave you in all the excitement?" I asked, scratching behind his floppy ears.

More tail-whipping and another attempt to wash my face.

It was so peaceful there that I sat down on a nearby tree stump and let silence wash over me. The dog sprawled at my feet, his big head resting on my shoe. Bluejays played Not-It in the treetops, and scarlet maple leaves drifted down around us. Beyond the ridge, I heard the lazy tinkle of Sam Haskell's cowbells. It seemed unreal that Noah's life could halt amid such peace and beauty. Winter winds had stripped these flaming trees and spring rains had reclothed them in green twenty times since Luke and I had raced each other up these slopes looking for chinquapins or wild violets, and now Luke's nephew might soon be gone, too.

I buried my head on my knees and the dog nuzzled my ear sympathetically. When I stood at last, I heard him frolicking on the rise above me.

Those city hunters had given Noah Good-Samaritan help; I could at least keep their dog for them. He answered my whistle with a woof but didn't reappear.

Wayne told me he'd closed Windy Ridge to hunters, so we had the woods to ourselves, I thought. Except for the cow-bells and birds and the sound of the dog running ahead through dry leaves, the place seemed silent and watchful.

I followed the dog up past a clump of red-leafed dogwoods until we were just below the last steep incline to the crest. Pulling myself around an outcropping of rock, I was startled to realize that this must have been the very spot where Noah fell. The ground was scuffed, and cigarette butts and bits of paper from an instant camera's film pack lay discarded from where Wayne's deputies had photographed the site.

Then I heard the dog bark farther up. He had stopped by a large fallen log; and when I approached, he pawed at the hol-low end and whined as if he'd cornered something. Field mouse or chipmunk, I hoped. It was a little late for snakes, but you never know.

I found a stick and raked aside the leaves that stopped the hole. As I probed, my stick touched something soft that crack-led almost like dry leaves. Gingerly, still thinking of timber rattlers, I pulled it out.

The bundle was long and heavy, wrapped in several layers of waterproof plastic, and it was worse than rattlesnakes. Even before I unwrapped it, I think I knew it was a rifle that had been bought for just one reason.

Abruptly, I was pushed aside, and Gordon Tyler snatched the gun from me, his eyes blazing with anger and fear.

"How the devil did you know?" he cried. "You weren't even here."

"The dog—" I said.

"What dog?" he snarled. "You came around the rocks and went as straight to that log as if you'd watched me yesterday."

I looked about and the dog was nowhere in sight; but in the

horror of the moment, one more oddity didn't register because I was suddenly remembering.

"Noah couldn't have pulled out a handkerchief! He left his with Julie. *You* dropped one there after you shot him, Gordon, to make Wayne think some trigger-happy fool saw a flash of white."

"And this evening, he'll think you stumbled across the killer hiding up here and got yourself shot for meddling."

The rifle barrel gleamed in the sunlight as he swung it up to aim. After that, everything seemed to happen in slow motion. The gun swung up; but before it could level, there was a blur of white and brown fur springing for Gordon's throat, then both plunged backwards onto the rocks below.

By the time I slipped and skidded down into the ravine, the gash on Gordon's temple had quit bleeding and there was no pulse.

I thought the dog would be nearby and I whistled and called, fearful that he might be lying somewhere among the rocks, hurt and dying, too.

Eventually, I had to give up and climb out of the ravine; yet, though dazed from my brush with death and from learning that Gordon had shot Noah deliberately, I was vaguely soothed by a sweet fragrance and was even able to wonder what autumn-blooming plant could so perfume the air.

Now Wayne and I waited on my deck and watched twilight deepen the blue mountains while Gordon's body and Gordon's gun were examined in distant laboratories.

At dusk, one of Wayne's deputies stopped by. "Sorry, Miss Ruth, but we looked under every log and rock in that ravine and there's no sign of your dog."

"I appreciate your looking, but he wasn't mine," I said. "He belonged to those other hunters yesterday."

"They didn't have a dog with them," Wayne said gently. "I asked. And Sam Haskell says he hasn't seen any stray pointers up that way, either."

I shrugged and didn't argue. Gordon had denied the dog, too. Maybe I was getting senile.

Once more, Wayne called the lab, and this time he learned that a test bullet from Gordon's second gun matched the one removed from Noah's lung. Ten minutes later, the medical examiner phoned to report that Gordon's death was from a broken neck and, no, except for the gash on his temple, no other marks; certainly no teeth marks at his throat.

The phone rang again and this time it was Julie. "Noah's blood pressure's stabilized and they think he's coming out of the coma!"

Her voice sparkled with radiant thanksgiving, and a huge weight rolled off my heart.

I've heard that people often don't remember the actual moment when they were hurt; but someday soon, I will ask Noah whether or not he heard a dog bark just before Gordon fired at him. *Something* up there had thrown Gordon's aim off just enough to save his life.

Yet, even if Noah doesn't remember, it won't really matter because I suddenly identified the sweet fragrance I'd smelled earlier. All around me, trees and vines flamed with October colors; but in that ravine up on Windy Ridge, the air had been heavy with the honeysuckle and wisteria of May.

<< The Dog >>

by

Pauline C. Smith

THE MORNING AFTER Aunt Sue called, Trudy phoned her office.

"I can't be in today," she said. "My uncle died and I must go back home. Could I have a week off?"

Her boss said of course. Was there anything he could do? He was so sorry.

There was nothing he could do and really nothing to be sorry for, thought Trudy. She had never liked Uncle Fred, her Aunt Sue's husband, and she was sure no one else had.

She packed her bags, had the Masda gassed, and took off.

She thought about Aunt Sue as she rolled off the miles. They had given her a home during her last two years of high school and the one year of community college. Aunt Sue took the place of the mother she had lost, but Uncle Fred? Well, he was just someone married to Aunt Sue.

She arrived in the early evening and parked her car at the curbing. She leaned on the steering wheel and looked at the house she hadn't seen for more than a year. A small, white house, shaded by old oak trees and surrounded by a chain link fence.

She picked up her bags, opened the gate and walked up the path to the house.

Aunt Sue led her to the kitchen and talked about food.

"But I've eaten," said Trudy. "I stopped along the way."

"Oh well, then, some cake and milk?" urged Aunt Sue. "You had a very long drive."

With Aunt Sue's chocolate cake in front of her, Trudy asked about Uncle Fred.

"You know he'd been sick for many months," said Aunt Sue. "He knew he was going to die. He talked about it a lot. And he read everything he could get his hands on about death."

Trudy shivered. "He read about *death?*"

"Yes. He sent away for these books. Piles of them. And he read them all. He told me that after he died, he would be back."

"Be *back?*" cried Trudy.

"That's right," said Aunt Sue. "Those books he read on transmigration, reincarnation, and I don't know what all made him sure that he would come back somehow, some way. He said he didn't mind dying now that he knew he'd be back."

"Well," said Trudy. "Well, maybe that helped. Maybe it helped him face the end."

"Maybe it did," said Aunt Sue. She smiled. "I'm glad you came."

"Of course I'd come," said Trudy. "Have you made all the arrangements?"

"What arrangements?" asked Aunt Sue.

"For the burial. The funeral."

"Oh yes," said Aunt Sue. "It's tomorrow afternoon."

"What will you do now?" asked Trudy.

Her aunt looked startled. "You mean now that Fred is gone?"

"Yes, now."

"Well, I suppose I'll stay on right here. I've got the house and Fred's insurance. I'll probably do a little volunteer work at the hospital and the church. See people. Do things. Fred never liked to have me go anyplace or see anyone except him. Maybe I'll even learn to drive the car. . . ."

"Good," said Trudy.

"He never really wanted me to do anything except stay right here at home and take care of him."

"I know," said Trudy.

"Another thing—" Aunt Sue trembled with excitement. "You know what I'm going to do? I'm going to get a dog."

"A dog?" said Trudy. "For protection?"

"No, no, no," cried Aunt Sue. "I mean a dog to love. You know I always wanted a dog. Fred hated them. That's why he built the chain link fence around the yard. 'To keep the dogs out,' he said.''

It was during the graveside service the next day that the sky darkened and the thunder began to roll. The minister shortened his already short eulogy, and with a sympathetic pat on Aunt Sue's shoulder, he left just before the rain started.

Workmen in slickers stretched a tarp over the still-open grave and took off, at a run, for one of the buildings on the cemetery grounds.

Trudy hurried her aunt to their parked car. "Well," she said, "this looks like it's going to be a bad one." She turned on the motor and switched on the lights. "Imagine! It's almost as dark as night."

At that moment, the storm broke.

Rain came down in blinding sheets. Thunder roared. Lightning forked. Trudy switched on her wipers. She drove the cemetery grounds slowly, peering through the wiper swipes of her windshield, and came out on Cemetery Road.

"This will lead me to the old back highway, won't it?" she asked her aunt.

"Yes. Turn left here."

Trudy turned and crept along the road, the wipers swishing across the windshield. "Aunt Sue," said Trudy, "lean back over the seat and see if I don't have an umbrella there on the floor. I usually carry one."

Her aunt leaned back and reached down. "Here it is," she said.

"Good," said Trudy. "It'll help us a little when we have to run from the car to the—" and slammed on the brakes. The car skidded to a stop. A dog right-angled in front of her and galloped down the road.

"Oh boy," groaned Trudy, "where did he come from?"

The dog had become a blur in the downpour.

"He was there. All of a sudden, there he was." Trudy let out her breath and went limp. "I almost hit him." She put her foot lightly on the accelerator and inched forward.

She turned toward her aunt. "Did you see him?" she asked.

"I saw him," said her aunt.

They reached the old back highway. Trudy was relieved that there was no traffic. "Who'd want to be out in a storm like this anyway," she muttered. "Maybe a dog, though," her mind still on the dog she'd almost hit, "but the dog would just be trying to find a dry place. Right? I just hope he doesn't get killed doing it."

"He won't," said her aunt.

As they turned from the back road to Center, the rain slackened. "Not much, though," said Trudy. "Just enough so it isn't coming down in sheets. How do you feel, Aunt Sue?"

"What do you mean, how do I feel?"

"Well, now that the funeral is over—"

"It's over," said Aunt Sue. "That's all. At least I think it's over."

"What do you mean you *think* it's over?"

"Just that," said Aunt Sue. "Nobody can tell when anything's over."

"Of course they can," said Trudy. "Something happens. Something's done about it. Then it's over."

Aunt Sue did not answer.

Trudy turned from Center to First. Then onto Elm. "We're almost there," she warned. "Got the umbrella ready?"

Aunt Sue nodded her head.

"Front door key?"

"Yes," said Aunt Sue.

"All right." Trudy slowed to a stop at the curbing. "Now, make a run for it," she said.

Her aunt opened the door on her side and raised the umbrella. Trudy opened her side and ran around the car. Together, they unlatched the gate, squeezed through, and raced, bent against the rain, up the walk to the porch.

And stopped dead.

For there was the dog!

His brown coat was caked with mud, his mouth half opened in a fanged grin. He waited at the top of the porch steps just as if he belonged there.

"It looks like the dog that ran in front of the car," cried Trudy.

"It is," said Aunt Sue and took off, around the house and to the back door. Trudy followed at a dead run.

"Here." Aunt Sue threw the umbrella at her and twisted the keys on her key ring until she found the right one.

She unlocked the back door and yanked it open.

"But, Aunt Sue," cried Trudy.

"Get in here." Aunt Sue grabbed her, jerking her inside. The umbrella, still open, flew from Trudy's hand and rolled on the grass.

"Why did you *do* that?" demanded Trudy as soon as her aunt slammed the door. "Why did you tear around to the back? Look, you're soaked. So am I. . . . And my umbrella—"

"It was the dog," said Aunt Sue when she caught her breath. She was pressed against the door as if to form a barricade. "I won't go near the dog on the porch."

"Oh, come now." Trudy took off her aunt's coat and sat her down in a kitchen chair. She took off her shoes. "That dog won't hurt you. You said you liked dogs. Remember?"

Aunt Sue shuddered. "That's another thing," she said. "Maybe because I like dogs he became the biggest, meanest looking dog he could so I'd have something that scared me and something I didn't want." Aunt Sue started to cry.

Angrily, Trudy yanked off her own coat and stepped out of her shoes. "I don't know what you're talking about. Look, I'm going to make us some hot chocolate. Now you just sit there, Aunt Sue, and calm down. The dog'll go away. He was just trying to find some shelter from the rain. He happened to find your front porch."

"My front porch," said Aunt Sue. "There are many, many front porches between the cemetery and here, so he finds mine. Behind a fence and latched gate."

Trudy turned from the stove. "Maybe he jumped over the fence. And who says he came from the cemetery?"

"You did. You said, 'He looks like the dog that ran in front of the car.' And that was way out on Cemetery Road just before we turned off on the old highway."

Trudy turned back to the stove. "Lots of dogs look alike."

"Yes. Yes, they do," said Aunt Sue. "But this one left the cemetery right after we did. Then he ran in front of your car. Then he worked himself through a latched gate and found my front porch. Doesn't that mean anything to you? Don't you think he's telling us something?"

"No, I don't." Trudy felt a chill travel along her spine. "What's he telling us?" She poured the chocolate into two cups and took it to the table.

"He is telling us he's Fred," said her aunt.

The cups clattered. Chocolate spilled. A scratching noise sounded from the front door.

"He wants in," said Aunt Sue. "Fred wants inside his own house."

"Stop it!" cried Trudy. "He's just a stray mutt that wants in any house."

Her aunt shook her head.

The scratching became frantic. The rain beat down. Thunder roared. Trudy cleaned up the spilled chocolate. . . .

"You see," said Aunt Sue, "I learned a lot during those months your Uncle Fred was dying. I learned about reincarnation; that is when people come back as people. I learned about transmigration; that is when people come back as anything, a bird, a plant, an animal like Fred. Fred told me about it. He said I could never be rid of him. He said I'd have to go on taking care of him as I had always done."

The scratching was loud and grating as if the claws were digging deep into wood.

"Do you believe it?" asked Trudy.

"I didn't then," said her aunt.

"Now?" asked Trudy.

"Well, now I know that Fred is here."

The scratching stopped.

The rain poured. The thunder roared.

But the scratching stopped.

"Aunt Sue," cried Trudy, "the dog has stopped."

"For just a little while," said her aunt.

"I think he's gone."

"No, he isn't."

"I'll go look."

"Don't open the door," cried her aunt.

"I won't." Trudy raced to the front hall. She pulled the curtain aside and looked through the narrow window beside the front door.

She saw the dog as he stepped carefully down the porch stairs. She remembered how Uncle Fred always walked carefully down those stairs. He used to say: "They're dangerous. The risers are too high. The treads are too narrow. . . ." but

Uncle Fred complained about everything. Anyway, this was a dog, not Uncle Fred.

She lost sight of the dog in the rain, and returned to the kitchen.

"He's gone," she told Aunt Sue.

"Did you see him go?"

"I saw him go down the steps. But the rain—"

"Well, he hasn't gone. Just wait."

They waited. And it came.

The sound of scratching. This time on the kitchen door.

Trudy screamed.

Then she jumped as the dog gave two sharp barks, sounding like "Gertrude," the name Uncle Fred used to call her, which she hated.

"I'm going to phone the dog pound," she told her aunt and slipped into her shoes.

"What for?"

"To come and get the dog," said Trudy. "There's a leash law, you know. That dog shouldn't be running around loose. The pound'll pick him up and that'll be the end of him."

"I hope so," said Aunt Sue. "But I don't think it will happen."

"It will. It's got to."

Aunt Sue put her shoes back on and walked to the window in the back door. She could look down on the dog as he scratched away. There was a bald spot on his head exactly like Fred's bald spot.

She walked back to her chair and sank wearily into it.

The storm gathered force. The winds blew.

Trudy walked from the kitchen to the hallway and flicked the wall switch. The lights did not go on. So—the electricity is out, she thought, and wondered if Aunt Sue had candles. Of course she did. The hall was dark. It was early evening, but black as night.

Trudy found the telephone on its stand. She inserted her finger in the last hole of the dial and circled it.

She told the operator she wanted the pound. "The animal-whatever. The animal shelter."

"One moment please," said the operator.

Then—"Here's your party."

"There's a dog," Trudy said quickly into the phone. "He followed us—he's scratching at the doors. Can you come and—"

A streak of lightning brightened the hall and the phone went dead.

"No, no," cried Trudy and clicked the receiver. But the phone was gone.

She groped her way down the dark hall to the kitchen. There, gray light came through the windows.

"What happened?" asked Aunt Sue.

"The phone conked out."

"Of course," said her aunt. She cried out as if it hurt. "It's Fred. He won't let any outsiders in. The dog's even got a bald spot, Trudy. He's got Fred's bald spot. I looked out and saw it."

The dog growled from the back door. Trudy remembered how her uncle used to grumble when anyone reminded him of his bald spot.

"All right, Aunt Sue," she said. "Enough of that. You're bugging me. That's a dog out there, a common ordinary dog. If he's got a bald spot it probably means he's got the mange—"

The dog scratched at the door.

"Stop it," screamed Trudy. "Stop that. Go away. Get out of here." She turned to her aunt. "Look, Aunt Sue, I think we've got to get out of here. Go somewhere and get someone to come and take the dog away—"

"Not out there," cried Aunt Sue, horrified. "We can't go out there."

The rain was easing off. Lightning no longer flashed. The thunder did not roar. Trudy edged toward the door. She pressed her face against the window and looked down upon the dog. Sure enough, he had a bald spot . . . which doesn't mean a thing, Trudy told herself.

He scratched deeply on the door again and again. Then, abruptly, he turned and trotted away.

"He's gone," breathed Trudy. "This time, maybe he's really gone." She raced for the front door and, pulling aside the curtain, peered out, waiting for the dog to return to the porch.

He didn't come.

The rain had abated so that it no longer poured but dripped. But she was still unable to see as far as the fence, so she didn't know if he'd left the yard. Oh, he has, she thought—and back in the kitchen she told her aunt, "He's probably gone off to scratch on someone else's door."

Aunt Sue wasn't as sure, even after minutes passed without a sound of the dog. "What he's really done is he's gone off to figure out another way to get into the house."

"Oh, Aunt Sue, an ordinary dog can't figure out things like that."

"No," she agreed. "An ordinary dog can't . . ."

At that instant, a crash sounded within the house. Then a heavy thump.

Trudy tore across the room to the stove. She looked wildly about.

Aunt Sue sat straight in her chair. Not a muscle moved. "He remembered the loose screen in the bathroom," she breathed. "He climbed through the open window."

Trudy spied a heavy iron skillet and grasped it.

The dog bounded from the bathroom down the hall and sat, filling the doorway, the half grin on his face, fangs sharp and bright.

As close as he was, Trudy thought how much bigger he appeared—and fiercer.

The three were frozen in the faint light.

With the dog barring the way into the hall, Trudy and her aunt were trapped. If they tried to make it to the back door, the dog, in one leap, could mow them down and chew them to shreds.

Trudy didn't doubt but that he would do just that. His eyes blazed in the shadows of the kitchen. Spittle drooled from the sides of his mouth and turned to froth.

While the dog watched Aunt Sue, Trudy slowly lifted the skillet.

The movement, the deeper, shadowed movement, caught the dog's attention.

He turned and sprang.

Trudy hurled the skillet. She heard the crunch of bone. She felt teeth dig into her thigh and the spongy chill of froth slide down her leg.

The dog dropped. She edged around him and backed her way across the room. Thunder grumbled. The dog's body thumped convulsively against the floor. A lightning streak lit the windows. . . . In that moment and during that instant, the dog's body appeared to be haloed by that of a man which faded as the kitchen turned dark.

Trudy caught her breath and groped behind her for the table edge—something to hang onto, something to lean against. Thunder rolled through the sky again. Lightning flashed and the dog, just a dog now, lay quiet on the floor.

"So it was a dog after all. Just a dog," says Aunt Sue today.

"That's all." Trudy laughs with a quaver. "Of course, the dog happened to be mad and of course he happened to bite me so, of course, I had to go through all those rabies shots, but it was a dog after all. For that I am thankful. Just a dog."

"You said that all the time," says Aunt Sue.

"I did, didn't I?" Trudy answers. "I didn't know he was rabid, though, until I saw that froth. Then I knew," she shudders. "Hydrophobia means morbid fear of water. Did you know that, Aunt Sue?"

Aunt Sue nods. They had repeated this same conversation so many times that of course she knew. . . .

"So there it was—raining," continues Trudy. "The dog must have been *desperate* for a dry place. And *that's* the reason he followed us home."

"And we found him on the porch when we got there."

At this point in their reiterated discussion, Trudy wonders if her aunt realizes she has blown the practical, sensible, factual dog story all to bits and supplanted it with a theory, a legend, a myth of an Uncle Fred who, knowing where his home was, beat them to it.

She wonders.

She wonders if Aunt Sue saw the haloed image of Uncle Fred over that of the dog in the lightning flash that terrible funeral night.

Or did she see it herself?

She wonders if Aunt Sue sold her house and moved close to Trudy because she feared the return of something that might be a man.

She wonders.

She wonders about every stray animal she sees. Every plant her aunt buys and hangs in her apartment—the ferns with their fast-growing tentacles, the cacti with spines . . .

Trudy wonders and becomes impatient with herself for wondering. Because, of course, it was a dog. A stray dog looking for a dry place. A dog with mange. A mad dog. It just happened, that's all.

But still Trudy wonders.

And she wonders if her aunt wonders, too.

<< The Light Next Door >>
by
Charlotte Armstrong

HAVING LOAFED ALL morning, Howard Lamboy was improving the holiday afternoon, but Miggs, the dog, thought that raking leaves in the back yard was a jolly game, and a part of the fun for him was to scatter all the piles. After much haranguing, and gesturing with the rake, Howard had just conceded that he was never going to get anywhere until Miggs was banished indoors. He had his hand in the dog's collar when the pouched face of his neighbor poked around the back corner of the garage. It was followed by the thin body, which stationed itself on the other side of the knee-high hedge.

"Hi," said Ralph Sidwell, with his usual gloomy diffidence.

"Oh, hi, Ralph," said Howard. "How's every little thing?" Then he bit his tongue, because the man was a bridegroom, and his bride, whatever else, was certainly not little; and while Howard was filled with normal human curiosity he hadn't meant to be crude.

"Fine," said Ralph absently. "Say, by the way, that dog of yours made off with a pillow from my place. Seen any traces?"

"What?" Miggs was writhing, head to tip of tail, like a line of light on choppy water. Howard let him go and the dog gamboled over to the hedge to sniff welcome. The neighbor looked sourly down at the Dalmatian.

"Now, what's all this?" said Howard genially. "What the devil would Miggs want with a pillow? He's got a pillow. No, I haven't seen any traces. What do you mean?"

"Francine," said Ralph coldly, "put a bed pillow out on

the back balcony to air and it fell off the railing. Your dog hauled it away."

"I don't believe it," said Howard. "Where is it?"

"That's what I was asking you."

"*Bed* pillow?" Howard was incredulous. "I doubt he'd bury a thing like that, you know."

"Well, it's gone," said Ralph gruffly.

"Well, I'm very sorry," said Howard, "but I don't know a thing about it and neither does my dog."

"How do you know he doesn't?" said Ralph. "My wife saw him."

"She recognized him?" Howard was stiff.

"Black and white spots," said Ralph in triumph.

"Well, well! Only black and white dog in the world, eh? I can tell you, Miggs didn't bring any bed pillow home, and you tell me where else he would have brought it."

"He did *something* with it," said Ralph stubbornly.

"I don't think so," said Howard. "Excuse us, please?"

He grabbed the dog's collar again and dragged Miggs off to the kitchen door.

"What's the matter?" said Stella.

"Oh, boy!" said Howard eloquently.

After a while he told her.

"Okay," Stella said, "Miggs didn't do it. So it's a mistake. But, Howard, what makes you so mad?"

"Aw, it was his attitude."

"In what way?"

"So damned unreasonable."

"Listen, he's only been married two days," said Stella. "It's whatever her little heart desires, for gosh sakes."

"Fine way she's setting up diplomatic relations."

But Stella said, "A second marriage, at their ages, is probably pretty upsetting. Have a little human understanding."

"Well, it's Miggs *I* understand," said Howard. "I know him better, for one thing."

The fact was, he didn't know Ralph Sidwell at all. Howard was 44 years old and his neighbor must be in his middle fifties. Howard preferred to think of this as a whole other generation. Ralph and his first wife, Milly, had been living next door when the Lamboys moved in eight years ago. While the Sidwells had not called, they had been pleasant enough over-the-fence;

but the relationship had never become more than a hot-enough-for-you or sure-need-rain sort of thing.

Milly Sidwell, a personality of no apparent force, had taken a notion to die in the distance, having succumbed, according to the newspaper, while visiting relatives in Ohio. When the widower had returned, without a wife or her body to bury here, the Lamboys had bestirred themselves to make a condolence call. This had evidently either surprised or alarmed the man to the point of striking him dumb. It hadn't been a very satisfactory occasion.

Later Stella had asked him over to dinner, three separate times, which invitations Ralph had refused, as if he couldn't believe his ears, and they must be mad. So the Lamboys had given up. For the last three years Ralph Sidwell had lived alone, next door, taking his meals out somewhere, coming and going with a minimum of contact. The Lamboys, being involved in warm and roaring communication with their neighbors on the other side, didn't miss what they had never had.

Now, suddenly, Ralph had taken unto himself a second wife.

The Lamboys had not been invited to the wedding which, indeed, scarcely seemed to have been a social occasion. Wednesday morning (only yesterday), Ralph had been standing in his own driveway when Howard drove out; Ralph had hailed him, and had announced, rather stiffly, that he had been married on his lunch hour the day before. He wanted the Lamboys to meet the bride.

Howard had shut off his motor and got out of the car in honor of the news. (The least he could do!) Stella had come running out in her morning garb of robe and apron, and Francine Sidwell—the widow Noble, that was—had come out of her kitchen to be presented.

She had been dressed neatly. (Stella confessed later that she had felt mortified, herself.) But there was no better word for Francine than "fat"—unless it was "enormous."

Stella reported that after Howard had driven off to his office they had told her that they had first met in a laundromat. "She's a marvelous cook," Ralph had said, and that was the end of the conversation.

Although Stella said mischievously that probably Ralph only wanted to make sure they didn't think he was living in sin, she was prepared to accept and adopt a neighborly approach. But it was only right to let them severely alone for "a while"—a period that would correspond to the honeymoon they evidently were not going on.

This was only Thursday. Howard was thinking, with human understanding, that a second "honeymoon" might not be all honey when Miggs, that lovable clown, placed his jaw in warm devotion on Howard's ankle. "That's my fella," said Howard. "Love me, love my dog."

This wasn't what he meant. He didn't expect the Sidwells to *love* him, but they ought to notice what *he* loved.

On Saturday, Howard was out, moseying along the line of the scraggly hedge between the lots and wondering what the hedge disliked about its situation, when Ralph Sidwell came out of his own back door, marching, to accost him.

"Now," he said, with no other preliminary, "you are going to have to tie that dog up." He pointed at Miggs, whose name he ought to know perfectly well, with a shaking finger. "We have a right," he sputtered, "to hang anything we like on our own clothesline and have it safe. Your dog—"

"His name," said Howard coolly, "is Miggs."

"Your stupid animal," said Ralph, "has taken my great-grandmother's patchwork quilt! And that's a priceless heirloom! It can't be replaced." He was shouting. "My great-grandmother made it when she was a *girl*!"

"Hold it," said Howard. "Now calm down, will you?"

"By *hand*!" yelled the neighbor.

"Listen, I'm sure she did," said Howard. "But what has that got to do with Miggs? He wouldn't take a quilt off your clothesline."

"If he didn't, who did?"

"How would I know? I suppose your wife saw him again? She must have spots before her eyes."

"Don't you insult my wife!"

"Then quit insulting my dog."

"Where is my great-grandmother's quilt?"

"I haven't the faintest idea and I couldn't care less!"

Miggs, getting into the spirit of things, began to growl. Stella came running out of the house. "What are you bellowing about?"

By now Howard was speechless. Ralph was still pointing at Miggs.

"Oh, honey?" Out of the back door of the other house (identical in floor plan except that right was left) came the bride. Francine was hurrying and her flesh jiggled and bounced. She had in her arms a patchwork quilt, all blues and whites and greens. "Oh, honey," she panted. "Look, I found it. It's all right, I found it."

"Well!" said Ralph hotly. He turned and gave Howard a hard glare. The look said: Don't you dare say I shouldn't have been so mad at you, because I am *still* mad.

Miggs, who understood hostility in every language, even the silent ones, barked, and Francine clutched the quilt and began to walk backward. (Was she afraid?) Howard rose in his wrath and simply strode past the hedge. "Let me see that," he demanded.

Francine screamed lightly.

"Hey, Miggs, whoa!" cried Stella, grabbing the dog's collar and hanging on with all her weight.

Ralph Sidwell said, "Don't touch it. That's *mine*."

"Yours, your great-grandmother," yelled Howard. "You show me my dog's toothmarks or his claw prints or *any* evidence—" He snatched up the quilt by a corner. It was a lovely old thing, on the fragile side. Francine kept backing away, and Howard had to let go to keep from tearing the treasure. "For your information," he howled, "*my* dog doesn't eat tomatoes."

"Okay, I apologize," Ralph screeched, as angrily as he could.

"Oh, honey, I'm sorry," Francine was saying to her bridegroom. (She was afraid?) "Oh, listen, Mrs. Lamboy, I'm so sorry—"

Stella bent her head as if she were the Queen and Francine the commoner. "Come, Miggs. Come, Howard," she said, rounding up her own fierce creatures.

They persuaded Miggs into the house. Howard flung himself down in his den and poured some beer and did it wrong and caused too big a head and swore and blew out his breath in a long "Whew!" The dog lay down at his feet and thumped the floor with his tail, waiting for praise. "That's right, pal," said Howard. "You didn't do it, did you? Darn idiots!"

Stella was cooling off, by herself, in the kitchen, and it didn't take her long. She came in and said, "We're not going to have this, you know."

"Darned right."

"I mean we're not going to have any feud on," she said grimly. "Of all the miserable things in this world a feud with neighbors is the stupidest. And *we* are not going to have one."

"Okay. Let them lay off my dog."

"What's this 'my dog' all the time?" she said. "He's my dog too, and I love him dearly, and I know he's not guilty, as well as you do. But I am not going to get into a silly fight with neighbors. Ralph apologized."

"Yeah, some apology," Howard scoffed. But he saw her point. He wasn't really as childish as this. So it was agreed that Stella would call on her neighbor, as soon as seemed correct, and—well, just do the right thing and *be* neighborly.

So on Monday morning, Howard being at work, Stella made a luscious pie. She phoned Mrs. Sidwell and announced that she would like to come over and call. Would three o'clock be all right? Francine, in a fluster, said it would, of course.

So Stella dressed herself nicely, but not too formally, and went down her own front walk and around on the public sidewalk to the neighbor's walk and up to their front door and rang the bell. She had been in this house only once before. She had no way to assess what changes the new mistress may have made in the décor or the atmosphere. The house was neat to the point of seeming bare. It "felt" like a man's house. But Ralph was not there.

Francine had dressed herself more or less "up" for company. She made exclamations over the high pie, delicate under its burden of whipped cream. She took Stella into the dining room and produced coffee with which she served generous portions of the peace offering. Stella, eating her own pie (and she wished she didn't have to because *she* did count calories), made the normal approaches.

The weather. Bright days. Cool nights. How long the Lamboys had lived here. That they had a daughter away at college. Just the one child. That the houses were small but comfortable, weren't they? A development, yes. You would hardly know any more that they were all alike, what with each owner using paint and trellis, shrub and vine, in an individual way. This had always delighted Stella. But Francine wanted, she said, the recipe.

Oh? Stella recited the recipe for her pie. And how did Mrs. Sidwell like the neighborhood?

Well, Francine thought it was very nice and the house was very nice and the market was very convenient and the pie was *delicious*! Oh, yes, she had been a widow for some years, all alone, yes, and she *was* enjoying this pie. Would Mrs. Lamboy take another piece? No? Then Mrs. Sidwell would.

Stella, smiling and murmuring, watched and listened and thought to herself: No wonder she's so fat! She also was getting a strange impression that the woman beside her was, in truth, a gaunt starving creature, and the flesh in which she was wrapped was a blanket to keep cold bones from shaking apart—an insulation to keep fine drawn nerves from splitting and shattering at the slightest sensation. But everything was going smoothly, on the surface, so Stella brought up the matter of the quilt.

She was so glad it had been neither lost nor damaged.

Francine said, "I washed and ironed it and it's as good as new."

This seemed to Stella to be an odd way to speak of an antique, but she went on to deplore any misunderstanding about the dog. "We know his habits so well, you see. He is really a harmless old fellow. Wonderful with children. Oh, *he* loves *everybody*, including burglars, I'm afraid. Of course, maybe you are a cat person? I seem to remember Mrs. Sid— Oh, I'm sorry."

Francine was staring at her. Her features were lost in the rounded flesh. It was hard to imagine what kind of nose or chin she had. But her eyes were peering out of their rosy nests, and surely there was fear in them.

"All I meant," said Stella, "some people adore cats and can't stand—" (She hadn't meant to mention the first Mrs. Sidwell—she must be more careful.)

"I don't care for pets, not much," said Francine and stuffed and totally filled her mouth with whipped cream.

· · ·

After a decently brief interval Stella went home, thoughtful and a little dismayed. She told Howard at dinnertime that there was now peace, and for pity's sake not to break it. Because peace, she went on to confide, was about all there could ever be between Stella Lamboy and the woman next door.

"It's not that I don't *like* her," Stella said. "It's just that I didn't find one thing—there's just no— Well, maybe it isn't fair after only fifteen minutes but there wasn't *one* spark! The only thing she seems to care about is food. She didn't want to know what I care about."

"Obviously," said Howard, "she doesn't care about being fashionably slim."

Stella shuddered and wondered why she did. "She admitted she doesn't care much for pets," she said. "But she's not— well, aggressive about it."

"Miggs can coexist," said Howard loftily, "as long as there is no aggression from out across the border."

But he was thinking: Who would spill tomato juice on an antique patchwork quilt? Or was it something else that I saw on it? The color of—blood? He shivered at such nonsense.

That night Howard got himself trapped in the Late Show. When he took Miggs out on his leash it was after midnight. The street was quiet; the tweedy dark was fresh and cool. As he ambled down the block, with the dog's eager life tugging, kitelike, on the leash in his hand, Howard fell into what he sometimes called, to himself, his "cosmic" thoughts.

Suburban, ordinary, these undistinguished rows of boxes, set among the trees, all silent now. What have we here, he mused. Everything commonplace. You betcha! *Commonplace* stuff—like birth, death, love, hate, fear, hope. In his imagination he could lift the lids from some of these boxes, lift them right off. He knew one box that held patient suffering, another that rang with music all day long. He couldn't help telling himself that every box on the street was a package of human mystery—which was quite commonplace, he thought complacently.

When he turned at the end of the block it was his fancy to cross over and come back on the other side of the street. Suddenly, in the upper story of the house next door to his—the Sidwells'—he seemed to see a wash of light. No room lit up. But something paler than the dark had washed along the windows from the inside. Burglars, he thought at once. There it went again. Howard began to walk on his toes, although now the house remained dark, and Miggs hadn't noticed anything.

Howard crept on until he was directly across from the Sidwell house and there, again, came that washing light, from inside, but now on the ground floor.

He hauled on the leash and struck across to his own house, keeping an uneasy eye to his right. Stella was asleep in her bed, trusting and innocent and *alone*. He must be careful. But his own house seemed to breathe in peace, so he stood quietly on his own porch until Miggs whined a question. Then he unlocked the door and took the dog in.

Miggs curled around on his own cushion in the kitchen and Howard patted the freshened fur, meanwhile peering out the window. There *was* a light of some sort in the kitchen over there, across the two driveways. But there was a shade, or drawn curtains. He couldn't quite see in. And he couldn't hear anything.

Nothing was happening. No more mysterious glimmers.

Finally, Howard locked all his doors and went up to bed. But he kept his ear on the night, until he remembered there was a better ear than his, downstairs.

The next morning, as Howard went to get out his car, he heard a futile whirring and whining in the Sidwells' garage. So he leaned over the hedge. "Trouble?"

It seemed that Ralph was going to work (so much for honeymoons!) but his darned battery— He wasn't going to drive Francine's old crate, either. So Howard offered him a lift. They discovered a useful coincidence of routes, Ralph ran into his house to give Francine his Auto Club card, then got in beside Howard, breathless and grateful.

Ralph worked for the Gas Company. He'd get home all right. A fellow worker lived not too far from here.

"Say," said Howard after a while, "anybody prowling around in your house last night?"

"What?"

"Well, I just happened to be walking the dog. Wondered if you had a burglar," Howard went on cheerfully.

"I wake up once or twice," said Ralph, bristling. "I'd know if we had a burglar."

Howard felt sheepish. "Well, I was really wondering if any-body felt sick. You know, had to get up and take medicine or something?"

"Not at all," said Ralph angrily.

Howard was sorry he had said anything. Whatever intimate ceremonies might take place at night in his neighbor's house were *not* his business. He said, "Maybe you ought to keep a dog. I was thinking, last night, he'd hear the softest burglar in the world. Trouble is, you take Miggs, he's all the time hearing things no man can *ever* hear. This can be upsetting, too."

"I am not," said Ralph furiously, "superstitious. And I don't intend to get that way, either."

Howard judged it best to change the subject.

He said to his wife that evening, "They're bugging me."

"Who are?"

"Next door. I don't know."

"What don't you know?"

"I don't know *anything*." Howard stared at her somewhat hostilely, because he was feeling foolish. "I don't know what he meant by 'superstitious.' And there's something else I can't get out of my head."

"So put it into mine," she invited.

"It bugs me that I saw a red stain of some kind on that quilt."

"*What* kind?" she said.

"Okay," he confessed. "You know the classics. Ever think of this? How do we know what *really* happened to Milly Sidwell?"

When Stella did not laugh it occurred to Howard, with a familiar surprise, that he loved her very much, darned if he didn't. She said in a minute, "I don't see how he could have buried Milly in his back yard without *Miggs* knowing all about it, do you?"

"That's right," said Howard, relaxing.

"Of course, in the cellar—" She raised an eyebrow at him.

"They've got no cellar," said Howard at once. All these little houses sat on concrete slabs. There were no cellars. How-ard could think of nowhere to hide a body in *his* house, so he felt cheered.

"Anyhow, that's silly," Stella said indulgently, now that he was cheered. And then she added, "Ralph didn't *care* enough about Milly to murder her." She hoped he wouldn't want her to explain. She wasn't sure she could.

But Howard said, "I'll tell you what, Stell. Why don't we ask them over for a barbecue on Sunday? Out in the back yard? Real informal?"

"Why?" she asked calmly, trusting him to know that she was only wondering, not saying "No."

"Because," he answered, "they bug me."

"Me, too," said Stella in a minute.

Stella extended the invitation over the phone, coaxed a little, saying that it was right next door, just the four of them, no special trouble would be gone to, everything very informal, just wear any old clothes. Howard was very good with steaks on charcoal. Francine said she would ask Ralph.

On Wednesday morning, when Howard appeared, Ralph was backing out his revived vehicle. He stopped. "Say, Howard?"

"Yeah?"

"Listen, Francine would like to come over on Sunday. The only thing—"

"Yeah?"

"I'm wondering, could you lock up your dog?"

"What do you mean, lock him up?"

"Well, Francine, she's nervous about coming over. She's afraid, I guess, of dogs."

"Well," said Howard, "Miggs isn't going to think much of the idea, but sure, he can stay in the house. You come along over, both of you."

So the invitation was accepted.

Sure enough, on Sunday, Miggs saw no reason to conceal his anguish at being incarcerated while something interesting was going on behind the house. Howard and Stella did their best, carrying trays of food out to the redwood table, lighting the candles in their glass globes, offering drinks and tidbits, Howard fussing over his coals.

The guests didn't help. The meal was uncomfortable, speech stiff, dull, pumped up. No spark, as Stella had said before.

Ralph was an unresponsive man, Howard decided. That was a good word for him. He seemed to be locked up inside himself. Lonely, you could say. As for Francine, she ate well.

When it was time for dessert, Howard went into the kitchen with a trayload of dirty dishes. Under full instructions he was trusted to return with a trayload of sweets, the ice cream and cake, while Stella poured the coffee and kept the lame talk limping along.

Howard stood over the sink, rinsing off the plates while he was at it, with Miggs coiling and curling around his legs. Begging and apologizing. Whatever I did to offend you, forgive me? Please, I would so like to come to the party?

Howard felt bad about this. He couldn't explain, could he? Staring out into the deepening dusk he saw, across the two driveways, that wash of light in the upper story. He stepped nimbly to his own back door and called, "Oh, Ralph, could you come here a minute?"

When Ralph came in, to be greeted with delight by Miggs (in whose opinion things were looking up), Howard was standing quietly by the sink. "I just saw something funny in your house. Same as I saw before. Come and look."

The older man was the shorter. He came up beside Howard. His head, at Howard's shoulder, was held in tension. Nothing happened for a moment or two.

"Well, I guess," said Howard, "it's like your tooth won't ache at the dentist's."

Then the light happened again.

Miggs began to bark suddenly. "Listen, Miggs, shut up, will you?" shouted Howard. Ralph was pushing against the sink. But his mood was not what Howard expected. "*You* saw something funny?" Ralph said firmly, when the dog was quiet. "*You're* not having hallucinations, are you? So whatever it was is real?"

"Whatever it is," said Howard cautiously.

But Ralph went rushing out the back door and Miggs tumbled after. Howard hurried to follow and saw the man jogging on the grass toward the candlelit picnic table with the dog bounding in pursuit.

Francine screamed in terror.

Howard swooped to catch the dog, and Stella began to soothe, and Ralph sat down.

When the noise and confusion had abated, Ralph said to his wife, "*He* just saw something funny. So now you tell *him* he's being haunted."

Francine began to cry. The oddest thing was that in the midst of her bawling she took up a piece of roll, buttered it, and stuffed it into her mouth.

"What's the matter?" cried Stella. "What did you see?"

"I don't know. Some car's headlight, maybe," said Ralph contemptuously, "but *she* says my house is haunted. She thinks we've got a ghost in there. Listen, I thought I heard something funny, a couple of times. But she didn't hear it, so she said that whatever is there must be haunting *me*. She said it must be Milly—Milly not wanting another woman in her house."

"Oh, come on," said Stella. "Really!" She was shocked, not so much by the idea of the supernatural as by the husband's ruthless betrayal of his wife.

"Well, I don't know," Francine was sobbing. "I don't know. I don't know."

Howard said, "Why don't we take Miggs over there? I told you, dogs can sense things out of our range. If *he* says it's okay, you can relax."

"No," yelled Francine. She stood up. Her great bulk, in the growing darkness, was uncanny. "No," she screamed. "I won't *have* a dog in the house. No!"

Miggs, who knew somehow that he was being insulted, replied in kind. So Howard dragged him back to his kitchen prison. What the hell, he was saying to himself. The worst of it was, he couldn't help thinking it might *be* hell.

The party was now definitely over. Francine kept blubbering and Ralph Sidwell was in a rage. He seemed to be a man who cast out whatever anger he felt, to ripple off on all sides, fall where it may. He seemed to be angry with the Lamboys. So the Sidwells went home.

Howard, stubborn to be kind whether they liked it or not, walked with them to the front sidewalk. Something made him say to them, "If you need any help, any time, just remember, will you? Here I am, right next door."

But they left without answering.

In the back yard Stella stood among the ruins. Howard went to let the dog out. Miggs raced around joyously for sixty seconds. He had been forgiven? That was fine with him. All was well.

But it wasn't.

The Lamboys ate dessert indoors. They didn't talk much. Stella could not be rid of the impression that somewhere beneath Francine's flesh there was a small, frail, and very frightened woman who had *not* been afraid of the dog. Stella was almost sure now that Francine hadn't wanted to come at all. But Ralph, unable to read the crooked signal of a false excuse, had fixed it so that she'd had to come. But what *was* she afraid of?

Howard kept wondering about that light, and what it had really been, and why Ralph had seemed, at first glad, and then angry, that somebody else had "seen something funny." What was Ralph afraid of?

Bedtime came and Howard let Miggs out briefly (no walk tonight), then checked the house and climbed upstairs. He went into their daughter's room that was always waiting for her, silent, vacant, but in sweet order. It was on the side toward the Sidwells. He looked out. The house over there had a light on somewhere—on the other side, downstairs—but as far as he could tell, all was peaceful.

Howard gave the whole thing up and dropped into bed.

At one o'clock in the morning the Lamboys' front doorbell rang and kept ringing in the manner that says *panic*. Howard leaped up, put on his robe and slippers, ran his hand over his rumpled hair, and went steadily down the stairs. Miggs, naturally, was curious too, and Howard could not but feel glad that the dog came to press his weight against his master's leg.

The porchlight fell on the white face of Ralph Sidwell. He was fully dressed. He said, "I'm afraid."

"What seems to be the trouble?" asked Howard quietly.

"I heard her scream. I think she—I don't—I'm afraid to go and see."

"Where is she?"

"Upstairs. I— Well, we had a fight. I couldn't— I didn't want to go up to bed. Then I heard the scream. I don't know what to do."

"I'll come with you," said Howard. "We'll take the dog. Let me get his leash."

Stella was halfway down the stairs and had heard. Howard

snapped the leash on Miggs's collar. He took his flashlight thinking of it vaguely as a weapon. But the weapon he relied on was the dog.

Ralph Sidwell could hardly stand on his puny legs. "I don't know if I c-can." His jaw shook.

Stella said, "We'll follow, Howard. You go and see." She bent in womanly compassion to this trouble. Howard walked toward whatever the trouble was, over there.

Strange night. The street was quiet. The little boxes stood in rows among the softly sighing trees, and how many civilizations—the insects, the little creeping creatures, the birds, the dogs and cats, and what others unknown—were coexisting all around the little boxes?

Howard went around the walks and up to his neighbor's box, the door of which stood wide open. He entered cautiously. The dog, keeping close, was silent.

He called out, "Francine? Francine?"

There was no answer. The lights were on in the living room to his right. The room was empty. The rest of the downstairs seemed dark and quiet. Howard led the dog toward other doors. He knew the floor plan. But Miggs made no sound.

So Howard started up the stairs. The dog, seeming nervous now, crowded him toward the railing. The upper-hall light switch was in a familiar place. Howard flicked it on and saw a pale blue mound on the floor.

Francine seemed neither conscious nor unconscious. She moaned but did not speak. She was bleeding from a scalp wound.

The ladder to the attic, that hinged from the hall ceiling, was down, and the square hole in the attic floor gaped open. Darkness lay beyond it. Howard's neck hair stirred. He didn't want to climb that ladder and turn his flashlight into that darkness. Wiser to check elsewhere first?

Now Miggs began to growl. Howard turned nervously and heard Stella's voice below. So he called down, "She's been hurt," keeping his voice not too loud, because more ears might be listening than he knew. "Not too badly, I think. Don't come up yet."

"Shall I call a doctor?" said his wife's clear voice.

"Good idea. Or else—no, wait."

Miggs was still growling and doing a kind of dance, advance and retreat, advance and retreat. "In here, eh?" said Howard to the dog. He pushed on the door of the back upstairs room that, in his house, was Stella's sewing room. It was a bedroom here.

Howard whipped the beam of his flashlight around the four walls. Nothing. No one. There was no clothes closet, so nobody could be hiding behind another door. Behind the door he'd come through? Howard shoved it flat against the wall. Nothing.

It was Miggs who saved his reason. (He said so later.)

Howard walked into the small room that seemed so empty. The dog went with him. But the dog *knew*. And the dog rushed and skittered, advanced and retreated, and his knowing muzzle, questing, knew *where*. So that when a hand of thin bone came out from under the bedspread's fringe and took Howard by his bare ankle, Howard did *not* fly up to the ceiling or out of his wits.

Oh, he jumped. But Miggs went at once into an uproar. So Howard, sheltered by the noise, dared to crouch and send the light under the bed and into a face—a face the like of which he had never seen before.

"Guard. Stay." he said to Miggs, kindly but firmly. "Good boy. On guard."

He went into the hall. Francine, huge in her pale blue robes, had lifted herself on one arm; her other hand was on her bloody forehead. "Lester?" she said, in a childish piping.

Howard called down the stairs to Stella. "Call the police, hon. That's quickest." Then he looked at Francine.

"My baby? My boy?" said Francine, making everything a question, as if she were sure of nothing. "Never right? Nobody knew? Hungry? Ladder? Hit me?" Her bulk seemed to shake and then flow back down to the floor.

Stella was already on the phone. At the bottom of the stairs Ralph Sidwell was staring up at his neighbor.

"We have a problem here," said Howard quietly. "You've had a kind of stowaway, I think."

He went back to where Miggs was. The dog backed off, obeying. Slowly Howard persuaded the creature out from under the bed. A boy? Anywhere from fourteen to twenty-four. Who could say? He was deformed and stunted, wire-thin, incredibly pale, almost witless. He did not know how to stand up. He clung to the floor like a spider.

People came . . .

It was 3:30 in the morning when the Lamboys returned home at last. Stella said it was unthinkable to go to bed without breakfast and set to work creating homely scents of coffee and bacon.

Howard sat down on the dinette bench and Miggs jumped enthusiastically beside him. This was forbidden, but Howard was in no mood to scold.

"How did she ever sneak the Thing into the attic?" he said, because he was too filled with horror and pity to mention feelings: the brain was safer. "That's where the pillow was. She made a mistake about the quilt, eh? What do you know about that candle! Dangerous, whew! That alone!" (Alone, he thought, a living thing, ever alone, alone.) "She'd have to bring its food by night, on Sundays. But last night Ralph wouldn't go to bed. The ladder hit her."

Stella said sternly, "*Her* shame. So hide it and everything is dandy. And when the money is running out, go after some ordinary lonely man."

"What did *he* want? Home cooking?" said Howard as sternly as she. "How come he didn't notice this woman was sick and off the beam—'*way* off, and so desperate. If it wasn't in his mind to pay any attention to her or to help her—"

In a moment Stella sat down and said, "If you're off, so far, and always getting farther, you'd have to have some little tiny pleasure. Something sweet in your mouth, at least?" She held her cheeks. They were feeling hollow.

Howard was thinking: In how many little boxes are there people, locked up, all alone, and in how many different ways? And how should we know? And what could we do? And why should that be?

Miggs was licking his master's left ear. We love. We love? And here we are together. So all is well. All is well?

Howard put his arm around the meat of Miggs, this warm loving creature who gave his heart in trust, even unto another species. "Miggs," he said, "what happens to people shouldn't happen to a dog." And he snuggled into the live fur.

<< Late September Dogs >>
by
Gene KoKayKo

STANDING IN THE waves, Rube figured everything he had
had gone south already—his hair and his chest and the arches
in his feet. So why should he, Barney Rubekowski, follow
them? His friends had gone south, too, most to Florida, and
Rube had wanted to start over somewhere new, somewhere
warmer than the East Coast but not quite so far south . . . so
retired. Somehow southern California still seemed too south
and too much a copout, so Rube had settled for the central
coast of California, west but right in between. This way he
could see the big O, the Pacific, not that dribble the Atlantic,
or some Gulf of Something, but the big P, the real ocean.

And so what if he couldn't swim? And so what if he no
longer looked quite so good in a bathing suit? He could wade,
couldn't he? He could wade and splash a little way into the
great surf. He had his pension and his new apartment and his
number fifteen sunblock; and the sun was bright and not too
hot and the world belonged to him and the big old dog who
was the only other creature on the beach this early in the
morning. He had beaten the odds, made it out of the rat race,
found home—in spite of what old what's-his-name had said
you couldn't do again—and by damn he was going to—

What did that dog have in his mouth?

Rube felt a flush of curiosity, then a flash of apprehension
as he saw the human hand. The dog was big, a yellowish
Labrador, and even from where Rube stood in the waves, he
could tell the dog was careworn. His tail was ringed with
scabs, as if some greater animal had taken small chunks along
the way, had chewed the tail when the Lab wasn't looking. It

gave the tail a diseased look, like some aging raccoon that was losing its fur. The dog stood on the shore, but Rube could still clearly see the human hand. The big Lab had it between his teeth as if worrying a snack, and he was trying to pull the hand from a huge clump of greenish seaweed. Rube could tell the dog was a he, too, the dog all spraddle-legged like that, and Rube shook his head at the observation, wondering why, at times of stress, he always noticed things like that. It was a character flaw, he felt. One he'd always had. If there was a terrible accident in the street, he would not only see the accident but all the attendant sights and sounds on the periphery. He'd see the car make, the color, the license plate number. He'd remember later the kind of day: cloudy or bright, approximate air temperature, number of clouds. Everyone else would be screaming, "Oh my God, the blood!," and good old Rube would be checking out the details. Inside, Rube thought, where no one could see. There was something wrong with him. He had no real compassion, perhaps, for humanity and its tragedy.

Rube splashed toward the dog. As he did, his focus frayed again and he saw: almost deserted beach, one flock of gulls a hundred yards down picking over some trash; a sky misty with alto cumulus; a sun melting through the clouds, still rising toward zenith; and a breeze softly tossing more trash along . . . the breeze plucked at the sweat on his forehead.

The dog saw Rube coming. He growled around the hand, then started to back, with the hand still in his mouth. The clump of seaweed shifted slightly.

"Easy now," Rube said, splashing up on the sand, "easy boy," as though he were trying to settle a big horse that was about to buck. Hell, the dog was big as a horse. But that wasn't the real reason—that wasn't the real fear. Rube was trying to settle himself because he didn't want to see what the dog had—not really. From a distance this was all very interesting, but from up close there was a chance it would get gruesome. Worse, it might interfere with Rube's new life. If what was attached to that human hand was a human body, then he'd be involved. And he hadn't come to the coast of California to get involved. He'd come here to retire.

The big dog lowered his head, as if to hide the contents of his mouth.

"Don't you swallow that!" Rube shouted.

The dog's eyes were big and white and they seemed to turn in the great head and accuse him.

"Drop it, now!"

But the dog didn't. He pulled instead, a muscle-wrenching heave of a pull that suddenly exposed a white arm. The rest of the body was tangled up in the big clump of green seaweed, and Rube told himself he couldn't really see. Couldn't really see the white, bare shoulder, and exposed breast, and the big gaping hole.

Rube turned away and put his hands on his shaky knees. "Ah, Jesus Holy Jehoshaphat."

His arms shook, and the sweat spilled down his forehead. Salty, it burned its way down his face like a track of guilty tears.

He could hear the dog worrying the hand, a small whimper through his large white teeth. Rube realized he'd bitten his own lower lip so hard the blood ran down his chin. He ran the tip of his tongue over the spot, licking it back like a wounded animal. He felt wounded.

But alive. And breathing.

The body tangled in the seaweed was not. The body tangled in the kelp was way past any thought or consideration for such mundane physical needs.

How to get the dog away?

Rube straightened and wiped the smear from his chin. He stomped toward the dog, big splashing steps in the sand. Pebbles flew, but the dog stayed. Whimpering.

"You gotta let go of that," Rube begged.

The dog growled around the fingers of the hand.

Rube backed off and picked through the sand until he had a neat handful of sharp stones. He started pegging them at the yellow Lab. The first fell short. Rube grimaced and bore down and fired the next, hard, at the dog's flank. The dog yelped, hitching sideways, but he held onto the hand. The dog seemed to grin around the shredded flesh like some demon from hell. Rube started throwing rocks as fast as he could: one, two, three, striking the dog along the body; and *finally*, the dog romped sideways, dropping the shredded hand. He stood with his big head hanging, looking back as if mournful over his loss.

"Just stay now—just stay." Rube waggled his finger at the dog, and the dog dropped to his haunches. Still whimpering. Still looking mournfully at the body.

Rube didn't want to look down, but he'd earned the right. On top of the kelp now, he could see more. Her hair was long and darkened by the sea, but her eyes were open and light, the color of green he remembered from old Coke bottles in his youth. They stared up but past him with a look of accusation and shock, a "how dare you look at me like this" look that made him glance toward the dog. The dog started to whine.

Rube started to whine, unknowingly, a soft whimper that sounded angry with the gentler sounds of the sea. He'd seen death before, but all of it in hospitals, where the smell and sights were antiseptic. Everything controlled, everything nasty beneath sheets. Her body lay tangled in the kelp, but it was bloated, the flesh too pale to be real and alive, the look from her eyes changing in the twinkling morning light, a look that filled him with sorrow, then shock as he saw the gaping hole between her breasts. Rube heard it then, the sound he made, a sound he remembered until the last: piteous and sorrowful and low and moaning—a sound like a worshipper at the wailing wall, a sound almost prehuman, a whimper of such mixed emotions that he felt lust and hate and fear all wrapped up into one. Rube shut his mouth and the sound died.

The dog whined again.

Rube opened his mouth to shush the dog but once again heard the moan start from his own mouth. He clamped his teeth together, reopening the cut on his lip. "I shoulda gone to Florida," he said to the dog.

The dog hung his head but stopped whimpering.

Her dress was in tatters, little left . . . no blood though, just the ugly gaping wound. Rube felt the strangest compulsion to reach out and touch—

Those peripheral senses again, intruding. Rube heard the crunch of big tires on sand, and he smelled something not of the sea, or of death, but of machinery. He jerked his head up.

The Jeep was almost touching him, a big chrome bumper near his face. Rube could smell the hot radiator and see the specks of rust on the front fenders.

He heard the door shut. Heard the crunch of sand beneath hard soles.

"Don't move, mister."

Somewhere close there was a crackling sound of voices, and Rube realized it was from a radio transmitter. But he couldn't focus on what the voices said. He was too busy looking down the barrel of the gun.

Waves crashed behind him. The air smelled of salt and . . . bloat? No. The body didn't have an odor. The kelp did. It smelled of decay, as if the ocean were dying.

Rube found his voice while he stared down the bore of the gun. "We found her in the surf. Well . . . he did, actually."

"Figures," said the man holding the gun. "Old Buddy's always into something he shouldn't be."

Rube shook and sweated in the warming sun. "You have to point that thing at me?"

The sheriff's face creased, almost a grin. "I guess not."

The sheriff knelt down beside Rube.

"Jesus," he said, looking at the wound. "Woulda killed two her size."

The sheriff's office was a corner of an already small building on Main Street, and it smelled bad. Rube was tired by now; they'd stood around for an hour waiting for the forensics team before the sheriff would leave the scene.

"Have a seat," the sheriff said as they entered the room. Rube saw that the paint was new, some neutral pastel between beige and cream in color. A painting of an old windmill hung crookedly behind the steel desk and leather executive chair. A wooden-backed straight chair stood in front of the desk. There was no carpeting, just a hard-textured floor, as if thinly veiled, wood-covered concrete.

Rube sat. The paint stank and Rube's legs ached. Jesus Jehoshaphat, what a mess. He wanted to slip off his shoes. He'd put them back on at the beach, but they were wet inside. They squished slightly when he wiggled his toes.

"Damned painters," the sheriff muttered. He filled the leather chair arm to arm. He sniffed. "Makes my nose run." His face was wide and almost chinless, the lines smoothed out with flesh, but there was a hint of hollowness beneath the

deep-set brown eyes. The plaque on his desk said SHERIFF
JOHN BOGGERT. Nothing more.

"You wanna go over it one more time, Mr. . . . ?"

"Rubekowski," Rube said. "And no, I don't. I told you
how I found her twice, and that's all there is. My story won't
change with a third telling."

Sheriff Boggert muttered something about tourists, how
they were more trouble than—

"I live here," Rube said. "I'm not a damned tourist. And
I've told you all I know. Book me or let me go."

Sheriff John glared at Rube with his haunted eyes. "Oh
now, don't get excited and swallow your gum. This is just
procedure until I get the coroner's report."

Rube stood. "Which is it to be?"

"You live here, huh? Funny, I don't remember seeing you
around town."

"Just moved," Rube said. "A week ago."

"Current address?"

"Three fifty East Main, that old house back by the creek."

The sheriff scribbled on a pad. "Yeah, the old Huffinton
place. You renting or buying?"

"Renting. For now. Why?"

"Just curious."

They stared at each other after that, in the ensuing silence.
Finally the sheriff sighed, then stood. Rube held his stare.

"Go on home. But I'll be in touch."

Rube nodded and stood himself. He backed out the door.

And that's that, he thought. He threaded his way through
the tourists with a sense of anger. He'd only done his civic
duty. Why was Boggert so nasty?

But then Rube thought of the woman in the kelp, the big
dog gnawing possessively on her hand. God, she was so cold.
She radiated cold. Colder than the sea had been when his bare
feet hit it early that morning.

The thought cooled some of Rube's anger, but the images
playing in the minefields of his brain made him wobble a bit
and he strayed into a fat lady with a big sack and almost tipped
her over. He caught himself and bowed and made apologies—
though she glared at him in anger, beady little tourist eyes like
two stones fitted in a bowl of fat—and Rube wobbled on over

to a bench in the plaza off the street and let his head down
on his arms.

He wondered, as he buried his head, where the big old dog,
Buddy, had gone?

Rube would have been all right if it weren't for the other
memory. He shook off most of the day's effects, made a light
supper of tuna on French bread, with a nice salad; he cleaned
the apartment—it was a house, not an apartment, but he
couldn't shake his East Coast mentality. The place had one
bedroom and a living room-kitchenette, with the inevitable
sliding doors that led to the little deck looking out upon nothing. Actually there was a view back there, a wispy tree that
loomed high over the garden plot and cut the afternoon sunlight to a drizzle. Beyond there was a hill that towered and
cut the morning sunlight, but that was okay. Rube could live
with a few shadows.

But then he'd lain down to rest and he'd almost dozed off
when that old memory kicked in to reveal a scene he thought
lost forever.

His only other visit to an ocean marched like a slideshow
past his inner eyes. Only this was the Atlantic, a long time
ago. He'd just received his first promotion from Mercer Chemical, a boost up from common chemist to research supervisor,
and the boss had taken a group of them out on his fishing
boat. The day was blustery and bright, the ocean a cruel, hard-
edged blue with waves that frothed and leaped against the
boat. The other supervisors were old hands, playing with their
fishing tackle, but Rube just held to the rail and stared out at
the sea. In front of the bow something long and sleek and
beautiful leaped and swam, and Rube was hypnotized by the
sight. He turned to ask his boss about this beautiful thing, but
his boss was leaning next to the rail, an ugly harpoon in his
big hands, yelling at the mate, "Close on it! Starboard now,
quickly!" and his big arm moved and the harpoon flew and
the blue-grey skin of the dolphin erupted with a flash bright
as a red flower. Bright as the red carnations Eleshia had grown
in their garden before the cancer took her. The harpoon ripped
the dolphin's flesh as the cancer had ripped Eleshia's. Only
there was something more terrible about the harpoon wound.
Something more insidious and needless because it was wielded

by a man who didn't need to kill. The cancer had been mind-less . . .

Rube sat up in a sweat and tried to shake off the mix of images. Two dreams in one, both horrible memories, both re-pressed; but that's what was bothering him. He'd seen a wound like that before, and it was definitely made by a har-poon.

Outside the late afternoon sun filtered weakly through the leaves of the big tree above his tiny deck. Someone had har-pooned that girl, Rube was certain of it now.

He put his shoes and socks back on and plucked a light-weight nylon jacket from the back of the chair and shut the house door behind him. Rube had never said a word to his boss about the slaying of the dolphin, had just stood open-mouthed and dumbfounded and shocked. He was afraid to spill out his anger, was afraid of losing his precious job and his new promotion. In some small way he'd hated his lack of courage for years now. But he'd have to talk to Sheriff Bog-gert again. He had to tell the man what he knew.

The tourists had thinned out, and the going was clear. To the west, over the Pacific, the sky was turning pink from the refraction of dust in the clouds. Rube cursed his scientist's mind as he thought it. Why ruin a pretty image like that, with the petty small knowledge of why it happened? But it was part and parcel of the animal he was, the mind he lived in, and he'd grown more accepting with age.

The pink in the clouds was quickly turning red, and Rube kept seeing the rent in the girl's chest. She'd probably been pretty, and she was obviously young. And now she's dead, a part of his mind screamed. Or was it some horrible accident? Was it some terrible mishap that no one wanted to report? Maybe by now someone had reported it.

Sheriff Boggert would know.

Much as Rube hated seeing the man again.

He almost missed the tiny office as he walked by with his head down, but the caustic smell of new paint made him fol-low his nose back.

No light inside.

Door shut and locked; he jiggled it to make sure. Hours listed said ten A.M. to five P.M. It was only a few minutes past five. Rube started to walk off, then thought better of it. He stepped back to the door and took out his notepad and pen, scribbled on it, and slipped the note beneath the door. No sense irritating the authorities any more than he had to. Sheriff Boggert looked like a man who was anxious to jail someone— like a man hard put by the demands of a one-man job. Rube didn't want to be his victim. Being new to a small town was a lot like a kid's first day at school. The bullies and the big guys had a tendency to pick on you.

Go home, he told himself. Go back to your little place and turn on the TV and shut the front door and let it all pass.

And he started to, had turned on the sidewalk and was heading back for the east side of town, when the horn beeped and made him turn his head. Boggert's big dog face stared at him from his big black and blue sheriff's Jeep.

"You're blocking traffic like that," Rube said, still walking as the Jeep followed him down Main Street.

"Don't matter," Boggert called through the window. "They can go around."

They moved on like that, a pair of old dogs sizing each other up. And in the city where Rube grew up, the people would have gone around. Here, though, in this tiny beach town, people just stayed behind the sheriff's Jeep, forming a line of cars back to the last street.

"I left you a note," Rube called, still walking.

"I ain't got time to go get it." The Jeep lurched ahead and pulled over, half blocking the sidewalk. The door popped open. "Get in, Rubekowski."

Rube stared at the open door as though it were the open mouth of a shark.

But Rube got in. He pulled the big door shut after him, but he left his seatbelt undone in protest.

The sheriff turned a corner, still cruising, his eyes moving left and right over the shops and people. "What the note say?"

"I know how she died," Rube said.

Boggert leaned his head back and chuckled, the sound as deep and vibrant as breakers against the sand.

"Something put a big damned hole in her, Rubekowski. That's how she died."

Rube shook his head in irritation. "Somebody harpooned her."

Boggert looked angry. He glared at Rube like he might at a precocious child. "The hell you say."

Rube stayed with the big sheriff's eyes: they locked like lovers in an ugly embrace.

"It's not a wound I'd forget," Rube said. "I saw it once before."

"You saw someone harpooned before?"

Rube hesitated. "Not exactly a person, no, but—"

"Yeah, sure," Boggert said. He shook his big dog head. "You know, Rubekowski, we got coroner's reports for this, and that's what we're waiting for."

Rube looked away, through the big windshield. The sun was lower now, dark plucking at the buildings, and the wind had picked up. A Dixie cup splattered against the glass and Rube twitched an inch in his seat.

"Won't the trail get cold, sheriff?"

Boggert's eyes stabbed at Rube from across the seat. "We don't even know, to begin with, how long she was in the water. Coulda been a couple of days. The trail is already cold." The sheriff let it go with a tiny shake of his head, as though castigating himself for talking to this man at all.

"Besides, what do you care, Rubekowski? What's your interest in all this?"

Rube continued to stare through the windshield. It was a Friday evening, and the tourists were starting to pack the sidewalks again. As though L.A. and San Francisco had emptied their streets, had set the wanderers loose to rape and pillage . . . the way Rube felt Mercer Chemical had raped and pillaged, with methods too insidious to bring to trial. Subtle hurts upon the public. Subtle acts against nature. And what was his interest in the case? What answer could he give this bulldog of a man who worked for the public good?

"It's the indecency of it." Rube moved his hands in the air as though he could draw a picture the sheriff could understand. "The way someone just punctured her body with a harpoon, as if she were a fish—something less than human."

For the first time, Boggert smiled. It wasn't a smile that Rube would have liked over a friendly lunch, was more of a contemptuous sneer. "You think death is pretty, all wrapped in neat motives and easy death? Some sigh where the actress turns her head left and quietly passes away?" The big man snorted and burst into a quick but nasty laugh of derision.

Maybe Rube did. Maybe that's what he expected. Something from a TV tube or big screen where the blood was makeup and the actress opened her eyes and walked away. But this lady wasn't walking, had lain bloated and violated, and no one even knew her name. Rube remembered her tattered green dress, a sheath that was torn too badly even to serve as a shroud.

"Do you know yet . . . who she is?"

Boggert snapped his gaze back to Rube's. "Was, you mean?"

Rube met his eyes with shock that quickly wore to a sad kind of moisture, as though he'd picked up a small piece of dirt in the corner of his eye. At least he explained it to his inner self that way.

"Yeah, was," Rube said. "Who was she?"

The sheriff's face went stone hard and cold. "Somebody's little girl. Somebody's loved one." His voice, gruff now and husky, skipped a beat. "Somebody's . . . hate. I'm not gonna tell you who she was; there's no reason for you to know."

The sheriff coughed to cover his emotion, as if feeling were a mistake he wouldn't make again. Not soon.

Rube could only nod and blink his wet eyes as the twilight sun closed in on the tiny tourist town and its evening shoppers.

But Boggert softened then, and a small, friendly smile twitched at the corner of his mouth. "I'll let you know as soon as I find out more. Meantime, you go home. Get some sleep. Rearrange your furniture or tinker in your garden. But stay outa mine. Okay?"

Rube stayed silent. He felt grim and patronized.

"Sure, sheriff," he said, stepping out after Boggert stopped the Jeep.

Rube walked away without looking back.

The trouble was . . . Rube couldn't sleep.

At first he thought it was his new place, the strange way the night wind blew the tree against the railing on the back deck. The rustling was like a yearning, a soft silky sound, like cloth against flesh. Green dress, tattered dress, rent with the hate of someone's child. The thoughts were night thoughts, and they chased the real night sounds across the pictures in his mind with a frightening clarity.

He remembered the wound so clearly because it had shocked his middle-class values. Rube had never been to war or done battle in a squared off circle as some men had, and his lifetime of toil had come not in a sweatshop or a factory but a modern day laboratory where he played with chemical combinations that sometimes healed and sometimes—he feared—killed. But that had been his life and he'd cherished those values, and when his boss had shown him the array of harpoons, each designed a bit differently, each with a more vicious type of head to gouge or bite into the flesh of the fish, Rube felt a bit squeamish. He should have shaken it off, would have, eventually, would have accepted the killing as part of everyday living, except the fish wasn't a fish but a mammal— an intelligent creature. The dolphin had been off the starboard bow, playing, teasing the waves and the sun when his boss blasted him from the water like so much detritus—so much cheap trash.

Rube rolled over. Emotional old man, he chided. In the night his voice sounded cold and lonely and a little creaky.

Someone had torn a hole through that young girl.

Emotional old man?

Rube had no children. And his wife was long dead. And now he had no work. At sixty-two he could see it all stretch out before him, too many good years left and not enough to do. "Good an excuse as any," he mumbled. He sat up and rubbed his face and strained through the darkness with eyes accustomed to more light. He couldn't see the tree that sounded so much like cloth against flesh, but he could smell the night, the salty core of it blowing from the ocean. All that life below the waves. Struggling to survive. One big mouth closing over a smaller tail. Eat and thrash and survive because the world made you that way?

But who made a world that harpooned young girls?

"Jesus Jehoshaphat, next I'll be crying in my beer and going to revival meetings and . . ." But he couldn't shake off the image of her body lying in the surf with that big hole through her chest, as though someone had performed an Aztec ritual and ripped her heart loose the hard way.

"Do something else," Boggert had warned. "Rearrange

your furniture or tinker in your garden, but stay out of mine.''

But he couldn't. He stood by the bed and wobbled for a moment as the feeling returned to his legs, then he reached for his clothes draped over the chair back.

Except for the Salty Dog, the village looked deserted. As Rube walked toward it, the breeze washed his face with a tangy fog as heavy as cigarette smoke. Rube could hear the twang of a steel guitar and the high tinkle of glasses followed by garish laughter. Light, soft and gold and warm looking, seeped through the open door. Rube padded down the sidewalk in his brown chinos and black nylon jacket, rubbing at his stubbled face. He should have shaved, but he'd been too restless and shaky not to cut himself.

Inside, the bar looked like mahogany, running full length from rear to front. Bright red leather sparkled with chrome trim, though only half the seats were full. Rube took a stool near the end and winced as the bartender stuck his big ugly face across the distance between them. His breath was bad—onions and bourbon and cigarettes, with a touch of garlic.

''What'll it be?''

''Just a draft beer.''

Rube sipped and glanced around. The tiny dance floor was empty except for a pair of young people in cowboy hats. They nuzzled each other's necks as they danced close, their bodies wiggling like upright snakes in some intricate mating dance. Beyond them, in the back, old men sat hunched together in one of the booths. Their clothes were rough-hewn, and their faces were bearded. They talked in low tones, like conspirators, but their whispers carried.

''It's that po-lution, from the big chemical plants—you know there's a power plant right next to the Morro Bay Fishery?''

''Well, whatever, the fish ain't running. It's take tourists out or starve. On bad days I begin to think I'd rather starve . . .''

Their accents were flat and hard, no accents at all.

Rube sipped his beer. The music played again. The same couples danced.

Maybe coming out had been a mistake. What was he doing? Looking for clues? Maybe the sheriff was right. Tend your own garden and stay out of his.

Something big and furry and yellow caught his eye.

Rube turned on the bar stool. In the golden light from the bar, the dog's eyes looked feral and ancient and judging. He sat like a huge, fur-covered lump just outside the door—sat way back on his haunches—but his eyes seemed to search the smoky room.

Rube remembered the way the big dog had worried the girl's hand. As though he could bring her back to life if he could just pull her from the clump of seaweed.

The boogie brass rumbled through the bar's stereo system, a sound so loud Rube thought he saw the smoke quiver with the vibrations.

The dog whimpered.

"You wanna 'nother brew?" Smell of garlic laced with rum.

"No, thanks," Rube said, turning to the barkeep. "You know that dog?"

"Personally?"

Rube wasn't in the mood. It was nearly midnight and he was suddenly more keyed up than ever. He needed to do something that would at least allow him to go home and sleep. Just one little fact would do it. Such as—why the dog sat there.

The bartender started to turn away, then changed his mind. Almost wistfully, Rube thought, the big man with the garlic breath looked at the yellow dog. "That's . . . that used to be Betty and Jesse's mutt."

As though that was enough in the way of explanation.

"I don't understand 'used to be,' " Rube said softly.

The barkeep played with his bar rag, mopping at a damp spot. When he looked up, his eyes were redder than before, as though something painful had kicked him from the inside of his skull.

"That girl you found this morning . . . her name was Betty Sturgis. She was engaged to a guy named Jesse, a local fisherman. Buddy was their dog." His eyes had gone deeper now, seeking out whatever hurt inside. "The dog used to wait for them out there—just like he is now."

Rube stared stupidly at what was left of his brew. Then he asked what seemed the logical question. "Why doesn't Jesse take him home?"

The bartender gulped at something invisible in his throat. "You don't know why?"

Rube shook his head. "I wouldn't ask if I did."

The dog whimpered.

The bartender seemed to make a decision, and his face turned angry and red. "Damned tourist. Drink your beer and go on back to L.A. or wherever you came from."

"I'm not a tourist," Rube said softly.

But the bartender was beyond reasoning. "Then you should know, dammit."

Rube sat stiffly.

"Jesse's dead," he said. "Been dead a week now."

Rube felt like someone had clubbed him. "I'm sorry," he finally managed, but the bartender had already turned and gone.

Rube stood and stared past the bar, then walked out into the night.

The dog stumbled up to all fours, tongue lolling.

"So we meet again," Rube said in a whisper.

The dog whimpered, then shut his mouth and followed Rube down the sidewalk.

Every time Rube stopped, the dog stopped behind him. Rube finally turned and pointed back down the street. "Go home, Buddy. Do you hear me?"

Rube realized the stupidity of his words. The dog no longer had a home. His owners were dead.

The knowledge haunted Rube as he walked toward his house. The street forked here, the left tongue of the fork slanting off at a steep angle that rose to Saint Anne's Cemetery. Up there, above the town, was a small wooden chapel painted white, its stark crucifix like some Celtic dagger that hung askew above the double doors. A big spotlight lit the front of the chapel. Like a used car lot, Rube thought painfully.

Rube was staying to the right, trying to shake off the night's bad feelings, when the dog growled behind him. The growl was sinister, and Rube tensed, thinking perhaps the dog was going to run up his heels and take away some hide. Instead, the dog blew past Rube so fast his pants cuffs rose in the breeze. Rube watched as the snarling Labrador streaked up the hill.

On top of the hill the shadow of a man danced down the

road, the shadow thrown long and sticklike from the large spotlight. Buddy was almost invisible in the night, blending with the yellow bushes on the side of the road, but his shadow too was finally caught and projected, until both shadows came together.

Then the shadows broke, the man's shorter as he turned and ran off. Down the other side? Rube found his feet turning to the left fork, starting up the hill of their own accord.

Buddy had paused at the crest, dropping his haunches to the asphalt. His leonine head went back, and he wailed.

The man's stick-figure came back, the shadow growing from nowhere, and the dog rose on his haunches, head lowered, the growl almost a hiss.

Rube tried to hurry, but the hill was steep and his legs wobbled.

Shadows crashed together, then disappeared over the crest of the hill.

Rube's heart pounded. The big spotlight caught him, and he stopped and shaded his eyes and stared up at the crucifix. Shadows played there, a halo formed from insects buzzing the light. "Give me strength," he muttered. He stopped for just a moment to rest his palms on his thighs, fighting for air. Past the light he could see the edge of a steel fence. There was a gap there, where someone had slid back a gate. Beyond, in the dim slice of moon, he could make out tombstones. Like huge teeth they curved away and down. The air felt colder suddenly, as if a door had opened on some Nordic hell. Rube shivered and rubbed himself. What was he looking for—besides the dog and the sticklike shadow of a man? Then he saw the dog. Buddy lay sprawled across the length of a grave. The earth was freshly turned, and there was no headstone yet. But there were stones on either side.

Rube moved gingerly, muttering to Buddy as he went. "Easy, boy. It's okay."

The words echoed.

Buddy sniffed and shuffled to his feet. He moved off the grave, just a few paces, and sniffed at the ground.

Darker here, the spotlight pointing the other way, down the long hill.

Rube fumbled in his jacket pocket for a book of matches.

The wind blew out the first.

"Damn." His voice sounded hollow and old.

He cupped the next and held it to the nearest tombstone.

Before he could read what it said, he noticed a fresh bouquet of flowers by the head of the mound. Buddy had half crushed them, and now the wind threatened to blow them away.

Rube stared at the tombstone next to the fresh mound. "In Loving Memory of Maria, Mother of Jesse, Husband of Walter. May all your seas be fair."

He died a week ago. The bartender's words, still fresh in Rube's memory. They were engaged.

The dog whined.

The few facts Rube knew gnawed at his mind. What were the odds, he wondered, of such a coincidence? Dying within a week of each other? And how had Jesse died?

The match almost burned his fingers then, and he lost his concentration. He closed his eyes tightly for a time, balancing himself with one hand on the tombstone of Jesse's mother. When he opened his eyes again, he could see better. With age, he'd noticed, everything took longer, even his night vision. Now, as he looked around on the ground, he noticed the new grave was scuffed and torn, as though a pitched battle had taken place.

"Buddy? Are you all right?"

He slowly moved toward the dog, who put his head between his paws and looked mournful.

Rube felt the big dog's head. Wet! His first thought was blood, and he lifted his hand to his face, expecting the worst. But it was just water with a slight floral scent. He knelt down and searched around the head of the new grave. A shard of pottery caught the moonlight. A larger shard lay a few feet away. And another.

"He hit you with the vase, didn't he?"

Buddy sniffed.

Rube picked up the bouquet of flowers now loosely strewn across the mounded earth. Pretty little things with pointy petals. Early poinsettias, he realized. From someone's garden. And something else. At first he thought it was another flower, a stray, very dark red petal. But then he felt it between his fingers. It didn't shred like the flesh of a plant. Cloth. And the red was blood. He was sure of it even before he brought it to his nose and sniffed. Fresh blood. Just a hint of metal there—

copper or iron. Blood had a smell. He had worked in enough labs to know that.

"You got a piece of him, huh, boy?"

Buddy whined, then lifted his head. Rube dangled the piece of cloth in front of the dog's nose. The dog rose unsteadily, back legs wobbling. He leaned forward, though, and sniffed the cloth. Then he let out a yowl that made Rube jump.

"Easy, you'll wake the—"

Then Rube remembered where he was.

Go home and go to bed, he told himself. In the morning he would take the cloth down and give it to Boggert, a gift from the town's newest resident. Hell, it wasn't his job.

And he almost had himself convinced. He made it to the bottom of the hill with Buddy trailing him. A little dazed, but the dog was starting to get his legs beneath him again. At the bottom, Rube started to turn left, toward home, but Buddy's growl stopped him.

Worse, his old habit of noticing details kicked in. Like a bad habit.

Rube turned to see the dog sniffing at spots on the walkway. Could be anything, Rube told himself. Some kid dripped his milk nickel in the heat of the day. Some tourist had a leaky beach bucket. But he knew better, even before the dog started to seriously sniff and follow the spots. Whoever had hit Buddy on the head had gotten past him in the dark. Wouldn't be hard to do. And Buddy had gotten a piece of him before whoever it was conked the old dog on the head. Now Buddy smelled his blood on the sidewalk.

Buddy started to trot, an ungainly thing seen from Rube's perspective. But the big dog ate the distance like a racehorse, even trotting.

"Buddy!"

No use.

Go home and go to bed.

But he couldn't.

Wait and tell Boggert tomorrow.

But he couldn't. He felt responsible somehow.

Rube turned and started after the dog, running a little.

The saloon was almost empty as Rube trotted by. He craned his neck and saw the big bartender leaning over to jaw with a lady holding a pool stick. Even the old fishermen in back had left.

Call me a tourist, huh?

At the end of the street the sheriff's office sat dark and closed. The Jeep was missing from the lot. Rube knew too little about the town or sheriff. His landlord had said the sheriff was new, that they shared him with Morro Bay and another tiny town along the coast. This wasn't New York, he reminded himself.

He slowed to a walk, blowing hard.

The marine layer found Rube before he found the turnoff to the harbor. First the slice of moon disappeared, as though a hungry gray sky had devoured it. Then the street lights started to blink out, nothing left but a fuzz of light through the heavy mist.

Rube shivered as he walked, fingering the bloody patch of cloth. The fog was too thick; he couldn't see. He turned to go home.

Buddy howled—only this time there was anger in the howl, the sound of a predator.

Rube moved through the fog toward the sound.

A hull creaked against a dock, water slapped—but he couldn't see a foot in front of him. Stumble around like a foolish tourist and fall in the water and get washed out to sea and drown yourself. My God, Rubekowski, what would old Sheriff Boggert and the bartender say to that? Think of the laugh they'd have at your funeral, you old—

And then he heard something he'd hear again and again, many nights, in his worst dreams. A thwock of wood on bone, a heartrending, terrible sound. Only to be surpassed by a worse sound, an awful whiny little dog sound, like a puppy lost and alone.

Rube tried to part the fog as Moses must have the Red Sea. If sheer will had been enough, the night would have cleared. But as it was, Rube just stumbled forward, his hands waving helplessly in front of his body, like a man batting at a smoke-screen. His foot stumbled on something, something that was solid and rose at an angle from the ground. He walked up the gangplank, realizing as he did so that he was almost blind. The thought hadn't cleared his mind when he stumbled over the edge of something and went flailing forward to land on all fours. Pain shot from a knee up through his hip, but he clenched his teeth and kept the whimper to himself. He'd just caught his balance when the boat lurched and he lost it again. What fool would move a boat in this fog, he wondered, grabbing for the deck. He hugged the deck and tried to breathe deep while listening once again for the dog's whimper. Instead he heard a bell. A buoy marker, he realized. He'd heard them earlier when he was wading. Beneath his body there was a thrumming now, a deep engine sound as the boat moved toward the marker.

This is crazy. He can't see. He'll crash and—

As they moved, someone shuffled through the fog. Rube could see a disturbance in the misty textures, like a ghost passing.

Buddy whimpered. A soft, hurt kind of sound. But then it grew and he started to howl.

"I'll shut ya up." That awful *thwock* again.

Silence.

Rube stood. His balance was bad, but he was determined to stay up. He moved toward the last sounds he heard.

The late September onshore breeze picked up and plucked at the fog, thinning it, and light streamed from an open cabin. Rube could see a figure hunched over something. The man's hand was raised.

A belaying pin, Rube realized, as thick as a man's forearm and shorter than a Louisville Slugger. The man was waving it above Buddy's head. Buddy lay on his side, one paw up, as if to defend himself.

"Ya had to have a chunk of me, huh? Again? You're worse than the little bitch that owned ye. She had to have it all, too. Killing my boy wasn't enough. She wanted the captain's boat. My home. My home since Maria died."

The voice was a slow rave.

"I couldn't do it. I couldn't, you see? I had to—"

Rube stepped on something loose on the deck, a corner of a tarp. The sound wasn't much, but the old man spun.

Rube thought of at least three things to say but couldn't get them out of his mouth.

"What are you doing on my boat?"

"I heard the dog whimper," Rube said. It sounded lame, and he knew it. Then again, it was the truth. Or most of it.

Rube stared at Buddy. The dog's head leaked blood.

"He's a bad dog," the captain said.

"I don't understand," Rube said.

"He attacked me at my son's grave," the captain continued. The way the old man went on, Rube almost felt he was talking to himself. "The dog's old, and he's gone quite mad, I'm afraid."

The boat still moved toward the buoy marker, out to sea, and Rube wondered how he steered. An automatic pilot setting, maybe? The mist was just that now, no longer heavy enough to call fog, and Rube could clearly see the old captain's face, the potato nose and the reddened, wrinkled skin. The chin was hidden in a thatch of heavy beard. But the blue eyes held Rube's, and they accused.

"Look," Rube said, "he's an old dog. I'm an old man, too. I understand the madness of retirement. Let me take the dog."

The captain glared at him—the way they all did at tourists.

"I've got room at my place, and a yard." And a garden I haven't started, he almost added, thinking he'd start one, thinking of the sheriff and how much he wished Boggert were here. Wish you were here, to protect the tourist? Like a joke message on a bad postcard. But Rube meant it. There was something lethal in the captain's eyes and stance. The man wouldn't let him go, and Rube knew it.

The captain moved from his position over the half-conscious dog. "You followed me, didn't you?"

Rube backed up clumsily. "No. I followed the dog."

"You're clever, no?"

"No," Rube said.

The captain's eyes changed for just a second. He seemed unsteadier than the deck should make him. Fatigue or drink or grief?

"She thought she was clever, too," the captain said.

Rube tried to look stupid. Hell, he felt stupid enough, swaying on the deck of a fishing boat next to a sad old dog half unconscious on the deck. Trouble was, he knew what the captain was talking about. Kind of. She had to be the girl Rube had found in the seaweed. And it must have shown on his face.

"It's too bad," the old captain said.

The light from the pilot's house seemed to surround him as

he thwocked the club heavily into one hand. "She thought she could steal Jesse from the sea, from me and his rightful heritage. She thought she could steal an old man's life."

Rube backpedaled clumsily toward the center of the deck. But sea legs must take time or special practice because he stumbled and fell backwards over a row of crates. His head banged hard, and the night darkened for a second. When his head cleared, the captain stood above him.

"She had no right to any of it," the captain said.

"Of course not," Rube agreed.

Rube felt like he was floating on the deck; he was dizzy even lying down, and he reached out for something to grab, something solid. His hand wrapped around a pole as round as a broomstick, in a rack. He grabbed the stick and pulled himself up, at least halfway, before the stick pulled loose and Rube clattered back to the deck. He still held the stick, though. The end gleamed in the light from the cabin, like a spear.

Later, there would be thought. Too much thought. But for now, as the captain stepped forward, drawing back the big club for the kill, Rube didn't think. He sat up and launched the big harpoon like a man born to it. He'd once played softball, once thrown a javelin, and this was not much different. Except this dug its way into the captain's stomach, right below the ribcage. The big steel end made a deep sound, like an animal sucking at meat. The shank quivered from the captain like an exclamation point as Rube scrambled to his feet. He stood there watching the captain grab at the wooden shank. The captain's face beaded with sweat. Muscles spasmed, and then blood spurted from the captain's mouth.

"She wanted it all. By damn, no!" and he crumpled onto the deck.

"Jesus Jehoshaphat."

And Rube still didn't really know what the captain had done. But he knelt beside him, shaking him with horror and revulsion.

The captain curled around the shank, as though it gave him comfort.

"Did you kill her?" Rube realized he was screaming.

No answer. Maybe a slight grin at the corner of the old man's mouth? The captain died curled tightly around the shank of the harpoon.

Rube stood and tottered toward the pilothouse. There was some kind of automatic pilot, and Rube didn't want to mess with it. He found the radio and got that working easily enough. A shoreside operator mumbled from the receiver.

"Get me Sheriff Boggert," Rube said. "It's an emergency. Wake him up if you have to. And I need to know how to drive this boat."

They sat in the stinky, newly painted room. Alone finally. There had been many people buzzing about and many questions. But not enough answers, Rube thought. Though what he had would have to do.

Boggert looked as fierce as a bulldog who'd lost his last fight. "If you'd a just waited," Boggert said, "I was gettin' on out to talk to the man. But I didn't have the damned report yet."

"If I'd waited, the dog would be dead."

Boggert just stared. "Oh for Christ's sake." He paused. "Then again, you can't be sure of even that."

Rube was too tired to hear it. But he knew he would.

"Maybe if you hadn't let that dog up to the cemetery, well—maybe he'd a gone on home. Or to someone's home. Or . . ."

Rube stood up. "Are you through with me?"

Boggert scratched at his leg. "Just about, yeah. Come sign this affidavit."

The sun was up, hard and bright, as Boggert drove Rube home. "You get some sleep, Rube. It's been a hard day and night."

"For a tourist?" Rube said.

"For anyone," Boggert said.

They drove up Main, trying not to hit the new day's tourists.

"It was self-defense, Rube. We matched the harpoon wound with one from the rack."

Rube was horrified for just a moment. "Not the one I killed the captain with?"

"No," Boggert said. "A different one. The captain was from a long line of oldtime whalers. Guess he kept them as—memories."

"Memories," Rube muttered, knowing he now had too many.

"Well, the old man was bonkers. No doubt about that. Betty had broken up with Jesse—some big fight over money—and Jesse, he just couldn't handle it. The old man found him hanging in a cheap hotel room."

"Memories," Rube muttered.

"And then she must have braced the old man for money. Probably said Jesse had promised her half the business. It fits, Rube."

"I guess," Rube said.

They stopped at a crosswalk, the closest thing in town to a real stoplight.

"And he was gonna kill the dog and you and drop you over the side."

"Dropping me over the side would have been enough," Rube said. "I can't swim."

Boggert shook his head. "Maybe you are a tourist, after all."

They pulled up in front of Rube's driveway, a winding stretch of asphalt that led to the house in back.

Rube got out. Opened the car's back door and called.

"Come on, Buddy."

The big old dog had a bandage on his head, but he stuck out a giant tongue and licked at Rube's hand, then jumped down from the back of the Jeep and started to follow Rube to the house.

Rube had a garden to start, things to plant. Maybe something good and green would grow. Maybe something green and alive.

<< The Dogsbody Case >>

by

Francis M. Nevins, Jr.

THE OAKSHADE INN had been touted to me, Milo Turner, professional con man, as the most restful place to stay in Barhaven, and during the first three nights of my visit to that drowsy and affluent community I had no cause to dispute the assessment. Floorboards buffed to high gloss, homey maple furniture, bright chintz curtains, view of lush meadows from my second-floor window, fine classical music from the local university's radio station, breakfasts in the hotel dining room that were a trencherman's delight, and a scam that was progressing fantastically. No con man with a taste for the finer things could have asked for more.

Until that fourth night when the phone jolted me awake.

I sprang bolt upright and groped for the night table. The digital clock beside the phone proclaimed the time to be 1:14 A.M. I found the receiver and jammed one end to my ear. "Yes?" I spoke into the mouthpiece, fighting to make the word come out calm.

"Fritz!" replied an all too familiar voice, low and menacing like the growl of a German Shepherd on guard duty. "Get your pants on and wait downstairs for a prowl car to pick you up. You've got four minutes."

For an awful moment I was convinced he'd tumbled to the scam and was arresting me over the phone. Then my brain came into gear and I exchanged a few sentences with my caller, hung up, and dived for the clothes closet. Fully dressed and with my Vandyke brushed, I had all of ten seconds to wait in the dim empty lounge of the Inn until the black-and-white braked in front of the picture window, the domelight whirling bloodily.

The scam had been going velvet-smooth till now. In fact, the only sour note in the orchestration was that Chief Knaup for some private reason kept calling me Fritz. My actual *nom de scam* this time was Horst—to be complete, Professor Doktor Horst Gerstad, formerly criminological consultant to the national police of the Federal Republic of Germany, currently president of Gerstad Security Systems, a corporation which analyzed and improved on existing security arrangements for businesses that were uptight about crime.

Professor Gerstad was one of my favorite identities and one of my most lucrative. The close-cropped military brushcut, the little Vandyke, the accent honed to a fine edge by hours of listening to tapes of Henry Kissinger's press conferences, all added up to the quintessence of a walking Teutonic efficiency machine.

I would present myself at a likely corporate headquarters, speak to its top management, learn its security arrangements, punch a few simple holes in them and offer to lease the corporation my own comprehensive security system, which of course had as much real existence as a hippogriff. If the corporation didn't agree, I could always recoup my losses by selling the information I'd picked up to a potential thief.

I had come to Barhaven to make my pitch at the university, and it was in the office of its president, Herbert J. Stockford, A.B., M.A., D.Ed., that I had chanced to meet Stockford's brother-in-law, the chief of the Barhaven police.

E. W. Knaup preferred to be called Duke—I gathered because the E. stood for Elmer or Ethelbert or something equally unmacho. He was a short, tubby, gravel-voiced, genially pushy specimen, and he had a blind spot wide enough to drive a semi through. He was a gun nut. No man or woman who encountered him, however casually, could escape one of his monologues on weaponry. One might glance at the sky and remark that it looked like rain, and Knaup would say, "If you want to see a rain of lead, buddy, try the VC-70 Heckler and Koch automatic pistol. Nineteen shots, double action, comes with a stock you can use for a holster *and* which you can attach to the pistol and turn it into a submachine gun. Brip brip *brip*, brip brip *brip*! Love those three-shot bursts."

The chief's personal police cruiser sported a rear-window sticker attesting to his life membership in the National Rifle Association, three separate anti-gun control stickers, a God

Bless America tag, a Support Your Local Police tag, and a flag decal. No ambiguity about ol' Duke's sympathies.

After that first meeting in Stockford's office I hadn't expected to see Knaup again, but the very next day, a little before noon, while I was in a conference room on the third floor of the university administration building, poring learnedly over security plans with the chief and deputy chief of the school force, he came striding into the room in full uniform, the polished butt of his Colt Python protruding from his buttoned-down leather holster.

"Fritz!" he barked, like an actor trying out for the voice of the Lord in a DeMille movie.

I looked curiously around the room to see if any of the security guards happened to be named Fritz. Nobody even looked up.

"No, *you*, dummy," he growled at me. That was the way he spoke to people he liked. "We're lunching."

"May I point out that my name is not Fritz?" I said in my most unruffled Kissinger tone.

"We in the law enforcement community eat Mex food for lunch. I hope you like tacos, Fritz," he said, and led me out by the elbow.

Over the guacamole salad at Panchito's he explained his sudden interest in me. "Now here's what it is, Fritz." He wolfed down great gobs of guacamole on taco chips between sentences. "As head honcho of the college, my brother-in-law Herbie Stockford is the one who has to decide about this security package of yours." Chomp crunch. "Only he doesn't know enough about security to hit the dirt when a Remington High Standard Model 10 goes off at him, so he's asked me to sort of help him make a decision." Crunch chomp. "Those retired village constables he uses for campus security aren't much better than Herbie, so he's relying on the only pro in town." Crunch crunch. "Me." Burp.

So I repeated my well-rehearsed pitch to the Duke, being careful to throw in as many gun references as I dared. And before we had demolished our quesodillas he had unsubtly switched the subject to weaponry. "What kind of contacts you got in Charter Arms, or Ruger, or Dan Wesson? I've got a little proposition for you."

When I modestly lied that my connections with several of

the firms he'd mentioned were at moderately high levels of management, his eyes brightened. "We in the law enforcement community appreciate the work of the arms manufacturers," he said. "And now that we're getting a lot of federal money from LEAA, we'd like to show our appreciation by placing some big orders. Like maybe a gross of M-16 or Armalite 180 rifles, a few dozen folding stock shotguns, all the Glaser Safety Slugs we can lay our mitts on. Say, if I get some of the chiefs in the neighboring towns to come in with me on a shopping list, you think you can get us, say, a thirty percent discount on a $200,000 order?"

He wasn't so crude as to make it explicit that his recommendation to his brother-in-law depended on my help in fixing him up with an arsenal, but I got the message loud and clear and assured him of my fullest cooperation. And that was how things stood between me and the gun-loving chief when, thirty-six hours later, the black-and-white whisked me through the sleeping streets of Barhaven to I knew not what destination.

We skirted the edge of the university grounds and swung north into the low foothills which sheltered the $100,000 homes. The black-and-white made a sharp turn into a private lane and then into the driveway of a fieldstone and redwood showplace halfway up the slope. Half of the house's windows were lit, and floodlights blazed across the broad lawn.

Duke Knaup strode tubbily into the path of the black-and-white and thrust out his palm like a crossing guard. The cop behind the wheel slammed the brakes and I emerged from the rear with what dignity I could muster. Behind the chief shuffled a slim balding man in silk dressing gown and slippers whom I recognized as none other than President Stockford of Barhaven University. His face looked ghastly, as if his best friend had turned into a cheese Danish before his eyes. Without a word they led me across 50 yards of grass still wet from the early evening storm to the foot of a stately old elm. The body of a large reddish-yellow dog lay beside the trunk.

"Someone poisoned the poor mutt," Knaup muttered. "Can't tell what was used—lab will give me a report in the morning. About an hour ago Herbie heard the dog whining and came out to investigate and found him lying here. Looks like he'd crawled under the tree to die."

A short dumpy woman in a blue wrapper trotted out of the house to join us. "My sister, Mrs. Stockford. This is Dr. Fritz Gerstad, a visiting criminologist," Knaup introduced us.

"Oh, are you going to help my brother find the—the animal who did this to Thor?" she demanded as we shook hands.

"It is possible I can be of assistance?" I murmured, wondering what the hell I was doing here and how best to stay in character.

"Tell Fritz what you told me about the dog's routine after dark," Knaup directed his brother-in-law.

"He was a trained guard dog," Stockford replied dully. "We let him out every night at sundown and he'd roam the grounds. We haven't had a burglary here since we got him three years ago."

"And have you had a burglary tonight?" I asked.

"No, nothing," Mrs. Stockford said. "I've just finished checking to see if anything is missing."

"Someone probably threw a poisoned meat patty onto the lawn to get rid of Thor," her husband added, "but he hasn't come back yet to break in."

"He'd probably wait till the wee hours before he came back," Knaup pointed out. "But with all the lights on and cops around the house, he won't show now. I'll assign a car to stand by the rest of the night just in case."

"Do I assume correctly, sir, that neither you nor Mrs. Stockford observed any strange automobiles on the private road this evening?"

"The storm was quite heavy up here for a while," the shaken president replied. "We couldn't see as far as the road during that period. That was probably when he came by and threw out the poisoned meat."

Chief Knaup clawed at my arm. "Come over here with me, Fritz." He led me across the squishy grass to a rose arbor behind the house. "Want to explain why I sent for you," he whispered. "You see, I don't believe Thor was killed by somebody who was out to burglarize the house. I think whoever did it wanted to kill the dog and that was all."

"A crazed dog-poisoner in Barhaven?" I clucked mildly, trying to suggest his theory was ridiculous without actually insulting the man.

"It makes sense if you know the background," Knaup went

on. "Thor was trained as a killer, the kind of dog they use for night security in big empty stores. When the college was going through the anti-war riots six years ago, Herbie hired an outfit that trains these dogs to let some of them run loose at night in the administration building and the ROTC building and some other vulnerable spots. A few long-haired kids broke into the ROTC building one night with a can of paint to put peace symbols on the walls. Couple of them got chewed up pretty bad by the dogs. Caused a big stink, the school went on strike for two days, and Herbie had to cancel the contract for the dogs. When the outfit went bust three years ago he bought one of those same dogs for his personal protection."

"Thor was one of the dogs involved in the incident in the ROTC building?"

"That's right. Half Irish wolfhound and half Pyrenean bearhound. Weight about one ten, a shade bigger than a full-grown German Shepherd, and a hell of a lot meaner."

"I'm sure he was an excellent guard dog," I murmured, "but I fail to see why you wish to involve me in the matter." And, like a tyro swimmer who suddenly realizes he's drifted two miles out from the beach, I was becoming distinctly queasy.

"Herbie loved that dog like a son," Knaup explained, "and I owe him a lot of favors, like my job for instance. He wants me to pull out all the stops to nail whoever poisoned Thor. Trouble is, if I give the case any more than routine attention, the papers will stomp all over me about misusing police resources. I can do without that grief."

I knew exactly what he meant, having taken the trouble to read the back issues of the Barhaven newspapers before I had made my appearance. Last year Knaup had come close to being removed from office over a little matter of assigning three patrolmen, while on duty, to paint his house and oil his gun collection. "That's why you're here, Fritz. You're going to be my dogicide squad for a while. Let's see how good a criminologist you really are."

I do not shy away from new experiences but this one made me fight hard to repress a shudder. Very few con men have found themselves drafted into the police force while on a scam. I was far from enthusiastic but saw no way to extricate myself short of blowing town. I made an instant decision and held out my hand to Knaup gravely. "So be it," I pronounced as we shook. "Although I wish it explicitly understood that my success will guarantee a favorable recommendation by you of my security system."

Duke Knaup stuck thoughtful fingers under his chin. "I don't know if you have a saying for it in sauerkrautland, Fritz, but here in America you scratch my back and I'll scratch yours."

It occurred to me, as the black-and-white sped me back to the Oakshade Inn, that there were two dogsbodies in this case. I was the second. The old English word dogsbody, meaning an insignificant underling, a lackey, fitted my present situation like pantyhose. Even worse, I had become a detective in spite of myself. But I had had enough experience putting myself in the shoes of the authorities to make me believe I could pull the thing off—with a large dose of luck.

It was too late to start on the case tonight, so I decided that tomorrow morning I would visit the college administration building, get the names of the students whom Thor had maimed six years ago, and then try to learn if they or anyone close to them still lived in Barhaven. And if someone in that category happened also to have access to the college chem lab, we might have our poisoner before the next nightfall.

The mellow sunlight of Friday morning was drenching my room when the phone exploded again. The digital clock read 7:12 and I was not yet in any mood to face the day. I made a kind of glunking noise into the mouthpiece.

"Fritz!" Even half awake it did not take me three guesses to identify my caller. "Get your rear end down to the station, *mach schnell*. All hell's broke loose!"

Thirty minutes later I stumbled out of a cab into the city hall and down a marble staircase to the basement, which was the police headquarters. I informed the fat asthmatic desk sergeant that Chief Knaup was expecting me, but before the sergeant could pick up the interoffice phone, a door flew open behind me and there he stood, posing with his hand on his holster for all the world like a short pudgy version of Randolph Scott playing marshal of Tombstone.

"Get in here!" he roared, and stalked ahead of me through the detective squad room and into his own office.

"Read this, and that, and this one." He tossed a stack of

police reports across his desk at me. "We've been getting calls all night. Some nut's been driving around the county making war on the dog population of the area!"

On a first reading of the reports I almost agreed with the sputtering chief. Our devotee of the spiked hamburger had cut himself a wide swath last night.

Winston, age 5, Boston bull terrier, property of Mr. and Mrs. Horace Burgess of Newcomb Heights, found dead in the service pantry of the Burgess home at 6:00 A.M.

El Toro, French poodle, age 2, owned by Miss Lucretia Runcible of Barhaven, found dead in its basket in the kitchen when Miss Runcible woke up hungry at 3:25 A.M. and went to the refrigerator for some yogurt.

Cincinnatus, mutt, age 7, belonging to Professor Featherstone of the classics department at the college, found dead behind the professor's front door at 1:30 A.M. when the professor returned home from the annual banquet of the Lucullus Club.

Including Thor, a total of seven canines had been transported overnight to that Big Kennel in the Sky, four within the Barhaven city limits and three in outlying communities.

"Has it been confirmed that the cause of death in each case was poison?"

"Only in the first three so far," Knaup told me. "County lab's been working all night on it. The others will prove out the same. This is a pattern, Fritz."

"Perhaps not the pattern you thought," I murmured, and shuffled through the police reports again. "Observe the addresses of the late dogs' masters and mistresses. Five seem to be private homes, but Miss Runcible is 243 Westview, Apartment 18-D, and Mr. Henry Wampler is 4576 North Wood Avenue, Apartment 907. Does this suggest anything to you?"

Before the chief could figure out what to say, his phone buzzed and he made a grab for it. "Knaup," he barked. "Yeah, Sergeant, I . . . *What?* . . . No, no, I'll go out on this one myself." He slammed down the phone and groped for his visored cap. "Let's go, Fritz."

"Dogsbody Number Eight?" I inquired.

"Catsbody Number One," he snarled. "Our nutcake's started zapping the cat population too!"

•   •   •

Knaup drove us in his own cruiser, the one with all the gun stickers on the bumper. Ten minutes out of town we turned in between a pair of stone pillars and onto another one of those private drives. The cruiser splashed through a mud puddle in a depression of the road, then sped along clean smooth macadam until the drive ended in a parking circle at the side of a huge Victorian stone monstrosity of a mansion.

"Who is the owner of this establishment?" I asked as Knaup rang the symphonic chime beside the front door.

"Used to be Franklin Bagnell, the big steel manufacturer. He died five or six years ago."

"Ah, yes, I remember seeing him on television—when he visited the Federal Republic of Germany, of course." I had almost blown my scam with that careless remark. I did remember seeing old Bagnell several times on TV newscasts, a cadaverous old reactionary who was forever ranting about Communist-inspired legal restraints on the American businessman. When he was upset a muscle in his cheek would twitch—a Bagnell family trait, I remembered having read in the news magazine.

"Ever since the old man died," Knaup continued, "the lawyers have been fighting in court over who owns the house and the money. For all practical purposes the dog owns it, I guess."

Before I could ask him to clarify that last enigmatic remark, the door was inched open and a trim tired-looking young lady in a pink pantsuit inspected us, made a lightning deduction from the chief's uniform that he was fuzz, and threw the door wide. "Hey, Mama!" she bellowed into the depths of the house. "Cops here!"

A gray fiftyish woman descended the oak staircase to meet us in the foyer where she stood under a huge oil portrait of skeletal old Bagnell and threw out her hands to the Duke. "Oh, Chief Knaup, it's *so* good of you to come. It's not many high officials who would come in person when a cat is murdered."

"We in the law enforcement community love cats deeply," Knaup orated. "Oh, this is Dr. Gerstad, the famous criminologist. Fritz, may I present Madge Slocum, the caretaker here, and her daughter Lila. What happened to the cat, honey?"

Her mother answered for her, sniffing back the hint of a tear. "I just don't know what happened, Chief Knaup. I put Kikimora's supper out for her at 5:45 yesterday evening the way I always do, and then I whistled for Barnaby to come in from the yard for *his* supper, and around then it started raining, and Lila and I ate at 6:30. We watched TV together and went to bed early and I found poor Kiki when I came down this morning to get her and Barnaby breakfast. She was lying in her little cat box so stiff and still I knew something was wrong with her, so I picked her up and listened for her little heartbeat and she was dead.''

"Is Barnaby your husband, madam?" I asked the sorrowing caretaker.

"He gets better care than a lot of husbands I know," Lila answered pertly. "He's the dog that more or less owns the place."

I took a casual stroll the length of the hallway to a parquet-floored conservatory at the back of the house. A riot of potted plants, hanging ferns, and crawling greenery almost suffocated me. I looked out the rear window on broad landscaped terraces stretching for a few hundred yards, dotted with bright flowerbeds. A large gray dog of indeterminate breed was romping in the middle distance, chasing a rabbit or something. Barnaby seemed a hell of a lot more carefree than most rich people of my acquaintance.

"It's the cat we're interested in, remember?" Knaup snaked an arm through the plant life and plucked me out of the conservatory, leading me through a side corridor and a butler's pantry into a barnlike kitchen and over to a wicker basket heaped with fluffy little pillows where the eighth victim lay. Kikimora was a broad-headed white Maltese with a black notch down the middle of her forehead.

"The cat was merely a personal pet of Mrs. Slocum, I take it?" I asked Knaup. "And the care of the dog is her job, like the care of the house?"

"You got it. Old Bagnell picked up Barnaby about five years before he died. Just a mutt, but the old man grew to love him a lot more than he loved the couple of relatives he had left. So he put most of his money in a fund to care for the dog as long as the dog lived. Honorary trust it's called. Dog's got the run of the house and grounds, eats better than a lot of people, vet comes out to look it over twice a week. The Slocum women's pay, the taxes on the property, everything gets paid out of the trust as long as Barnaby's alive.''

"And when he dies?" I murmured.

"The property and money get divided among seven or eight

charities and those two relatives. Second or third cousins, I think. Morton Godfrey, a lawyer in California, and a young kid named George Bagnell. They're the ones who started the lawsuit to knock out the will on the idea the old man was bananas. It's been in the courts for years.''

I paced back and forth across the spotless kitchen floor. The extent to which I'd become my own fictitious creation was beginning to frighten me, but with a wild sense of excitement I realized that I might be on the brink of actually solving this case. ''But why should the cat have died?'' I mumbled half to myself. ''Everything else I can account for, but not the cat.''

''Fritz, what the hell are you muttering about?''

''Last night you believed that Thor was the intended victim of someone who drove near the Stockford house and threw a poisoned meat patty for him to eat. The rash of dog deaths during the night established that animosity against Thor was not the motive. But you still believed that the killer was a person who spent yesterday evening driving through the area dropping poisoned meat on lawns. This cannot be so. I remind you that at least two of the dogs lived in high-rise apartments. Where do they roam? How does our killer deposit the meat in front of them? You have misconceived the technique of the crimes.''

''Now wait a minute, Fritz,'' Knaup objected, banging on the door of the walk-in meat keeper for emphasis. ''Why couldn't the cat over there have picked up something with the poison in it yesterday? It could have been out in the grass playing with Barnaby all evening for all you know.''

''We drove through a mud puddle,'' I reminded the chief, ''just inside the private drive leading here. The macadam between that puddle and this house was clean and unmarked until your own car traversed it. You will recall that it rained heavily last evening. No automobile crossed the puddle between its formation and this morning. This is at least circumstantial evidence that there is no madman driving around your community with poisoned meat. Kikimora was poisoned here in this house. And the seven dead dogs were poisoned in their respective homes also.''

Something like understanding was beginning to dawn over the chief's dumpy face. ''I submit that it was the food their masters served them that was poisoned,'' I went on. ''It is the only hypothesis that explains everything. Well, almost everything—everything but the cat. You must call your brother-in-law at the university and ask him where he purchases dog food. Then you must call each of the other owners and ask the same question. I predict you will receive the same answer. Go." I pointed to the phone extension hanging on the kitchen wall next to a memo board. To give orders to a police chief in his own bailiwick tickled my soul.

Knaup pressed touch-tone buttons, got the university switchboard, and asked for President Stockford's office. "Yeah, Herbie, it's Duke. Say listen, Herbie, Fritz here has got a nutty question he wants me to ask you. Where did you buy Thor's chow? . . . Four-footed Gourmet, huh? Okay, Herbie, buzz you later."

He hung up and turned to me. "Herbie fed the dog a special-quality ground chuck he bought at The Fourfooted Gourmet. That's a specialty shop we have in town—finest cuts of meat and other goodies specially prepared for pets. It's where all the pet pamperers go."

"Then that is the place where the poison was mixed with the dog food," I insisted. "Call your office, have your sergeant phone each of the others, and ask them the same question you put to Mr. Stockford, then report back to you. Meanwhile I must deal with the problem of the cat."

Knaup whirled back to the phone while I went through the swing doors in and out of the butler's pantry and down the long hallway into the drawing room where the Slocum women waited. They sat on matching armchairs upholstered in rich blue velvet, talking together in hushed tones.

"Excuse me, ladies." I stepped in front of them and executed a slight bow. "Where do you purchase Barnaby's meals?"

Madge Slocum stared up at me with a look of puzzlement behind her shell-rimmed glasses. "Why, what a strange question! Well, you know Barnaby is not what you'd call an aristocrat among dogs. He was just a stray that Mr. Bagnell found as a puppy and grew extremely attached to. After Mr. Bagnell's death I tried to get Barnaby to eat the finest foods available but he would always turn up his nose, so ever since I've just served him canned dog food I get at the supermarket."

"And where do you obtain the food for your cat?" I continued.

This time Lila Slocum did the honors. "That's a funny story

too. Like Mama said, she tried to get Barnaby to eat fancy food. There's a special grade of ground chuck she bought for him but he wouldn't eat the stuff. But Kiki went crazy over it, so ever since then we bought the ground chuck for her.''

"Every Thursday afternoon I did my weekly shopping for Kiki," her mother added helpfully.

"Did you follow this procedure yesterday as well?" I inquired. Both women indicated that they had.

I didn't need to ask the next question but I asked it anyway. "And the name of the establishment where you procured these culinary delights?"

"It's called The Fourfooted Gourmet," Lila said.

"Thank you." I practically clicked my heels at them Prussian-style, and wheeled back out to the kitchen where Knaup was just hanging up the phone. "Sarge made four of those calls so far. You were right, by damn! They all bought that special ground chuck at The Fourfooted Gourmet."

"As did Mrs. Slocum for her cat," I reported. "The pattern is now clear. Someone poisoned the food at its source. And the rest of a week's supply is sitting in that meat keeper at this moment, and no doubt in the refrigerators of every other bereaved pet owner in this case. Call headquarters and send men out to collect the meat at once. Then let us pay a visit to these canine caterers."

We rocketed back through the mud puddle and roared onto the state highway back to town. Knaup drove with one hand on the wheel and the other on the butt of the Colt Python in its holster. We turned into the main business district in the center of Barhaven and pulled up short in the middle of a tiny parking lot next to a low tan-brick building. "That's the place," Knaup said.

"Is it permitted to park this way?" I asked. Every slot along the sides of the lot seemed to be taken, and he was blocking at least a dozen cars the way he was positioned.

"Man, I'm the law in this town, anything I do is permitted. Let's go."

And casually as two dog owners about to pick up their pets' dinners we stepped into the premises of The Fourfooted Gourmet. A bell over the door tinkled as we walked in. The establishment looked more like a real-estate office than a food store.

Pickled-pine paneling, Muzak box bracketed to the wall near the ceiling, imitation brick tile on the floor, an occasional poster of a dog or cat carefully posed to look irresistibly cuddly.

Behind a gold-flecked formica counter at the far end of the shop there was a long line of refrigerator cabinets. A pale and very thin young man in a white apron, with hair the color of cooked noodles, was weighing meat in a scale for a customer. "What's your pleasure, gentlemen?" he began as he looked at us.

And then he registered Knaup's uniform, and a muscle in his cheek began to twitch. I studied his cadaverous face more closely, compared it with a painted face I had seen this morning, and made one of the rashest statements of my career.

"This is Mr. George Bagnell," I announced, turning to Knaup, "the animal poisoner."

And instantly the place was a madhouse. George flung the package of meat at us, scored a direct hit on Knaup's face, and sprang through a doorway to the rear. Dripping with meat juice, Knaup vaulted the counter and clawed for his gun shouting, "Police, halt!" as he and I ran through the rear storage area and out a side door into the parking lot.

George was gunning a blue Pinto out of the lot and smashed head-on into Knaup's cruiser. He flew out the door of the Pinto and started sprinting toward the street. Knaup snapped a shot at him, aiming low for his leg. He missed George but hit the right front tire of his own cruiser.

George was almost out of the long narrow lot when suddenly a two-tone convertible sped into the area with a fat blonde woman in the front seat and a huge German Shepherd in the rear. The kid had to swerve out of the car's way in a split second. He slammed against the wall as Knaup fired again and the dog leaped out of the car and dived for George as if the kid were a cat.

The fat woman floored her brakes and screeched, "Oh, my God! Down, Schnitzel, down!" and waddled out of the convertible just as Knaup was ramming his Python into the small of George's back and motioning him to assume the frisking position against the wall.

Knaup had to radio for another car to come and haul the prisoner away. While we were waiting for the nearest service station to send someone over to change the flat on Knaup's cruiser, I explained the rest of my conclusions to him.

"As long as Barnaby lived, Bagnell's cousins profited nothing. George Bagnell came to Barhaven for the express purpose of killing the dog. He probably shadowed Mrs. Slocum on her shopping trips, observed her weekly visits to The Fourfooted Gourmet for ground chuck, and reasonably but wrongly assumed that the food was for the dog.

"He proceeded to obtain a job at the shop and some poison elsewhere and waited his chance to impregnate a supply of the special ground chuck with the poison just prior to one of Mrs. Slocum's Thursday visits. Altogether a foolish and wasteful plan and one that betrayed its perpetrator's inexperience. Any other dog owner who picked Thursday to shop would find his animal dead too, but I suppose George was not displeased by that. The more dead dogs, the less it would appear that one particular dog was the target.

"And remember that you must arrange for announcements in the newspapers and radio and television that all patrons of The Fourfooted Gourmet must bring their meat in at once for analysis. We want no more dead animals."

"I know it was the twitch that told you the kid was a Bagnell," the chief asked, "but why couldn't he have been Morton Godfrey, the other cousin?"

Actually, of course, he could have been, and I had taken a 50/50 chance, but it wouldn't do to let Knaup know that.

"Being an attorney," I rationalized sagely, "Morton Godfrey would depend on his suit contesting the will, simply because if he should win, the entire Bagnell estate would pass by the law of intestacy, with the charities taking nothing and the two cousins everything. Would he have been so foolish as to try to kill the dog for a small share of the estate when by lawful means he stood to gain so much more? No, it was clearly not a legal mind that conceived these crimes."

"Sharp thinking, Fritz." Knaup clapped me on the shoulder. "And you can bet on it I'll make sure old Herbie signs that contract with your company for security services. Uhhh—provided you put through that little side deal we talked about?"

I looked at the hapless chief, with his uniform dripping meat juice and his tire flattened by his own well-placed slug, and struggled to keep from laughing aloud as I shook his hand again. "We in the criminological community," I assured him, "support a well-armed police force."

Souvenir
<<   >>
de Mme. H. Thuret
by
Robert Campbell

DAVID GREENING, COTTAGER, in his garden on a morning in early autumn, savoring the scent of loam and manure, aware of the sun upon his back, the scrape of trowel in earth; utterly content.

When he heard the voice, David Greening looked up from the hole he was digging to accommodate the Golden Ducat daffodil and felt his heart stand still at the sight of the woman at the gate.

Her hand was laid upon it as though she'd meant to walk right in and then had thought better of it. The pose lent her slender figure an attitude of vibrancy. He saw the larger impression that she made, but it was the shape of her hair blown somewhat about her face and the eyes that were clearly gray, even at a distance, and the mouth, generous and vulnerable, that fit so completely the portrait of the imaginary woman who had haunted Greening's dreams for many years.

"Please," called the vision, "I don't wish to intrude, but . . ."

She hesitated, swaying slightly as though faint.

Greening was on his feet and hurrying down the path as she tottered and seemed about to crumple.

". . . but I'm afraid my husband has been killed."

It was then Greening saw that the hand that had not lain upon the top of his garden gate was red with blood.

"Will you have another cup of tea, another tot of brandy?" asked Greening with a certain offhanded hospitality which did

not cater to her emotional fragility or do anything to upset
with excessive compassion the delicate balance of her command of self.

It was as though she was a neighbor come to call on him,
though he was a comparative newcomer to the village of Pummery, retired to the tiny country cottage and garden after many
years in London, only the year before.

She'd removed her jacket and while she'd used the lavatory
to wash the blood from her hands, he'd sponged the stains on
the sleeve (though failing to remove it all) and had it draped
over a kitchen chair before the fire to dry.

"So early in the afternoon? I think not," she said, accepting
the role he'd given her, pretending for the moment that her
visit was no more than social, postponing the inevitable storm
of feeling that would accompany her explication of the tragedy
when the police should arrive.

He regarded her with quiet intensity but did not remark
upon the bruises she'd covered with rouge and powder. Still,
his scrutiny disturbed her more than a bit, and she reached
down to touch a miniature gray poodle who had none of the
nervousness of the smaller breeds, as though seeking comfort
from it.

"I went to Fidelia first, but she wasn't at home," she said
in a lovely, husky voice. "I couldn't think for the moment
where else to go and found myself growing faint."

"Mrs. Enkworth is a relative?"

"Just my oldest and dearest friend in Pummery."

"I haven't seen you visiting."

"We've been away, my husband and I, for more than a
year, and Fidelia tells me you've only just settled in permanently though you've been a weekender and summer holiday
visitor for five or six years."

"Fidelia speaks of me?"

"Fidelia speaks of everyone," she said, smiling. "You must
know that. She's most curious about who you are and what
you were before retiring here."

"How I made my living?"

"I'm not sure she'd admit to being as rude as all that," she
said, "but it would certainly make her happier if she could
place you in your proper slot, Mr. Greening."

"David, if you'd rather," he said. "I haven't asked your name."

"Hawkhurst. Mrs. Malcolm Hawkhurst. Madelaine, if you will. And this is Souvenir."

"Souvenir de Mme. H. Thuret," murmured Greening.

The little dog lifted its head at the mention of its name.

"I beg your pardon," said Madelaine.

"Your two names together form the name of a rose. A very beautiful rose," said Greening.

Madelaine blushed and Souvenir cocked its little head, then perked its ears as a knock sounded at the front door, which was no more than two or three arm's lengths from where they sat.

Madelaine Hawkhurst started as though she'd taken a blow, and Souvenir, sensitive to his mistress's every mood, whined a bit until she soothed it with another touch.

"Will that be the police?" asked Madelaine.

Greening laid a steadying hand upon her shoulder as he went to the door.

Fidelia Enkworth stood there looking up at him, blue eyes peering out of a face that seemed not to have lost its childish innocence, yet displaying the wisdom gained only by long life and much experience.

"This is not how I planned your introduction to Madelaine," said Fidelia. "How awful."

"You know about it?" exclaimed Greening, not really altogether surprised.

"It's all over the High Street. A tradesman, Jack Ewen, the baker, passing by, heard the shot but went on his way. Then he thought better of it and went back to the manor house to see if anything was amiss. The front door was wide open and no one answered his halloo, so he went in and saw what he saw. Then he hurried to the police station, declaring his discovery all along the way."

"I've called in as well," said Greening.

"Yes, well, the police should be along any minute now," she said, slipping past him and going to her knees in front of Madelaine; reaching out to embrace and comfort her.

"Don't baby me, Fidelia," said Madelaine. "I'm only just holding on."

"Well, perhaps you shouldn't. Stiff upper lips are for fools. Wouldn't you say, Greeny?"

"No doubt tears can help on occasion, but there's much to be done and steady might well serve Mrs. Hawkhurst better until it's over."

Fidelia huffed and got to her feet, glancing at Greening as though he'd somehow betrayed her trust by not supporting her opinion.

Then the police, in the bodies of Detective Sergeant Sunderland and Constable Wiggins, appeared at the still-open door.

"Mr. Greening. Mrs. Enkworth. Mrs. Hawkhurst," said Sunderland, as though counting them out for a parlor game.

"Detective Sergeant Sunderland," said Fidelia, matching exactly his tone of voice.

"Shall we return to the manor, Mrs. Hawkhurst, or would you rather we repaired to the station house for your statement?"

"Can you take my statement here?"

"You've no objection to an audience?" asked Sunderland, casting a dubious glance at Fidelia in reference to her reputation as village gossip.

"I'd rather my friends were here to witness what I have to say."

"Very well, then," said Sunderland, taking the chair opposite, which had been occupied by Greening, after obtaining permission with a glance.

Fidelia pulled up a footstool and sat at Madelaine's feet. Greening went to stand on the hearth, and Wiggins stood by the door after closing it.

They made a crowd in the tiny sitting room.

"Now, then," said Sunderland, after removing his hat, "in your own time and in your own way, if you please, ma'am."

"I know so little," said Madelaine. "I'd just finished dressing to take Souvenir for a long walk. I'd asked Malcolm—my husband?"

"Yes, ma'am."

"I'd asked him if he'd like to come along. Our first day in the country after a year on the Continent. He said he'd rather not. He wanted to clean his guns in readiness for a shoot. It was the principal reason for our returning in autumn. We usually opened the house for weekends late in spring, resided here a month in summer, and weekended again in autumn until the shooting was done. That was why we had no staff, the house lying empty the rest of the year.''

''Were you intending to bring staff from elsewhere, or were you going to hire locally?'' asked Sunderland.

''We intended to bring our housekeeper-cook from London, but she'd taken ill. I knew that I could manage for a few weeks without help except for Mrs. Wiggins . . .'' She looked at the constable and smiled. ''. . . who's helped out with the cooking when we've had large affairs and who we hoped would lend a hand on the weekends until our own cook recovered.''

''But she'd not yet arrived?''

''She was to have come before suppertime today but it was early still.''

''Ah. So you were alone with Mr. Hawkhurst in the house?''

''As far as I know. Except for Souvenir, of course.''

''That little dog?''

Souvenir had lifted his head at the sound of his name once more.

''So you were on your way out,'' said Sunderland, prompting her to go on.

''I was walking down the central staircase, putting on my gloves. Souvenir ran ahead and darted into my husband's study.''

''Your husband called him?''

''No. My husband had very little to do with Souvenir. He didn't like pets around the house and merely tolerated my dog to indulge my desire for a companion. He only allowed me to keep him when I promised to train Souvenir to a rare perfection of obedience. My husband made fun of Souvenir all the same. He tolerated hunting dogs kept in kennels because they were useful to him, but even so he used local packs and kept none of his own.''

''It's often the case,'' said Greening, diffidently, ''that dogs and cats favor persons who seem openly to dislike them and want nothing to do with them. Was this the case with Souvenir and Mr. Hawkhurst?''

''How did you know that?'' asked Madelaine, quite impressed.

"Why else would the little dog have gone into your husband's study unsummoned? Either he wanted a goodbye from Mr. Hawkhurst or there was something or somebody else in the room that excited his curiosity."

Sunderland stood up as though Greening had asked his own last questions. "Mrs. Hawkhurst, I'm sure you've heard it asked a thousand times on telly mysteries," he said. "The reason it's become such a cliché is that it is, indeed, asked at least once in every homicide investigation."

"Yes?" said Madelaine.

"Do you know of anyone who had reason to hate your husband so deeply as to act to cause his death?"

Color flooded her face, rising from the neck of her blouse in a becoming rush, as though he'd paid her an improper but not altogether displeasing compliment. She turned her head away in some confusion and raised her hand as though to hide her face. When she turned to him again, she was quite recovered.

"There were a good many people who hated my husband, and not a few who would have conspired to kill him had they the opportunity."

"Then the next question must necessarily follow," said Sunderland. "To your certain knowledge, can you say that no one but yourself, your husband, and, of course, your little dog, was in the house this afternoon?"

"I would not swear to it," said Madelaine Hawkhurst.

"I was curious," said Greening, peering through the open French doors to the Hawkhurst study. "Am I trespassing on a crime scene?"

"Why do you call it that?" asked Sunderland.

"You asked certain questions about intruders in the house."

"Routine."

"And did not ask certain other questions."

"Such as?"

"You said nothing about the bruises on Mrs. Hawkhurst's face. She'd done her best to conceal them with makeup but they were plain to see all the same."

"Come sit down, Mr. Greening. Let me turn on some lamps and we'll have a chat."

Greening carefully walked around the welter still left on the large leather chair in the center of the room, though Hawk-hurst's body had long since been taken away, and sat down at one end of a matching leather couch.

"I didn't ask about the bruising because I already knew the cause of it. Hawkhurst drank and had a bad temper to boot. Apparently he sometimes took it out on his wife."

"You'd been called out on disturbances before?"

"Never, but I'd been given word by Dr. Crowstairs, who'd treated her more than once for . . . accidents, she called them. Has Fidelia Enkworth told you nothing about it?"

"Fidelia's a notorious gossip, I know," said Greening, "but I would bet a packet on her loyalty and discretion in all important and private matters concerning friends."

"Well, the cat's well out of the bag and wailing now," said Sunderland. "Give it time, and I'm sure we'll discover one of two things."

"And they are?"

"That Madelaine Hawkhurst finally had enough and either hired her husband's murderer or blew his head off herself whilst he slept."

"Sunderland's not quite a fool," said Fidelia. "Neither is he overzealous, but he's wrong in accusing Madelaine, and we must do all we can to prove it. You will put all your considerable wit and intelligence to work on it, and I will do what little I can."

"How's that?" remarked Greening, clearly startled at her excessive praise of him.

"You won't tell me, I know—sworn to secrecy, I've no doubt—but I would not be surprised to discover that you were, in the past, a member of one of the intelligence services."

"Really!" said Greening, amused and dismayed.

"Oh yes, you have the professional's way of deflecting inquiries about yourself."

"Really, Fidelia, you do have the most outrageous fancies."

"Be that as it may, you will do what you can, won't you? I thought you displayed a more than ordinary interest in Madelaine."

He felt color rushing to his own cheeks. Had he really been so transparent, or was Fidelia merely firing shots at random?

"Of course I'll help, if I can," he said.

• • •

When he went to visit Madelaine Hawkhurst three days hence, the day following Hawkhurst's interment in the village churchyard, Greening was wearing his Irish crush hat against the light rain that was falling and carried a walking stick to insure his footing on the wet leaves.

Madelaine was not at the manor house but had removed herself to a little garden folly that was fitted out as a self-contained guesthouse.

"This cottage suits me better than that cold house," she said, as she greeted him at the door. "It's about the size of your own little dwelling, is it not?"

"But mine is not as charming."

"I think it very charming indeed."

"Thank you for saying so," said Greening, inordinately pleased, but embarrassed by the compliment all the same. "Fidelia would have me redecorate."

"Fidelia has no one of her own to care for, so she picks up . . ."

"You were going to say strays, were you?" said Greening.

"I was going to include myself, I assure you. Will you have a cup of tea?"

"I think that will go down well."

"Please sit down."

Greening took a small overstuffed chair beside the fire, removed his hat and shook the drops off onto the hearth, then cupped it on his knee.

"I can put up your hat and walking stick," said Madelaine.

"I'm comfortable with them as they are," he said, settling himself with his hands placed one on top of the other and his chin on top of both propped up on the head of his walking stick.

She smiled without further encouragement and gave her attention to the kettle and pot.

"Where's your little dog? Where's Souvenir?"

"In the kitchen in the main house, with the cook."

"Mrs. Wiggins?"

"Yes, the constable's wife. She's been very kind and helpful. I take my meals there, though she's offered to bring them to me here on a tray. Will you stay for supper? I'm sure Mrs. Wiggins's pot roast can accommodate one more."

"That's a very tempting offer to an old bachelor," said Greening, soliciting another compliment which was not long in coming.

"Surely not old. One would say attractively mature," said Madelaine, gifting him with a dazzling smile.

There was a scratching at the door.

"Souvenir," she said, "come to call me in to supper."

"What a clever bit he is," said Greening, as she opened the door to let the little dog in.

"He's learned a dozen tricks or more. I'm sure he understands everything we say."

The little poodle, tongue happily lolling from its mouth after its scamper down the path, through the garden, and across the grounds from house to cottage, rushed at Greening and jumped up and down, clawing at the walking stick.

"Behave, Souvenir, behave," commanded Madelaine, scarcely raising her voice, and the dog immediately stopped his leaping about and went to ground near her foot, waiting for a praising pat.

Greening's eyes met Madelaine's and she read his thoughts.

"He's usually such a calm little animal," said Madelaine, "but that jumping at anyone holding a stick is a habit of which he will not be broken."

"Is it something he learned all on his own, then?"

"Oh, quite alone," said Madelaine and never dropped her eyes.

After a fine and simple meal taken in the kitchen, with Mrs. Wiggins gone to her own home and hearth, they sat over cups of Sumatran coffee laced with Devon cream before the fire in the parlor. Not the sitting room where Hawkhurst had met his tragic end, but another room that was most obviously her own.

Souvenir sat beside his mistress, his head in her lap as she idly stroked him.

"How are you bearing up?" asked Greening.

"There are strains and tensions. Keeping up appearances."

"I think I understand."

"Yes, I think you do. You notice things, David. The first time you laid eyes on me I think you knew my husband abused me."

Greening waved his hand in demur, as though reluctant to be the confidant of her private life.

"It's always been an open secret in the village, though I pretended few were aware of my condition."

"Why did you remain with him?"

"The properties and fortune were mine," she said. "I lived a privileged and sheltered life before meeting Malcolm. One might say that I'd existed in a time warp, a creature of another age. Malcolm Hawkhurst came highly recommended by my father and I married him without much hesitation or protest. After my father's death, Malcolm moved to make my property his own, and before I knew it, he had control of it and me. Were I to have left him, I would have been penniless, thrown out into the street with nothing but the clothes on my back."

Greening could not escape the notion that she was telling him a Victorian tale, overselling it more than a little. Still, that might have been—probably was—a substitute for the greater truth, that she had feared Hawkhurst's violence so greatly that she was willing to suffer some of it rather than risk the worst of which he might be capable. In this day and age, for an intelligent, educated woman to allow herself to be so abused and terrified might well be a humiliation too bitter to be endured.

"So, you see, when you ask how well I'm faring," she went on, "and I reply that there are strains and tensions, I mean only those that attend my position in the society in which I find myself. Were you to ask what I felt about my husband's death, I would say that I was much relieved, having been given back my life."

The challenge in her glance that said he must judge her if he would, the candor with which she regarded him with her clear gray eyes, squeezed Greening's heart. Were such a woman his, how he would keep and cherish her. Yet that was the very thing she did not need, another protector. What she needed was time and space enough to find herself.

"I think you have every right to rejoice," said Greening.

"Not rejoice. I am simply grateful to have it at an end," said Madelaine gravely.

The bell at the front door sounded.

They both started as though intruders had come upon them during an act of the utmost intimacy.

Madelaine got to her feet, sending Souvenir leaping to the floor, and hurried from the room, Souvenir at her heels.

She was back in moments with Detective Sergeant Sunderland in tow.

"Will you have a coffee or a brandy, Sergeant?" asked Madelaine.

"I'll only stay a moment," said Sunderland, nodding to Greening and no doubt noting for the future the comfortable domestic scene.

"You need more help with your inquiries?" asked Madelaine.

"We've had no luck at all finding anyone who saw a person or persons near the manor on the day and time of your husband's death. In a village as small as Pummery, there's rarely a move anyone can make without someone noticing."

"I've already said that I believed no one to be anywhere about," said Madelaine.

"I know you did. Still I hoped to find some visitor or trespasser."

His meaning was very clear. If there had been no one else about, then clearly Madelaine Hawkhurst was the only likely suspect, Sunderland apparently having ruled out suicide as a most unlikely cause of death.

"I came to inquire if you meant to return to London or to go elsewhere any time soon?" said Sunderland.

"Am I not to be allowed?" asked Madelaine.

"Not at all. You're under no restraint. But I would ask that you keep me informed of your whereabouts, if you please."

"Are you saying that Mrs. Hawkhurst is not quite on but not quite off the hook?" asked Greening.

They both looked at him as though he'd said something unforgivably rude, though there was the hint of a smile on Madelaine's soft lips at his rough audacity.

"Because if that's the case, I'd like to try an experiment that may settle the matter to your satisfaction once and for all," continued Greening. "If you would be so kind as to sit here, where I've been sitting."

Sunderland sat in the chair which Greening that moment vacated.

Greening handed Sunderland his walking stick, which had been lying on the side table beside his coffee cup.

"Will you hold it upright between your legs, one hand on top of the head and the other where you will?"

Sunderland placed his hands one on top of the other on the head of the walking stick as Greening scooped up Souvenir and went to the door.

"Just sit there as you are and watch what happens when I open the door again and set the dog down on the rug."

He popped out of sight and closed the door. Madelaine stood by the fire. Sunderland sat stock-still, waiting. The door opened and Greening set Souvenir down.

The little dog rushed at once to Sunderland and danced about the walking stick, scraping at it with his forepaws.

In came Greening. "And there you have him, Detective Sergeant, the culprit who pulled the trigger while Hawkhurst was cleaning his shotgun, butt-first upon the rug."

There were many more holes to be dug, the bottoms sprinkled with bone meal, the bulbs in papery gowns placed just so at the proper depth, four to seven inches for most varieties.

Greening was on his knees contemplating the attention a simple hole so often required, a cup of nothingness waiting to be filled.

"Well, Greeny, she's gone away," Fidelia chirped above his head.

Greening glanced up to see Fidelia peering over the fence, her blue eyes nearly obscured by the tulle mushroom hat she wore while gardening. She would be standing on tiptoe on a paving block to get a better view of him.

"Gone away?" he said, rising reluctantly to his feet and adjusting his kneeling pads.

"Don't play Old Dog Tray with me. You know perfectly well that Madelaine Hawkhurst's left for London."

"Yes, I do know," said Greening.

"Will you miss her much?"

"I scarcely know her."

"Well, you've seen enough of her of late. She's told me that she finds you very comforting."

"Oh? I've been the subject of conversations, have I?"

"Nothing too revealing, Greeny, not to worry. Just she feels you've done her a marvelous service."

"I merely pointed out to Detective Sergeant Sunderland

how Mr. Hawkhurst's unfortunate death may have come about.''

''You don't really believe an experienced hunter like Hawkhurst cleaned his shotguns muzzle up with the breech unbroken?'' said Fidelia.

''A momentary carelessness is possible.''

''Or that the weight of the little dog's paw could have depressed the trigger?''

''It might have happened, Fidelia. It very well might have. Who's to say?''

''Did you have much to do with long shots in your previous life?''

''I was not a bookie, if that's what you're wondering, but I did have many odd experiences . . . as do we all,'' said Greening and knelt again to his planting.